ONE-WAY TICKET

ONE-WAY TICKET

A BRADY COYNE NOVEL

William G. Tapply

St. Martin's Minotaur
New York

Tap

This is a work of fiction. All of the characters, organizations, and events portrayed in this novel are either products of the author's imagination or are used fictitiously.

www.minotaurbooks.com

LIBRARY OF CONGRESS CATALOGING-IN-PUBLICATION DATA

Tapply, William G.
    One-way ticket / William G. Tapply.—1st ed.
       p. cm.
    ISBN-13: 978-0-312-35829-7
    ISBN-10: 0-312-35829-6
  1. Coyne, Brady (Fictitious character)—Fiction. 2. Lawyers—
Massachusetts—Boston—Fiction. 3. Kidnapping—Fiction. 4. Boston
(Mass.)—Fiction. I. Title.
    PS3570.A568O53   2007
    813'.54—dc22

                                       2007019341

First Edition: September 2007

10 9 8 7 6 5 4 3 2 1

In Memory
Phil Craig
My partner in fiction, fishing,
and other frivolities

ACKNOWLEDGMENTS

As always, I am indebted to my indispensable support group:

Vicki Stiefel, my wife, my first and best critic, a terrific writer and teacher, and my love;

Keith Kahla, my editor all these years, and the most astute and hardest-working one in the business;

Fred Morris, my agent, who allows me the luxury of not worrying;

My kids and stepkids, Mike, Melissa, Sarah, Blake, and Ben, who give me incentive and claim always to like my books;

My students at Clark University, who inspire me with their talent and motivation and energy and enthusiasm;

The good citizens of Hancock, New Hampshire, who pay close attention and give me a lot of ideas;

And all my writing friends and acquaintances, professional and amateur both, who remind me that it's always hard, but we have no choice.

A lawyer's job is to manipulate the skeletons in other people's closets.　　　　—SOL STEIN

"How do you do Nothing?" asked Pooh.

"Well, it's when people call out at you just as you're going off to do it, What are you going to do, Christopher Robin, and you say, Oh, nothing, and then you go and do it."

"Oh, I see," said Pooh.

"It means just going along, listening to all the things you can't hear, and not bothering."

　　　　—A. A. MILNE, *Winnie-the-Pooh*

ONE-WAY TICKET

ONE

June bugs and fireflies were flitting around in the walled-in garden behind our townhouse on Beacon Hill. Overhead, an almost-full moon and a skyful of stars lit up the Boston evening. Now and then a myopic moth would alight on the screen of our little portable TV, which was sitting on our picnic table.

Evie and I were slouching side by side in our comfortable wooden Adirondack chairs with sweaty bottles of Sam Adams in our hands, as we often did on a pleasant June evening when the Red Sox were playing. Henry David Thoreau sprawled on the bricks beside us, his legs occasionally twitching with dog dreams. Baseball put Henry to sleep. From our backyard we imagined that we'd heard the roar of the Fenway crowd all the way from Kenmore Square when David Ortiz hit one over the bullpen in the third inning.

At the end of the sixth inning, Evie yawned, stood up, stretched, and said she was exhausted. She kissed the back of my neck and stumbled into the house and up to bed. Evie enjoyed baseball. She liked the geometric symmetry of it and the occasional remarkable feat of athleticism, but she wasn't really a fan. She didn't care enough about who won, and she didn't understand the passionate neuroses of lifelong Red Sox addicts such as I, who had seen the home team squander so many late-inning leads over the years that we were never comfortable until after the final out. We knew there was always a Bucky Dent or a Bill Buckner lurking around the corner, waiting to break our hearts. The aberration of 2004 would never ease our apprehensions.

"It's only a game," Evie would point out while I clenched my fists on every pitch. "And besides, they play about two billion of them a year."

"It's not only a game," I would say. "It's life in a nutshell."

One inning and half a bottle of beer later the Sox were clinging to an uncomfortable 9–6 lead. The Orioles had runners on first and third with only one out when the phone rang.

We'd brought the portable kitchen phone outside with us, so I was able to grab it on the first ring, before the one beside our bed disturbed Evie, I hoped.

When I answered, a voice I didn't recognize said, "Mr. Coyne?"

"Yes," I said, "this is Brady Coyne, and it's almost eleven o'clock on a Tuesday night. You better not be trying to sell me something."

Henry, hearing the tone of my voice, sat up, yawned, and arched his eyebrows at me. I reached over and scratched his forehead.

"This is Robert Lancaster," said the guy on the phone. "I don't know if you remember me. I'm here with my father. Dalton Lancaster."

"We met once," I said. "You were about eight. Your parents were in the middle of a divorce. You and your dad and I had lunch together."

"That's right," he said. "That was about twelve years ago."

I waited, and when he didn't continue, I said, "So where's 'here'?"

"Excuse me?"

"You said you were there with him."

"Oh. The emergency room at the New England Medical Center."

"Who's hurt?" I said. "You or Dalt?"

"Him. My father."

"Is he okay?" I said.

"They say he's going to be all right. He wants to talk to you."

"So what happened?"

"He got beat up."

"Who—?"

"I don't know. Three guys. He says he doesn't know who they were."

"Well, okay," I said, "put him on."

"He's wondering if you'd be able to meet with him."

"Sure. We can set something up."

"No," he said. "He means now."

"Listen," I said. "Whatever happened to your father, client or no client, it's late and I'm tired and I intend to watch the rest of the ball game and then crawl into bed with my girlfriend, who's waiting upstairs for me. Just put him on the phone and we'll set up an appointment."

"Thing is," said Robert Lancaster, "they jumped him in the parking lot, kicked him in the face, loosened a couple teeth, cut his tongue, banged up some ribs, and he can't talk very well. He's pretty scared, and he says he needs your help."

"They kicked him?"

"That's what he says."

"A mugging, huh? They robbed him?"

3

"I don't know. He says they didn't take anything."

"Just kicked him."

"I guess so," said Robert Lancaster.

"Did he call the police?"

"No."

"Tell him to report it to the police," I said. "That's what he needs to do."

He blew a quick breath into the phone. "Look, I'm sorry, okay? He called me. I said, 'Why are you calling me? You never call me.' He said, 'I got a problem, and I need you to come over here.' I said, 'What about all those times I had a problem? Did you come over?'" He paused. "Anyway, he called, I went. Now I'm here and I'm calling you."

"You're the one he called," I said. "You being his only son."

"Me being convenient," said Robert. "I live in Brighton. I go to BU. I took the T over. Look. He's hurt pretty bad, Mr. Coyne."

"So I should come right away, too," I said. "Since I'm his lawyer as well as his friend."

"That's the message. If you can't do it, I'll tell him."

I blew out a breath. "Yes. Okay. He's my client. That's what I do. When are they releasing him?"

"In a few minutes, I'd say. They've patched him up, given him a prescription. He's finishing up some paperwork."

I thought for a minute. "There's a little bar-and-grill on Tremont Street, place called Vic's, stays open late for the after-theater folks, five minutes from where you are. Know where it is?"

"We'll find it," he said.

"Just around the corner from Boylston," I said. "I'll meet you guys there in fifteen or twenty minutes. You get there first, grab a booth and order me a cup of coffee."

"You got it," said Robert Lancaster.

I clicked off the phone, verified that the Sox had not blown their lead, turned off the TV, and took the phone and the TV into the house. Henry followed behind me.

I went up to our bedroom and opened the door. In the dim light from the hallway I saw Evie mounded under the covers. She was lying on her side facing away from the doorway. The curve of her hip made me smile.

I went in, sat on the bed beside her, and touched her shoulder. "Hey," I said softly.

She didn't respond.

I leaned over, lifted the hair away from her neck, and kissed her on the magic spot where her neck joined her shoulder.

She moaned softly, then rolled onto her back. She blinked her eyes, focused on me, and smiled. "Did we win?" she mumbled.

"It's not over," I said. "We're ahead. Sorry to wake you up. I—"

"I wasn't really asleep," she said.

"You feel all right?"

"It's nothing."

"What's the matter, honey?"

"Little headache, that's all."

"Why don't I get you some aspirin."

"Sure," she said. "That's a good idea."

I went into the bathroom, shook a couple of aspirin tablets into my palm, filled a glass with water, and took them back to the bedroom. I sat beside Evie and propped her up with my arm so she could take the pills.

"Thanks," she said. She sighed, lay back on her pillow, and closed her eyes.

"You going to be all right?"

"Oh, I'll be fine," she said. "Overtired, I guess. You coming to bed?"

"Not yet. I've gotta go meet a client."

"Huh?" Her eyes popped open, and she frowned at me. "What's up?"

"I don't know," I said. "I'm meeting him at Vic's on Tremont Street. I'll be back soon. You go to sleep."

"Anybody I know?"

"Just a client, honey."

"This time of night?"

"A lawyer's work is never done," I said. I touched her cheek. "Feel better, okay?"

"Yes, sir." She closed her eyes and smiled. "Kiss me."

"Yes, ma'am." I bent over and kissed her mouth.

Her hand touched my face. "Come right back, please."

"I will."

"Be safe."

"Always," I said.

TWO

Dalton Lancaster and I were first-year students together at the Yale Law School twenty-something years ago. He quit after his first miserable year when his father died. He hated law school and only went because both of his parents were lawyers. His old man was a partner at Schilling, Lowe, and Lancaster on State Street and expected his only son to join the firm as soon as he passed the bar. His mother was none other than Superior Court Judge Adrienne Lancaster.

Dalt was convinced that he'd never satisfy his parents, especially his father. All he ever wanted, right up to the day that Frederick Billings Lancaster keeled over in the firm's washroom, was for the coldhearted prick to say something nice to him.

So after he buried his father, Dalt quit law school and used his patrimony to buy an upscale California-style bistro in Boston's South End, and when that failed he tried to make a go of a family restaurant in Arlington, but that didn't work out, either. He managed to keep it a secret for a long time, but finally it came out that he'd been investing more time and money in the blackjack and poker tables at the Foxwoods casinos in Connecticut than in the tables in his restaurants, and pretty soon Dalt's share of his old man's money was gone.

Along the way he married a dark-eyed waitress named Teresa. They had a son, Robert. When Dalt gambled away all their money, Teresa divorced him and took Robert with her.

I handled Dalt's end of the divorce. Teresa went for full custody of Robert on the grounds that Dalt was an addicted gambler, besides being an incompetent father and husband. I told Dalt I thought we could get fifty-fifty custody, but he said no, Teresa was right, he was not to be trusted, and we ended up settling for a weekend a month and a week in the summer.

For the past decade or so Dalt had been managing other people's restaurants, working for a salary, most recently at a seafood place called the Boston Scrod in the Faneuil Hall Marketplace in downtown Boston.

The last I heard, Teresa had married a Nissan dealer and was living in Acton.

I'd been Dalt's lawyer the whole time, through the purchases and failures of his businesses, his struggles with addiction, his marriage to and divorce from Teresa, and then through his remarriage, five or six years ago, to a pretty high school biology teacher named Jessica Laroche.

I'd always liked Dalt Lancaster, and I tried not to feel sorry for him. Even though his father had died many years ago, and even though the old man's money was long gone, Dalt still seemed always to be looking over his shoulder. His mother the judge seemed to love him well enough, although she'd never tried to hide her disappointment in the way his life had gone. Dalt had never really crawled out from under Frederick Lancaster's big paternal shadow, and that seemed to explain everything.

Dalt once told me that fatherhood scared him. He was afraid

he'd turn into the father that his own had been. That's why he let Teresa have Robert. He'd rather be no father at all than end up like his own old man.

The bar at Vic's was two deep with theater people in silk dresses and pearl necklaces and summer-weight suits and blazers, but when I shouldered my way through them and stepped into the dining area, I saw a face lean out and a hand wave from the booth in the far corner.

I went to the booth. I guessed it was Robert, although I hadn't seen him in many years. He resembled his Italian mother. A big mop of curly black hair, bronze skin, white teeth. He was a slender, handsome kid-almost-a-man. He wore the uniform of his generation—sunglasses, black T-shirt, and a gold stud in his left ear.

I shook Robert's hand. Dalton Lancaster and a man I didn't recognize were sitting across from him.

Robert gestured at the man sitting beside Dalt. "This is Mike Warner. My Uncle Mike. He just got here. He's going to drive my father home. The doctor said he shouldn't drive."

Mike Warner had curly sun-bleached hair, a tanned face, and startling blue eyes. I guessed he was a few years older than Dalt, late forties, maybe. He was cradling a mug of beer on the table in both of his beefy hands.

He took his right hand off his sweaty beer mug, wiped it on his pants, and held it out to me. "Hey."

I shook Warner's hand, said, "Hey," and slid in beside Robert. "You must be Jess's brother, then."

"No," he said. "I'm Kimmie's husband. Kimmie is Jess's sister, which makes me Dalt's brother-in-law." He grinned. "Got all that?"

I shrugged. "Either way you're Robert's uncle."

"Stepuncle," he said, "technically."

Dalton Lancaster was sipping a Coke through a straw. The entire left side of his face was red and beginning to swell, his left eye was bloodshot and half closed, and his left eyebrow was covered with a Band-Aid. Some dried blood had caked in one of his nostrils, and his shirt was torn and smudged with dirt.

"What the hell happened?" I said to him.

"Three guys," he mumbled. "In the parking lot." He talked through clenched teeth. His voice was so low I had to lean across the table to hear him. "Bastards punched me, knocked me down, kicked me."

I pointed at his wrist. "They didn't take your watch."

"They took nothing," he said, staring down into his glass of Coke. "They just kicked me. Loosened some teeth, bruised some ribs. The doctor said I was lucky." He tried to smile, but it didn't work, and he had to squeeze his eyes shut for a minute. "No broken bones, no internal injuries. Just a raging fucking headache." He looked up at me. "I know what you're thinking."

"It wasn't luck, you know," I said. "If they didn't break anything, it's because they didn't want to. This was to put you on notice."

He nodded. "Yeah, well, for what?"

"You tell me. What did they say?"

He shook his head. "I don't know. I was too busy getting my head kicked in."

"Did you get a look at them?"

He shrugged. "They were kind of short and dark and muscular. Italian, Hispanic, something like that. They were wearing suits. They followed me to the parking lot. I was kind of aware of them behind me, but I didn't think anything about it. Figured just some guys like me, heading for their car."

"Could you pick them out of a lineup?"

He shook his head. "It was dark. They came up behind me. They were just, you know, thugs. One of them had a big mole or wart or something on his face."

"So how much do you owe them?" I said.

He frowned at me, then lifted up his hands and spread them open. "Brady, honest to God," he said. "That's what I'm trying to tell you. I don't do that anymore. All I owe is the mortgage and the car loan. I'm not even behind on my payments. I don't think the bank sends goons, do they?"

I smiled. "Depends on your definition of goon, I guess. So what do you think? Sounds like they got the wrong man. They mistook you for somebody else, huh?"

"Well," he said, "they called me Lancaster, and last I looked, that's my name."

"They used your name?"

He nodded. "I was almost at my car, starting to get a little nervous about these guys behind me but trying to ignore them, and one of them says, 'Hey, you. Lancaster. Dalton Lancaster.' So I stopped and turned around, and he punched me in the chest. This was the one with the mole on his face. Felt like I'd been hit by a sledgehammer. Knocked me down, and then they commenced kicking me."

I slid out of the booth, then looked down at Robert Lancaster and Mike Warner. "Mike," I said, "Robert, give him a minute with his lawyer, will you?"

They both nodded, got up, and walked away.

I resumed my seat across from Dalt and watched Warner and Robert Lancaster move toward the front of the restaurant. They stopped when they got to the bar area and talked for a minute. Then Warner nodded, gave Robert a little punch on the shoulder, and made a left turn toward the men's room.

I turned to Dalt and said, "Your son has become a man."

Dalt smiled. "He's a good kid, Brady. Thank God I didn't fuck him up the way my old man did me."

"Something to be proud of," I said. "Warner seems like an okay guy."

He nodded. "Mike's a good guy. I called, told him where I was, asked him to come get me, and he came. No questions asked."

I put my elbows on the table and pushed my face at him. "I can see why there might be things you wouldn't want Mike and Robert to hear," I said. "But God damn it, Dalt, you can't lie to me. I'm your lawyer. We've been through all this before. You know it's all confidential." I looked hard at him. "So let's have it. Who do you owe money to, and how much?"

He blinked at me. "Brady," he said, "I'm telling you the truth. I promised Jess I'd quit when I asked her to marry me, and I've kept my word. I have no idea what those thugs wanted."

"Next time they won't pull their punches," I said. "You understand that, right?"

"Of course I do."

"They might kill you."

He gave his head a little shake. "Believe me, I understand that."

"So don't fuck with me."

"I'm not fucking with you," he said. "I have no idea what this is all about. That's why I need you."

"They must've said something."

He shook his head. "They didn't say much. They had me on the ground, kicking me and grunting and swearing, calling me a fucker and a cocksucker, and I've got my arms around my head trying to cover my face, you know? Trying to survive?"

"They didn't say anything about money?"

12

"It seemed like I was supposed to know what they wanted."

"Look," I said. "You had Robert call me at home, drag me away from my girlfriend and my ball game—why? So you could lie to me? What the hell is going on?"

"I don't blame you for what you're thinking," he said. "But I'm not gambling, Brady, I swear. I don't owe anybody anything." He looked down at the tabletop for a moment, then lifted his head and looked into my eyes. "It makes no sense. I don't know what's going on, and I'm scared, and that's why I called you. Because you're my friend and my lawyer, and I couldn't think of anybody else who could help me."

I stared at him. He looked right back at me. His eyes were full of innocence and outrage.

"What did you tell them at the hospital?" I said.

"About this?" He touched his face.

I nodded.

"I said I fell down some stairs."

"They believed you?"

He shrugged. "They didn't argue with me. What do they care?"

"If they knew it was an assault," I said, "they'd have to report it to the police. Which is what we're going to do. Right now. We'll go together. Give them the best descriptions you can. They'll probably have a good idea who these guys are."

"I can't give them any descriptions. What am I gonna tell them—three guys, one had a wart or something on his face, they attacked me in a parking lot and called me a fucker? They'll nod and take notes and make me fill out a report, and next thing you know they'll interrogate me, what I'm into, who I owe money to, and they'll figure out that I've got a history, and just like you, they won't believe me, and I'll end up being a suspect instead of a victim. You know that."

13

"We should report it anyway."

He shook his head. "Can't do that," he said. "No police."

"Why the hell not?"

He shrugged. "My mother, just for one thing. Not to mention my wife."

"Your mother the judge."

"Yes. Both of them. They'll believe I'm back into the casino thing again. They'll assume I'm lying. Getting beat up in a parking lot? Police reports?" He shook his head. "My mother's a judge. I've done enough to her. I can't do that to her reputation."

"You and Jess getting along all right?"

"Sure. Fine." He shrugged.

"Okay. None of my business." I leaned back in the booth and folded my arms across my chest. "Well, I just ran out of ideas. You don't want to make a report to the police, you want to lie to your wife and mother, not to mention your lawyer and your son, I don't know why you even called me, because I don't know how else to advise you. Get out of town for a while, I guess."

"There must be somebody you can talk to," he said. "You know everybody. Can't you figure out who these guys are, talk to them, tell them it's a mistake, make them understand it's not me they're after, get it straightened out?"

I smiled. "I'm just a family lawyer, Dalt. Divorces and estates. That's about it."

"You've been involved in lots of other things," he said.

"Not by choice," I said.

"You're my friend."

I looked up and saw Warner and Robert approaching us. I held up my hand, and they nodded and stopped.

I leaned across the table. "If I find out you're lying to me, I will no longer be your lawyer. Or your friend. Understand?"

He nodded. "Yes. I'm not lying."

14

I narrowed my eyes at him. He stared right back at me.

"Okay," I said.

"Okay, what?"

"I'll try to get a sit-down with Vincent Russo."

"Russo, huh?" said Dalt. "I thought he was—"

I nodded. "He's presumably retired. But if somebody orders his goons to beat you up because he thinks you owe him money, if it's not Russo himself, he'll know who, because he knows everything. If he can't tell me what's going on, you're on your own, and then you should seriously think about moving to Canada."

Dalt gave me a crooked smile. "Canada doesn't sound like such a bad idea, goons or no goons, except I doubt Jess will go for it. You'll talk to Russo?"

"I'll see what I can do."

"Thanks, man."

I waved my hand at Warner and Robert, and they came over and stood beside the booth. "You guys get it all straightened out?" Warner said.

"We're working on it," I said. I looked at Dalt. "So what are you going to tell Jess?"

"I guess I'll tell her I got mugged."

"That's not exactly the truth," I said.

"Close enough," he said. He gave Robert and Warner a crooked just-between-us-guys grin. "You shouldn't lie to your brother-in-law or your son or your lawyer, I know. But your wife's a different story. You guys'll back me up, right?"

They both shrugged.

On the sidewalk outside the restaurant, we all shook hands. Warner and Dalt turned left to head for the parking garage where Warner had left his car. I turned right to go home, and Robert fell in beside me.

We walked toward the Common. I assumed Robert was headed for the T station at Park Street.

"So what's going to happen?" he said.

"They got the wrong man," I said. "I'll try to get it straightened out."

"Can you do that?"

"I don't know. Maybe."

"I hope so," he said.

I handed him one of my business cards. "In case you think of something," I said. "Or just feel like talking. Give me a call."

He looked at the card, then stuck it in his pants pocket. "Okay. Thanks."

We walked in silence for a few minutes. Then Robert said, "I hated you for a long time, you know."

I turned and looked at him. "Me? Why?"

"I was just a kid. In my mind it was you who told him to give me up. I hardly ever saw my father."

"I was just the lawyer," I said.

"I know. It was easier to hate you than to hate him."

"And now?"

He shrugged. "I guess it wasn't your fault."

THREE

A little before eight the next morning, I was sitting at the picnic table with my second mug of coffee and Henry was sitting alertly beside me eyeing the chickadees in the feeders when Evie came out. She had a glass of orange juice in one hand and a half-eaten bagel in the other. Her auburn hair was brushed glossy and tied back in a loose ponytail with a green silk scarf. She wore an off-white blouse with a slender gold chain at her throat, a narrow blue skirt that didn't quite make it down to her delicious knees, and high heels that showed off her slim, strong calves.

I gave her a whistle, and she smiled quickly. "I'm late," she said. "Why didn't you wake me up?" She sat across from me and took a bite from her bagel.

"I figured you needed your sleep," I said. "You were tossing and turning and mumbling all night."

She looked up at me. "Sorry I ruined your sleep."

"That's not what I meant."

She shrugged. "I've got to run a damn staff meeting at nine. I hate it when I have to rush around in the morning."

17

Evie was an administrator at the Beth-Israel hospital. A big part of her job seemed to be holding meetings.

"Listen," I said. "How about we go out to dinner tonight?"

"How come?"

I looked at her. "Something bothering you, honey?"

"I don't think so. Why?"

"You don't seem very pleased at the idea of eating out. You didn't kiss me when you came out just now. You've seemed kind of grouchy lately."

"You didn't exactly jump up to kiss me."

I reached across the table and gave her cheek a caress. "You're right," I said. "I love you."

"I know," she said. "Where do you want to eat?"

"How about Nola's?"

"Huh?" She narrowed her eyes at me. "Nola's Trattoria, you mean? In the North End?"

I nodded. "We ate there once. You loved their food."

She narrowed her eyes at me. "What's up, Brady?"

"What do you mean?"

"Nola's is that Mafia guy's restaurant. Russo. You took me there because you wanted to talk to him about something. He gave me the creeps, the way he looked at me. He's got snakey eyes. I think you only brought me there for some kind of disguise or something, so it'd look like you weren't really there to talk business."

"Russo was utterly charmed by you," I said.

"Yeah," she said, "that's what I mean. That's what this is about, right? You want something from him, and you think he'll be more cooperative if I'm with you."

"Anybody would be."

She flashed me a quick, sarcastic smile.

"Come on," I said. "Lighten up. The food's good, right?"

"We can do it," she said, "but it'd be nice sometime to go out to eat without another agenda, you know? Just you and me?"

"I do have an agenda tonight," I said. "You're right about that. But we'll still have good food. It'll be a nice evening. I just have a question for Vincent Russo."

"This have something to do with where you went last night instead of coming to bed?"

I nodded. "It does, yes," I said. "If you don't want to go, you don't have to. I'll go by myself."

"No, no. I'll go. It'll be fine." She glanced at her wristwatch. "Shit. Call me a cab, would you? I've gotta do my eyes."

I spent the morning at the district court in Concord, had lunch with my client at the Concord Inn, and didn't get to my office in Copley Square until two-thirty that afternoon.

After Julie gave me my messages and a stack of letters and documents to read and sign, I went into my office and called Dalton Lancaster at his restaurant.

When he answered, I said, "You got home okay, huh?"

"Mike dropped me off at my door."

"So how are we feeling today?"

"I can't speak for you," he said, "but me, I feel like I got run over by a school bus. Luckily, the doctor gave me a prescription. Percodans. They're pretty nice."

"But you went to work."

"I had to get the hell out of the house," he said. "Jess was driving me crazy."

"What'd you tell her?"

"Told her I got mugged, like you and I agreed."

"I didn't agree to that," I said. "I'd never advise you to lie to your wife."

"She noticed I was still wearing my watch. She didn't say anything, but I don't think she believes me."

"Yeah, well," I said. "It *is* a lie."

"So what'm I supposed to do?"

"Avoid parking lots," I said.

"You gonna talk to Vincent Russo?"

"I've got a reservation at his restaurant for seven-thirty tonight."

"I don't owe anybody money, Brady."

"I'm curious to see what Vinnie Russo's gonna say about that."

The year's longest day, the summer solstice, was a week away, and at seven o'clock that Wednesday evening in June it was still as bright as noontime on Beacon Hill. A cool easterly breeze was blowing off the ocean and wafting through the city, and Evie and I decided to walk to Nola's—up the hill on Mt. Vernon Street and down the other side on Bowdoin behind the State House, along Cambridge Street, then past the JFK Federal Building and under the expressway to Hanover Street. It took less than half an hour to stroll from the old Boston Brahmin bricks and cobblestones and antique doorknockers of Beacon Hill to the twisty Italian streets of the North End, redolent of oregano and Parmesan and garlic, where, as the kids say, it was a whole 'nother world.

Nicholas, who was whatever the Italian equivalent of maître d' would be called, greeted us inside the door with a quick bow. "Mr. Coyne," he said, "and Miss Banyon. We are honored. Please, this way."

He led us to a table for two by the front window, the only unoccupied seats in the place that I noticed. He pulled out

Evie's chair and held it for her. She smiled up at him over her shoulder as she sat. Nickie was dark and smooth and young and ridiculously handsome in his white shirt and puffy sleeves and gold chain and tight-fitting black pants. A young James Caan, with black curls on his forehead and perfect white teeth and a dimpled chin.

Vincent Russo once told me that Nickie was his favorite nephew, his sister Estelle's youngest, a sweet, biddable boy, but not bright enough for the Business, by which he meant his various illegal enterprises, loan sharking among them. So Russo was setting Nickie up at Nola's, and as soon as the boy learned how to keep the restaurant profitable—and how to cooperate with the various Russo relatives and associates who might need to move money through it and preempt it occasionally for discreet meetings—Uncle Vin would turn ownership over to him.

Meanwhile, Vincent Russo occupied the office in back. He claimed to be retired from the Business. Maybe so. But I happened to know that the FBI had not removed the surveillance camera that they'd been running from a rented room across the street for the past six years, and they still had a tap on the restaurant telephones, even though they knew that these days everybody did Business on cell phones.

Of course, Russo had known about the cameras and phone taps from Day One. He would've been insulted if they ever removed them.

Maybe the old man himself was pulling back from the Business, but he was still consorting with Businessmen.

Nickie told us that our waitperson would be Diane. He gave us menus and a wine list, bowed, smiled at Evie, and oozed away.

Evie leaned across the table. "He's astonishingly pretty, isn't he?" she whispered.

"Gorgeous," I said. "Should I be jealous?"

"Oh, absolutely."

Diane, our waitress, brought us a bottle of expensive Chianti compliments of Mr. Russo. She was quite astonishing herself, in a big-brown-eyed, dimpled-cheeks, short-black-haired, busty sort of way. She wore a low-cut peasant blouse and a narrow midthigh black skirt, and she had not the slightest suggestion of an Italian accent. She told us she'd grown up in Peterborough, New Hampshire, spent two years at Brewster Academy in Wolfeboro, and was now a junior at Boston College majoring in math.

Diane uncorked the wine bottle, set the cork on the table by my elbow, and splashed a little Chianti into my glass. I sniffed the cork, stuck my nose into the glass, sniffed and swirled, took a sip, chewed it, and smiled up at her. "Exquisite," I said. "It begins with a wisecrack and finishes with a grin."

Across from me, Evie rolled her eyes at my pantomime. She knew that I didn't know squat about wine.

After Diane had poured the wine and left to fetch our antipasti, Evie said, "Okay. It's a draw. Nickie and Diane. They're terribly beautiful, both of them, aren't they?"

"Mere children," I said. "In the category of beauty, they are not to be mentioned in the same sentence as Evelyn Banyon."

Evie couldn't hold back her smile. "You'll be rewarded for that, I promise," she said. "Wait'll we get home."

"I'm just calling 'em as I see 'em, babe."

She rolled her eyes. "You gotta be blind."

I reached across the table and touched her hand. "Thanks for coming with me."

"It's nice," she said. "It's just . . ." She tilted her head toward the back of the restaurant, indicating Vincent Russo's office.

"We'll go to Hamersley's next week," I said, "just you and me, no agenda except wine and food and seduction."

She smiled and squeezed my hand. "The seduction part is working already."

I squeezed back. "Are you feeling better today?"

"Sure," she said. "I'm fine. Tired, that's all. Lots of stress at work. It fills my head, keeps me awake."

"That's all?"

"There should be more?"

"Have some more wine."

An hour later we were sipping our *cappuccinos* and nibbling from plates of melons and grapes and cheeses when Nickie came over and put two snifters on the table. "Frangelico," he said with a little bow. "Compliments of Mr. Russo."

"I'd like to thank Mr. Russo in person," I said.

"I'll let him know," said Nickie.

Five minutes later Nickie returned, this time pushing Vincent Russo in a wheelchair. Russo looked shrunken, as if his suit and shirt were several sizes too big for him. His skin was the pasty white of a man who spent his days and nights under fluorescent lighting.

Nickie parked him at our table. "Want something, Uncle Vin?"

Russo twisted his neck and looked back at Nickie. "Chianti," he rasped in a voice that sounded like slabs of concrete grinding against each other. Then he turned and blinked at Evie as if he were surprised to see her sitting there. "Miss Banyon," he said. "You are sunshine in the gloom of my poor establishment. Thank you for coming."

Evie gave him her best smile. Evie's best smile is utterly dazzling, and only I would notice the effort behind this one. "The food was wonderful," she said. "Thank you for the liqueur. It's so nice to see you again."

23

He turned to me, lifted his left hand off the arm of his wheelchair, and held it out to me. I noticed that his right hand lay motionless in his lap. It was twisted into a claw. "Mr. Coyne," said Russo. "You honor us. You and your beautiful lady."

I gripped his hand awkwardly in both of mine. It felt like a pigskin glove full of matchsticks. "How are you doing, Mr. Russo?" I said. "I heard . . ."

He took his hand back and wobbled it in the air. "Getting old is a sonofabitch, excuse me, Miss Banyon. If it ain't one thing it's something else, huh?" He tapped his head, still using his left hand. "Nothin' wrong up here. They tell me that's what counts. And you, Mr. Coyne? You are well?"

I shrugged. "My health is fine."

Russo looked at me from the depths of his black, hooded eyes. "I hear a *but* in your voice. Your business? Your family? I hope your family is well. Your two boys."

"My boys are excellent," I said, cringing at the idea that Vincent Russo even knew I had two sons, "and business is okay. I'm a little concerned about a friend of mine. It preoccupies me. I'm sorry that it shows." I waved it away with the back of my hand. "I don't want to bother you with my insignificant worries."

"Perhaps I know your friend?"

"Come to think of it," I said, "perhaps you do. Like you, he's in the restaurant business. His name is Dalton Lancaster. He manages the Boston Scrod."

"The Boston Scrod, eh?" Russo blinked, then shook his head. "No, I guess not. Your friend Lancaster, he has troubles, huh?"

"Three men jumped him in a parking lot last night," I said. "They kicked him in the face."

"They robbed him?"

"No," I said. "It was apparently a warning."

"A warning," said Russo.

"They didn't quite say it," I said, "but it probably had something to do with a debt."

"And he was badly hurt?"

I shook my head. "Not this time."

Russo shook his head. "Uncivilized," he said, "kicking a man in the face. But on the other hand, failing to pay a debt is also dishonorable. What a world, huh?"

"The thing is," I said, "my friend Lancaster swears he doesn't owe anybody any money." I waved my hand. "Well, it's no concern of yours. It weighs on my heart, that's all. I'm worried for my friend. He cannot pay off a debt he doesn't owe, and then what will happen to him?"

"I see your point," said Russo. "Please convey my best wishes to your friend, as one restaurant man to another. It's a hard business. You might suggest to him that it would be wise to take taxis, avoid parking lots for a while, eh?" He tried to smile, but only half of his face participated.

"Yes," I said, "I told him exactly the same thing. Coming from both his lawyer and a fellow restaurateur, perhaps the advice will make sense to him."

Russo chuckled. He reached over and gripped my arm with his left hand. Then he tilted his head toward Evie. "Come back soon, Miss Banyon. We will always have a table by the window for you."

She smiled. "Thank you, Mr. Russo."

He lifted his hand, then let it fall back on the arm of his wheelchair. "Mr. Coyne. Don't be a stranger, huh?"

I nodded. "I won't."

Russo half turned his head, and Nickie was there at his wheelchair in an instant. He smiled at us with those ridiculously white teeth, then pushed his uncle toward the rear of the restaurant.

When I looked at Evie, she was frowning at me. "Dalton Lancaster got mugged? That's what last night was all about?"

"Not mugged, exactly," I said. "They didn't take anything. It was a warning."

"They think he owes money and he doesn't?"

"So it seems."

"Does that make any sense?"

"Not much," I said.

"So," said Evie, "that's what this—this charade was all about. You and Russo not quite saying what you mean, all this polite concern for each other. You assume it's his thugs who beat up your client. You're asking him to lay off Dalton Lancaster."

"Not exactly," I said. "Russo doesn't do favors like that for people like me. Not favors that involve a debt. Debts are supposed to be matters of honor for both parties. If Dalt really is into him, there's nothing I can do about it. I was just asking Russo to be sure he had the right man before he decided to fracture his skull or rupture his spleen or shoot him in the ear."

"Jesus," she muttered. "Let's get the hell out of here."

FOUR

At four on Friday afternoon I rinsed out the office coffee urn while Julie shut down the computers for the weekend. Megan, Julie's eleven-year-old daughter, had a soccer game that Mommy wanted to see, and I was eager to get home, change out of my office pinstripe and into a pair of jeans and a T-shirt, and have a pitcher of gin-and-tonics waiting for Evie. I'd grill some burgers out on the patio, with bacon and cheddar cheese and Bermuda onion. Evie loved them. Called them Cholesterol Sandwiches. The hated Yankees were in town, and even Evie seemed excited about watching the game. We'd bring out the battery-powered TV, and she'd sit on my lap, and who knew what might happen between innings.

I said good-bye to Julie on the sidewalk, then crossed the street and ducked into the parking garage. I was walking down the rows of cars to where I'd left mine when somebody grabbed me by my right biceps and said, "Just take it easy, Mr. Coyne. You're gonna come with us, okay? Don't yell or nothing, please."

He was a couple of inches shorter than me and about twice as

27

wide. Black hair, black eyebrows, black mustache. He had a shiny round mole beside his nose. It was pink, about the size of a mothball. When you looked at his face, it was hard not to stare at the mole.

Dalt had said that one of the thugs who beat him up sported a mole on his face.

Then another hand grabbed my left arm, and I felt something ramming against my kidneys. This guy barely came up to my shoulder. He was half-bald, even though he didn't look much over thirty. His scalp was as deeply tanned as his face.

"If that's a gun you're poking at me," I told him, "you can put it away. I won't yell. What do you want?"

"We're gonna go for a ride, Mr. Coyne. Nothin' to worry about." The gun stayed there.

"I'm not worried," I said. "I'm annoyed. There's no need for this bullshit. You guys aren't planning to kick me in the face the way you did Dalton Lancaster, are you?"

They didn't answer.

They were hauling me along between them, one on each arm, as if I were a big sack of trash. I was tempted to go limp and let my feet drag, but I thought it would be undignified.

"If Vincent Russo wants to talk to me," I said, "all he has to do is ask."

My two escorts said nothing. I tried to twist my arms out of their grips, but they just held tighter.

They walked me over to a dark sedan that was parked a few slots past mine. It was puffing gray exhaust into the dim yellow light of the concrete parking garage. They opened the back door and shoved me in. The guy with the mole got in beside me, and the bald guy went around and climbed in the other side, so that I was sandwiched tight between two bulky thugs in shiny suits. The one behind the wheel made three.

It was useful, if not comforting, to know what they were capable of.

They might have been hoodlums who believed they were above the law, but they couldn't do anything about the bumper-to-bumper Friday-afternoon traffic on Boylston Street, and it took more than half an hour for them to stop-and-go a couple of miles through the city to the North End.

They continued past Hanover Street, where Vincent Russo had his office in the back of his restaurant, and took a right onto Salem Street. It was a winding one-way street barely wide enough for a vehicle to maneuver past the parked cars at the curb. After a minute, we took a left onto an even narrower street, then another left into an alley that paralleled Salem, and pulled up beside a Dumpster.

They steered me up onto a loading platform and through the back door, which opened into a storeroom lined with shelves of cardboard boxes and wooden crates and industrial-sized jars and cans.

A door opened to a steep stairway. We climbed to the second floor and stopped outside another door. The bald thug knocked, and a minute later somebody inside cracked it open. They exchanged a few grumbled words, and then the guy with the mole shoved me into the room.

Seated behind a desk was a bulky fortyish man. His scalp was tanned mahogany under his thinning black hair, and his eyes were close-set and piggy.

This was Paulie Russo, Vincent's son and, according to the rumors, his heir apparent, the godfather-in-waiting. He'd been working his way up the family career ladder since middle school. He started out collecting payoffs, got promoted to kicking people in the face, and graduated to capping them with a .22 automatic pistol.

A younger man leaned against the wall behind Paulie Russo's left shoulder. The bulge of a shoulder holster spoiled the drape of his suit.

My two escorts, the guy with the mole and the short bald guy, half-dragged me up to Russo's desk, still gripping me hard above my elbows.

Russo waved the back of his hand at them. "You can leggo of him."

They released their grip on me, moved away, and stood on opposite sides of the room with their backs against the wall. The third man, the one who'd been driving the car, had also come in, and he was standing with his back to the door we'd just come through. That made one lawyer, four thugs, and one godfather-in-training.

"Get Mr. Coyne a chair," said Paulie Russo.

Almost instantly a wooden chair without arms was shoved against the back of my legs, and hands pushed down on my shoulders.

I sat. "Where's Vincent?" I said.

"He's not here," said Russo. "I'm here. This ain't about him. We gotta talk."

"Paulie," I said, "your goons here, they treated me disrespectfully, and it pisses me off. Your father would never allow me to be treated this way."

He lifted his hand and let it fall. "Well," he said, "tough shit, okay? You want some wine?"

"No," I said, "I don't want to drink with you. I don't want to make conversation with you. I don't care how your family's doing, and I don't intend to tell you how mine is. Just tell me whatever you've got to tell me so I can get the hell out of here."

"There's no reason to be hostile, Mr. Coyne. It's just business. Come on. Let's have a drink, be civilized." There was an open wine bottle by his elbow on the desk. He filled two glasses and pushed one toward me. "Take a sip, Mr. Coyne. It's a nice Chianti."

I made no move to pick up the glass.

Paulie Russo stared at me.

I stared back at him.

After a minute he shrugged, picked up his wineglass, held it up to me, said, "*Salute,*" and took a gulp. Then he set the glass down on his desk. He leaned back in his chair and folded his arms. "Refusing to drink a little wine with me," he said. "That's not respectful. You would not disrespect my old man that way."

"Your old man," I said, "never sent goons to accost me in a parking garage."

"I don't disrespect you," he said. "If my associates treated you with disrespect, I'm sorry, okay?"

"They're your associates," I said. "They represent you. How they treat me is how you treat me."

He bowed his head. "I apologize for them." He touched my wineglass with his forefinger and inched it closer to me. "Come on, Mr. Coyne. Have a drink."

"No," I said. "Just say what you want to say."

He inhaled and exhaled deeply, as if he were struggling to keep his patience. "Okay," he said. "Fine. So listen. Your friend, there. Your client, huh? Lancaster. He's in some deep shit."

"I know," I said, "that these associates of yours"—I waved my hand to include the shiny-suited men in the room—"they followed Dalton Lancaster into a parking lot the other night. They knocked him down, and they kicked him, and they threatened to kill him. So, yes, that, by my definition, would be considered deep shit."

"I don't know nothing about anybody kicking somebody,"

said Paulie. "But that Lancaster has got an obligation, and if he was a man of honor he'd admit it, don'tcha think?"

"Lancaster says he doesn't owe you money," I said. "You or anybody else."

Russo shrugged. "I don't want to argue with you. Your friend, or client, or whatever the fuck he is, whatever he wants to tell you, nothing I can do about it." He shook his head as if it were all too confusing to comprehend. Then he narrowed his eyes at me. "But listen. Do you think I'm the kind of man who'd send three of my most important associates to escort you here so I could lie to you? That make any sense to you?"

"I'm not sure what kind of man you are, Paulie."

"I'm a man of honor. Like you."

"So you're trying to tell me that I should trust you and not my client?"

He put his forearms on his desk and leaned toward me. "He's got a fuckin' obligation, Mr. Coyne, and if he don't like it, maybe he should take it up with the judge." He straightened up, took a sip of wine, and narrowed his eyes at me.

"The judge?" I said.

Paulie raised his head and looked over my shoulder to where the guy with the mole was standing. "You explained to him about the judge the other night, right?"

I turned around.

Mole-face was nodding and shrugging at the same time. "Sure, Paulie. 'Course we did."

I turned back to Paulie. "You mean Dalt? When these goons beat him up?"

"Ask him, for Chrissake." He flipped his hand. "I don't know nothing about anybody getting beat up."

"So tell me," I said. "How did Dalton Lancaster incur this, um, obligation?"

Paulie Russo grinned. "Incur, huh?" He looked around at the four men who were holding up the walls. "You hear that? Incur? Smart fuckin' lawyer, huh?"

The four stooges all remained stone-faced.

When Russo looked back at me, he was no longer grinning. "Incur. Fuck." He narrowed his eyes at me. "When an apple falls off a tree, it goes straight down. You understand what I'm saying, Mr. Coyne?"

"I believe you intended a metaphor, Paulie. I'm impressed."

He grinned. "Good. Now it's up to you."

"Up to me? What the hell is that supposed to mean?"

He flapped his hands. "You're a smart lawyer. You can figure it out." He pointed his finger at me. "You got a week." He lifted his chin and looked over my shoulder. "Take Mr. Coyne wherever he wants to go. Be polite and treat him with respect, for Chrissake." Then he stood up and walked out of the room.

The thug who'd been holding up the wall behind Paulie glared at me for a minute, then followed him.

Once again the bald thug and the mole-faced thug gripped my upper arms. The thug who'd been driving opened the door and held it for us. They urged me out of the chair and steered me out of Paulie Russo's office, through the storeroom, and out the back door into the alley, where they shoved me into the backseat of the sedan.

It took about half an hour through the thinning late-afternoon Boston traffic to drive from Paulie Russo's office in the North End to the parking garage outside my office in Copley Square. From one world to another.

No one said a word the whole time.

They pulled over at the curb. The mole-faced thug slid out and stood there holding the door.

I got out, and Mole-face got back in, and the sedan pulled away and disappeared in the traffic.

I looked at my watch. It was ten after six. The whole event had taken about two hours, most of which was spent getting there and back.

I sat on a bench in the plaza by the public library, watched the secretaries and professional women in their high heels and short skirts stroll past, and waited for my blood pressure to return to normal. Then I pulled out my cell phone and called the Boston Scrod.

I asked to speak to Mr. Lancaster, and a minute later Dalt said, "This is Dalton Lancaster."

"It's Brady," I said. "How're you feeling today?"

"A little better, actually. My ribs are sore as hell, hurts to breathe, and my face is turning purple. It scares people, ruins their appetites. I'm mostly hanging out in my office. Hiding, you might say. You got some news for me? You talk to Vincent Russo?"

"Evie and I ate at his restaurant the other night," I said. "Didn't learn anything. This afternoon I had a sit-down with Paulie Russo, Vincent's son and heir. Paulie's the one with the three goons, including the guy with the mole on his face. Paulie says you have an obligation, by which I assume he means money."

"Jesus Christ," said Dalt. "I never even met Paulie Russo."

"I'm just wondering if you want to tell me anything that you didn't tell me the other night."

"You still think I'm lying to you, Brady? You think I'd lie to my lawyer?"

"People lie to their lawyers all the time."

"I'm not lying," he said. "I told you. I'm not gambling anymore, and I don't owe anybody any money, and I don't know what the hell this is all about. I don't know why you won't believe me."

"Did those three goons say something about your mother?"

"My mother?"

"They didn't mention the judge when they were whaling on you?"

He was quiet for a minute. Then he said, "I don't know. I don't think so. I'm not sure what they said. Mostly they just grunted and called me a fucker. I told you. I was on the ground with my arms around my head. I was just trying to survive. If they had some message, I didn't get it. Why are you asking about my mother?"

"Paulie mentioned her."

"Christ. What about her?"

"He said you should take it up with the judge."

"What's that supposed to mean?"

I said nothing.

"Oh," said Dalt after a minute. "Jesus." I heard him blow out a breath. "That's just great."

"You should talk to her," I said. "Tell her what happened."

"She'll never believe me," Dalt said. "I can't do that. Anyway, I don't see what the point is." He hesitated. "She respects you, Brady. Maybe you . . ."

"Sure, okay," I said. "I'll do it. I'll talk to her."

"This is all crazy," he said.

"Let's see if I can get it straightened out," I said. "I'll keep you posted. Take it easy. Oh, wait. Do you happen to have Robert's phone number handy?"

"Robert?"

"I walked with him to the Park Street station the other night

35

and we got to talking. We thought we might get together some time, but we neglected to exchange phone numbers."

"He's a pretty good kid, huh? Hang on. I got it right here on my cell phone." There was a pause, and then he recited a number to me. "Maybe sometime we can go fishing, the three of us."

"That would be fun."

"He used to love fishing," Dalt said. "When he was a kid."

"I'll mention it when I talk to him."

After I disconnected from Dalt, I tried Robert's number. When he answered, I said, "It's Brady Coyne. I'd like to buy you a cup of coffee."

"Oh, hey," he said. "Coffee, huh? Like when?"

"Like now. Where are you?"

"I just got out of my Russian lit class. I'm taking a couple summer courses, trying to get caught up. What's up?"

"We need to talk."

"This really isn't a good time," he said. "Let's make it next week some time?"

"No," I said. "Let's make it now."

He didn't say anything for a minute. Then he said, "Sounds ominous. This about my father?"

"Yes."

"Is he all right? Did something else happen?"

"Where can you meet me?"

"Where are you coming from?"

"Copley Square," I said. "I've got my car."

"Well, there's a Dunkin' Donuts right here on Comm Ave just before you get to the BU Bridge. Know where I mean?"

"I know it. I'll be there. Give me fifteen or twenty minutes."

"Is my dad all right?"

"So far," I said.

FIVE

I disconnected with Robert and called my home number. When Evie didn't answer, I tried her cell.

"Brady?" she said. She sounded a little breathless.

"Hi, hon. You all right?"

"I'm okay," she said. "What's up?"

"You're not home yet."

"Almost. Just crossing the Common. I'll be there in five minutes if I don't get beheaded by a Frisbee. Sorry I'm a little late. Can't wait to get out of my bra and pantyhose. Maybe you can help. You got the G 'n' Ts all made?"

"No," I said. "Something came up. I'm not home yet, either, and it's going to be another hour or two. I'm sorry."

"What's wrong?"

"Nothing," I said. "Just a client thing. Make yourself a drink, relax. I'll be there."

"Brady," she said, "it's Friday."

"I know, babe. Can't be helped. I'll be there as soon as I can."

I snapped my phone shut, stuck it into my pocket, got into my car, and headed for the Dunkin' Donuts on Commonwealth

Avenue near the BU Bridge. I took the back way out on Huntington Avenue and made a big loop, skirting Kenmore Square, which I knew would be gridlocked with Fenway Park traffic. The game would start in about an hour.

I got lucky and found a car pulling away from a meter on a side street off Commonwealth. I grabbed the slot, got out, locked up, fed quarters into the meter, and walked over to the Dunkin'.

The place was about half full. I spotted Robert Lancaster in his black T-shirt and sunglasses sitting at a table against the wall with two other people. One of them was a dark-skinned Hispanic-looking guy with a mustache and goatee and close-cut black hair. He was wearing a New York Knicks basketball jersey. Number 14. He had muscular arms and thick shoulders. Sitting between the two guys was a pretty blond girl wearing a backwards baseball cap. They were all sipping through straws from tall Styrofoam cups.

I went over and stood beside their table.

"Hey," said Robert.

"Hey," I said.

He waved at an empty seat. "Join us."

I remained standing and looked at the dark guy and the blond girl. She appeared to be about Robert's age. The other one looked older. "I'm Brady Coyne," I said.

"Sorry," said Robert. "These are my friends. Ozzie and Becca."

I leaned over the table and shook hands with both of them, then turned to Robert. "Reinforcements?"

He frowned. "Huh?"

"We need to talk. Just the two of us. You and me. I'm going to get some coffee. I want your friends gone by the time I get back."

Ozzie frowned up at me. "Hey, man—"

"Nothing personal," I said.

"These are my friends," said Robert. "I don't have any secrets from them."

"I do," I said.

He looked at me for a minute, then shrugged and turned to his friends. "I'll catch up with you guys later, okay?"

Ozzie and Becca stood up. Ozzie was a big guy, six-three or -four, I guessed. Becca, on the other hand, had the compact body of a gymnast. Mutt and Jeff.

Robert and Ozzie exchanged a complicated handshake, and then Robert hugged Becca and kissed her on the mouth.

I went over to the counter and got a cup of black coffee. When I got back to the table, Ozzie and Becca were gone.

I sat across from Robert. "That Ozzie's quite a large fellow."

"He's on the crew. He trains all the time." He looked at me through his sunglasses. "What's this about?"

"Tell me about your friends."

He shrugged. "Becca's sort of my girlfriend. She used to be Ozzie's. We hang out together."

"You and your girlfriend and her former boyfriend."

"We're all cool."

"You stole Ozzie's girlfriend and you're still friends?"

He grinned. "Something like that."

"And you figured if your friends were here you wouldn't have to talk about anything important with me, right?"

"It wasn't like that." He looked at me. "So I guess this isn't just some friendly cup of coffee here, me and my father's lawyer. You got some information for me?"

"No," I said. "You've got information for me."

"I don't know what you mean, Mr. Coyne."

"Take off your sunglasses."

39

"Huh? Why?"

I reached across the table and took them off.

The skin around his left eye was the greenish yellow of an old bruise. It was still puffy, and the eye itself was bloodshot.

"How much?" I said.

"How much what?"

"How much do you owe?"

He picked up his sunglasses and put them back on. "How did you know?"

"Something Paulie Russo said."

"Who's Paulie Russo?"

"The man you borrowed money from."

"Look," said Robert. "I don't know any Paulie Russo, and I don't want to talk about this, okay?"

"No," I said. "It's not okay. Paulie Russo is a mobster, Robert. A big-time mafioso. He's Boston's Tony Soprano, understand?"

"Jesus." He shook his head. "What did he tell you?"

"He said something like 'the apple falls straight down.' He was going for the cliché about the fruit not falling far from the tree."

"What the hell is that supposed to mean?"

"It means," I said, "that your father had a gambling problem, and now you do, too. So you got in over your head and they beat you up, huh?"

Robert looked down at the table for a minute. Then he looked up at me and nodded. "Three guys, just like with my father. Same guys, I guess. One of 'em had a big wart or something on his face. They punched me and kicked me, gave me three days to come up with the money."

"Obviously you didn't."

"So they went after my father?" he said. "That's what that was about?"

"Of course it was. I bet you figured that out all by yourself."

He looked up at me. "Truthfully, I've been trying not to think about it."

"If you ignore it, it'll go away?"

He shook his head. "I don't know what to do, Mr. Coyne."

"It's not going to go away," I said. "These people don't let debts slide. To them, it's business. They don't care who you are. They'll go after your family."

Robert nodded. "I guess they already did."

"So it's time to think about it."

"I tried to pay them back," he said. "I did my best. I cleaned out my checking account, and I borrowed from Ozzie and Becca and some of my other friends. I met those guys right here—it was Friday, a week ago today—and I gave them almost two thousand dollars, told them I'd get the rest when I could, they needed to give me some more time. They took the money and said it wasn't good enough. Said I'd be hearing from them. Next thing I know, my father's calling me from the emergency room."

"What did you think was going to happen?"

He shook his head. "I don't know. They'd beat me up again, I guess. I never thought they'd go after my father. I was just trying to figure out how I could get some more money."

"Did it occur to you to ask your parents? What about your uncle or your grandmother?"

"Jesus, no. That's the last thing I'd do. Are you serious? After what my family's been through?" He shook his head. "This is my problem. I'll deal with it."

"You're doing a helluva job so far," I said. "Tell me how it happened."

He gave me a crooked half-smile. "Maybe us Lancasters have a gambling gene or something. First my dad, then my cousin, now me. All my life, all I've heard is the evils of gambling.

You'd think it was heroin or something." He shrugged. "I didn't believe it, of course. I started playing poker online my freshman year. You can lose a shitload of money that way, and my credit card got tapped out pretty fast. It was addictive as hell, and you win just often enough to make you think you're pretty good and can win it back, you know?"

"Online?" I said. "The Internet, you mean?"

Robert looked at me as if I were illiterate, which I pretty much was when it came to computer technology. I used e-mail and knew how to look things up on Google, but I still preferred talking on the telephone and buying things in stores.

"There are, I don't know, a dozen or more poker games you can get into online," Robert said. "You sign up, come up with a handle, give 'em your credit card, and you can play. You can play all day and all night. A lot of my friends do that. I know some guys—girls, too, actually—who flunked out because they spent all their time playing online poker, never went to classes."

"What was your handle?"

"Orphan Eight." He shrugged. "I was eight when my parents got divorced. I felt like an orphan, you know?"

I nodded.

"Anyway," he said, "I heard about this live game in Brighton not far from where I live, and it was way better, playing with actual people you can look at, read their tells, figure out who you can bluff. I played there two or three nights a week. They fronted me chips when I didn't have any money, and I never paid much attention to what I owed them. We played no-limit Texas Hold 'Em. I started playing in that game in the spring of my freshman year, and I've been doing it ever since. Two years. Until a couple weeks ago, no one ever said anything about cutting me off or paying them back, so I didn't worry about it."

"You didn't?" I said.

He shrugged. "I didn't think about it. I just figured I'd end up winning as much as I lost, at least, and it wouldn't be a problem."

"That's the kind of thinking that comes with that gambling gene you mentioned," I said. "Did you ever think to ask yourself why they made it so easy for you to go into debt to them?"

Robert looked at me. "What do you mean?"

"Come on," I said. "You're a college man. Figure it out."

He didn't say anything for a minute. Then he nodded. "I know they know who I am. That's how they knew about my father."

I nodded. "And?"

"You mean my grandmother? You think . . . ?"

I shrugged. "They know who all their suckers are. An obligation, the threat of a scandal . . . they're always looking for leverage."

Robert was shaking his head. "I never thought about that."

"So they finally cut you off, huh?" I said.

"Wouldn't even let me in the door. I said, 'Hey, what the hell is going on?' And they just said, 'You better figure it out.'"

"So how much do you owe?"

"About fifty grand, I think."

"You think?"

He looked down at the table. "At least that." He shook his head. "I am fucked." He looked up at me. "What'm I gonna do, Mr. Coyne?"

"Let's convene a family council," I said. "We'll lay it all on the table, get it out in the open, deal with it that way."

"We?"

"I'll help."

He looked at me for a minute. Then he shook his head. "No. I can't do that."

"You got a better idea?"

43

"Any idea is better than that. I'll figure something out. I don't need your help. All I need from you is to promise not to tell anybody."

"It doesn't work that way."

"You're a lawyer, aren't you? You're supposed to keep things people tell you confidential."

"Clients," I said. "You're not my client."

Robert reached across the table and grabbed my wrist. "I wouldn't have told you these things if I thought you wouldn't keep them private between us. Please. Not for me. For my family. It would kill all of them, man."

"It might kill some of them anyway," I said. "Especially you. In case you didn't notice, your old man got the crap kicked out of him the other night."

"I'll take care of it," he said.

I shrugged. "A minute ago you mentioned your cousin. Tell me about him."

"Jimmy?" Robert shook his head. "He was five years older than me. Uncle Mike and Aunt Kimmie's only kid. Jimmy was my hero when I was growing up. Amazing athlete, brilliant student, great-looking dude. He was nice to me. Took me fishing, ball games, stuff like that. Taught me how to play chess. Everybody loved Jimmy. Got accepted at MIT, ended up getting involved with a bunch of math geniuses who invented some kind of system to beat the odds at craps. Jimmy tried to tell me about it once, but I didn't understand. It involved cheating, is all I know. They'd fly out to Vegas just about every weekend, make the rounds of all the casinos. Jimmy used to say the casinos cheated because they always had an edge, so there was nothing wrong with cheating right back at them." He blew out a breath. "You can figure out how it all worked out."

"It never works out well in Las Vegas," I said.

Robert nodded. "One of those MIT guys got beat up so bad he's in some kind of home hooked up to machines, a vegetable for life. A couple of the others are rumored to be living in London or someplace with fake IDs, afraid to come home." He hesitated. "No one knows what happened to Jimmy."

"He disappeared?"

"Uncle Mike thinks he got murdered and they buried him in the desert out there. Aunt Kimmie still believes he's alive somewhere. They've hired private investigators, but they've never learned anything. Now and then they hear a rumor, and they hire another PI, but nothing ever comes of it." He looked at me. "You see why I'm saying it would kill my family?"

I spread my hands. "All the more reason to come clean with them. Think about it."

Robert looked at me for a minute. "Yeah," he said. "I see what you're saying. You're right. Okay. I'll do it. I'll take care of it. It's not your problem. It should come from me."

"You better be serious."

"I am." He took off his sunglasses so that I could see he was looking me straight in the eyes. "It's my responsibility. I'll take care of it. I will. I promise."

"I'll be there if you want," I said.

"It's my thing, Mr. Coyne. My responsibility. Thanks, though." He slid his sunglasses back onto his face.

"You've got a week," I said. "Paulie Russo says he won't do anything for a week, so that's what you've got. If you haven't talked to your family by a week from today, I'm going to do it myself."

"I said I'll do it."

"One thing, though."

"What?" he said.

"I've got to talk to the judge," I said. "Your grandmother."

45

"Oh, God," he said. "Not her, of all people. You can't tell her."

"I won't tell her more than I have to," I said. "That's the best I can do for you. No promises."

"At least tell her not to tell my parents."

"You don't tell Judge Lancaster what to do," I said. "You should know that." I drained my coffee cup, stood up, and held out my hand to Robert Lancaster. "It's time to be a man."

He took my hand. "I know," he said.

As I walked back to where I'd left my car, I tried to convince myself that this was all going to work out, that Robert would actually stand up, take responsibility for himself, and do what he needed to do, and I tried to believe that if he did, Dalt and Jess, and Mike and Kimmie Warner, and Judge Adrienne Lancaster would all rise to the occasion, too.

But addicted gamblers, like drug and alcohol addicts, are victims of their own weaknesses. They lie and steal and rationalize and evade and betray the people who love them, and I had no particular reason to believe that Robert Lancaster would be any different.

And then there was Paulie Russo. I didn't even want to think about him.

Six

By the time I'd wended my way homeward through the Friday-evening traffic, deposited my car in the parking garage at the far end of Charles Street, and walked up the hill to our house on Mt. Vernon Street, the streetlights were winking on and dusk was seeping into the city.

I found Evie slouched in one of our Adirondack chairs out back. Henry was sprawled on the brick patio beside her. The only light came from the kitchen window and the darkening sky. A tall glass sat on the arm of Evie's chair. She was wearing a pair of cutoff jeans and one of my ratty old T-shirts. Her hair hung loose around her shoulders.

She turned up her cheek for a kiss, which I gave her. "Sorry I couldn't get here earlier," I said.

"Me, too. I made the G 'n' Ts." She pointed at the pitcher on the picnic table.

I filled a glass. The ice cubes had shrunk to the size of sugar cubes. I fished out a few and gave them to Henry. He loved to crunch gin-flavored ice cubes between his teeth.

"Mine, too," said Evie. She held out her glass.

I filled it and handed it to her. "How many is this?"

"Huh?" she said. "You got me on a quota?"

"Just wondering how fast I've got to drink to catch up."

"Oh, quite fast," she said.

I laid my jacket on the picnic table, pulled off my necktie, and took the chair beside her. "You must be hungry."

"Not anymore," she said.

I turned to look at her. "You okay?"

"Me? Why wouldn't I be?"

"We kind of had a date," I said. "It's Friday night. I was going to make the drinks, grill some burgers. I crapped out on you."

"It's all right, Brady. You gotta do what you gotta do." She took a long swig of her drink. "You want to talk about it?"

I shook my head.

"Come on," she said. "Tell me a story. Amuse me. Perk me up. Make me laugh."

"It's not a very amusing story."

"I don't care. I want to hear about somebody else's problems."

"You know I'm not supposed to talk about it."

"Yeah," she said, "but I'm your sweetie."

"You certainly are."

"So that makes it different."

"No," I said. "It really doesn't."

"Dalton Lancaster, huh?"

I nodded.

"Anything new?"

I wasn't going to tell Evie how Paulie Russo's goons had grabbed me in the parking garage. She didn't need to know that. "It's just client business, honey."

"You're an old poop," she said.

"I know," I said.

She reached over, touched my cheek with the backs of her fingers, then trickled them down my arm until she found my hand. She gave it a squeeze. "I need to talk to you about something," she said. Her voice was so soft I barely heard her.

I turned to look at her. Her head was bowed so that her long auburn hair curtained her face, and I couldn't see her expression. I reached over and touched her chin.

She turned to look at me. Her eyes were wet.

"Hey," I said.

She tried a smile. It didn't work very well.

I patted my lap. "Come here," I said.

She got up and sat sideways on my lap. She hooked one arm around my neck and pushed her face against my shirt.

I hugged her with both arms. "What is it, babe?" I said.

She shook her head against my chest.

"You're scaring me," I said.

"I'm scared," she said.

I held her tight against me. I could feel her shoulders shaking. I stroked her back. She huddled there, making herself small in my lap. I hugged her and didn't say anything.

After a little while, she picked up the bottom of her T-shirt and wiped her face with it. "I'm better now," she said. "Gin makes me weepy." She adjusted herself on me, reached into one of her pockets, and took out a cigarette box and a plastic lighter. She thumbed open the box, plucked out a cigarette with her teeth, lit it, and blew a long plume of smoke up into the darkness. "Want one?" she said.

"I quit," I said.

"Doesn't answer my question."

"Of course I want one."

"But Mr. Iron Will Coyne won't have one, because you quit."

"I thought you did, too," I said.

"I started again."

"How come?"

"Miss Jell-O Will feels like it, that's all."

"What's going on, honey?"

She puffed on her cigarette. It smelled good.

"I've been kind of grouchy with you lately, right?" she said after a minute.

"I guess so. Kind of."

"I haven't been sleeping well. Feeling shitty. Short-tempered. Complaining all the time."

I didn't say anything.

"It's not fair, I know. I'm sorry." She took another drag on her cigarette. The tip of it glowed orange in the gloom that was gathering in our walled-in backyard garden. "It's not you, Brady."

"Oh, shit," I said.

She tilted her head back and looked at me. "What?"

"Now is when you say, 'It's not you. It's me.' And then you tell me you can't do it anymore, that I'm a great guy but it's not working, or you—"

Evie put her hand on my mouth. "Stop it. I wasn't going to say anything like that."

"Oh," I said. "Well, that's a relief."

"I think it's working okay."

"Good. I'm glad."

"Don't you?"

I nodded. "Better than okay, I would've said."

"Even when I'm distant and grouchy?"

"Sure," I said. "That goes with the territory."

She was quiet for a minute. "There's a big fat *but* coming at you."

"Yeah," I said. "I figured."

"It distracts me. Preoccupies me. Makes me not pay attention to you. Makes me treat you worse than you deserve. I wish it didn't, but it does. It's how I am. That's what I mean when I say it's me, not you."

"What's the *but,* honey?"

She took a deep breath and blew it out through her mouth. "It's Daddy."

"Your father?"

She nodded. "He's . . . sick."

"Bad?"

"I don't know. Yes, I think so. I'm assuming the worst. I keep telling myself he's a rock, he'll be all right, but deep down, I know it's not true. He's not going to be okay. I'm brimming with worst-case scenarios. They keep me awake. They come in my dreams. I try to be positive, but being positive seems stupid and unrealistic. So I'm being negative. And it's eating me up."

I couldn't think of anything to say. So I said nothing.

"My mother called me at work a couple of weeks ago," Evie said after a minute. "I never talk to her, you know that. We don't like each other very much. I didn't know she and my father were even in touch. They've been divorced for almost twenty years. So this was a big deal, her calling me. So I answer the phone, and she says, 'It's your mother,' like that. And I go, 'Oh. Hi. How are you?' And she says, 'Your father's sick. I thought you'd want to know.' Just like that. She doesn't have a clue about other people's feelings. Anyway, she didn't have any details, so I called him. Daddy. I expected him to laugh it off with his usual macho bluster. But he didn't. He just said, 'Yeah, I haven't been feeling so hot lately.' He sounded depressed and scared and lonely, like I never heard him before. I mean, that's the opposite of him. He's always carefree and brave and self-contained, you know?"

I nodded. I'd only met Ed Banyon once, but that was the way

51

I remembered him, too. He was a strong, happy man at peace with his life.

Evie took a puff of her cigarette, then dropped the butt into her gin-and-tonic glass. "He didn't want to talk about it. But finally I got him to tell me. He's been losing weight. He's nauseated all the time. No energy. No enthusiasm for anything. Even talking to me, he didn't sound like he was happy to hear from me. You know how we are. Daddy and I always have fun."

Evie's father lived on a houseboat in Sausalito, just over the bridge from San Francisco. He was an old ponytailed hippie who wore sandals and seashell necklaces and knee-torn jeans. He kept a coffee can of marijuana in the refrigerator, and Jimi Hendrix and Buffalo Springfield posters hung in his bedroom. It was pretty obvious that the two of them, Ed and Evie, had one of those special father-daughter bonds that those of us with only sons envy.

"I wish you'd told me," I said.

"It's not your problem."

"Of course it is," I said. "Your problems are my problems."

"I didn't say that right," she said. "It's just, I needed to be alone with it, get my head around it. The idea that my father might die."

"Maybe you should go see him," I said.

"I know," she said. "I want to, but I don't want to, too. Do you understand?"

"It's not really about what you want," I said. "It's about what you'll regret if you don't do it."

"He's going into the hospital," she said after a minute. "To have tests. Then we'll know."

"It's better to know than not know."

"Yes," she said. "It's got to be." She snuggled against me.

"When you can't feel hope anymore, no matter how hard you try, even the worst thing is better than not knowing."

I waited until ten o'clock the next morning to call Judge Adrienne Lancaster. It was Saturday, so I tried her at her home in Belmont.

She answered with an abrupt "Yes?"

"Judge," I said, "it's Brady Coyne. I—"

"Attorney Coyne," she said. "This is most inappropriate. You should know better."

"I don't have any business before your court," I said. "This isn't a professional issue. It's a family matter."

"Hm," she said. "A family matter, you say? Your family or mine?"

"Yours, Judge. I'm wondering if I can see you this morning."

"This morning? Can't it wait?"

"No, ma'am, it really can't."

"It's that urgent, is it?"

"I think it might be. Yes."

She was quiet for a long moment. Then she said, "Very well, Mr. Coyne. I shall have to trust your judgment. You may come here to my house. You know where I live?"

"I do, yes."

"You'll find me around back pruning my roses."

"I'll be there in less than an hour," I said.

SEVEN

During the twenty-odd years since Frederick Billings Lancaster, Dalt's father, died, his mother, Judge Adrienne Lancaster, had been living alone in their big half-timbered Tudor on Belmont Hill near the Lexington line. It took me about twenty minutes in the sparse Saturday-morning traffic to drive there from my own house on Beacon Hill. You had to know where it was located, because it was screened from the road by a stand of hemlocks, and it was unmarked by a sign or even a mailbox.

A long peastone drive wound through flower gardens and rectangles of lawn and grape arbors and fruit trees and terminated in a circular driveway in front. I parked there and walked around to the back.

I found Judge Lancaster sitting in a wicker chair and reading a newspaper at a glass-topped picnic table on the fieldstone patio behind the house. She was wearing black high-topped sneakers, baggy blue jeans, and a long-sleeved white shirt with the tails flapping. A wide-brimmed straw hat and a pair of cotton work gloves sat on the table by her elbow.

She was about seventy and had sat on the Superior Court bench for more than twenty years. Among lawyers, she had the best reputation a judge could have: She was tough but fair, and she ran a tight ship. I'd been a Massachusetts lawyer almost as long as she'd been a Massachusetts judge, and I'd never once heard a whisper of scandal about Judge Lancaster. Not everybody agreed with her decisions, of course, and I'd never heard anybody accuse her of being warm and cuddly or of having a bawdy sense of humor. But nobody questioned Judge Adrienne Lancaster's integrity, or her commitment, or her intelligence, or her mastery of the law.

Over the years I'd argued a few cases before her. If Judge Lancaster believed that the lawyers—defenders or prosecutors, it didn't matter—were slacking, she didn't hesitate to chide them from the bench right there in the courtroom. She had a sharp tongue. It tended to keep you on your toes.

She looked up from her newspaper, poked at her glasses, and waved at me.

I went over. A pitcher and a couple of glasses sat on the table.

She held out her hand, and I took it. She shook hands like a man. She didn't smile. "Sit down, Mr. Coyne. Pour us some tea, why don't you."

I poured two glasses of iced tea, handed one to her, then sat and gazed out at the formal gardens and lawns of her vast backyard, which sloped away behind the house and disappeared down the hillside. It was June, and everything seemed to be blooming. The mingled scent of dozens of varieties of flowers and the almost subsonic drone of bees filled the air. From her spot on top of Belmont Hill, the Prudential Building and the John Hancock Tower, the tallest buildings in Boston, loomed side by side through the thin city smog on the horizon.

"You've got quite a view, Judge," I said.

"After a while you don't notice it," she said. She peered at me. Her eyes were the color of ice. "Well? What did you want, Attorney Coyne, that you had to come here to see me on a Saturday morning?"

During the drive over, I'd thought hard about what I should and shouldn't say to her, and how I should say it. It was delicate, and I hadn't worked it out very well.

"Please don't ask me to explain what I'm going to tell you," I said.

She shrugged. "Go ahead."

"Here it is." I cleared my throat. "If you have a case on your docket involving the Russo crime family," I said, "I'm here to urge you to recuse yourself. It involves the safety and well-being of your family."

Her smile was without humor. "You don't think a statement such as that deserves an explanation?"

"Of course it does," I said. "I just cannot provide it."

"Can't, or won't?"

"Won't."

"My family, you say. Meaning . . . ?"

I shook my head.

She gazed past me toward her gardens. She took an absent-minded sip of her iced tea, then put down her glass and shifted her eyes to me. "You're asking me to trust you on this."

I nodded.

"You are my son's attorney, Mr. Coyne. This must involve him." She arched her eyebrows at me.

I took a sip of tea and avoided her eyes.

She was silent for a long moment. Then she said, "A judge might be called upon to risk the hypothetical well-being of a family member to perform her duty. But no judge should ever permit the integrity of her courtroom to be questioned or compromised. That's what this is really about, isn't it, Attorney Coyne? My integrity, the integrity of my courtroom? The integrity of the law?"

"Yes," I said. "I believe so."

She nodded. "Fair enough. I won't ask you any more questions. I respect your discretion."

"Thank you, Judge."

"I blame Frederick, you know," she said after a minute. "My late husband. He was a hard man, and Dalton was a sweet, sensitive, rather ineffectual boy. He had no calling to the law. He only wanted to please his father. It was inevitable that he would rebel. Restaurants, of all things." She smiled at the very thought of a Lancaster in the restaurant business. "Even since Frederick died, my son has continued to wrestle with his father's demon." She shook her head. "What could he have done this time?" She looked at me. "That was rhetorical. I did not mean it as a question."

I smiled. "I didn't intend to answer it."

"Was there anything else you wanted to say?"

"No," I said. "That's it."

She picked up her straw hat and fitted it onto her head. Then she pulled on her gloves and stood up. "Let me show you my roses, Attorney Coyne. They are especially spectacular this year."

A half hour later we were standing beside my car in the gravel turnaround in front of Judge Lancaster's house. I was holding a vase containing two dozen long-stemmed yellow rosebuds.

"I know it took courage for you to do what you did today,"

said the judge. "I'm not pleased with what you had to say, but I do appreciate it."

"Not courage," I said. "It was just something I had to do."

"Sometimes simply doing one's duty demands more courage than most people have," she said. "Don't underestimate doing your duty. And now it seems that I must determine what my duty is." She cocked her head and gave me a little cynical smile. "I've got you to thank for that."

"I'm sorry," I said.

She held out her hand. "As am I," she said.

I shook her hand. "Thanks for the flowers. Evie will love them."

"Roses are good for whatever ails you," said Judge Adrienne Lancaster. "I don't know how I would survive without my roses."

When I walked into the house bearing a giant bouquet of yellow roses, Evie smiled hugely, took them from me, and buried her face in them. Then she put them on the table, wrapped her arms around my neck, and gave me a long, deep kiss. "You are the sweetest man," she murmured.

"They're, um, actually from Judge Lancaster," I said. "From her garden. She's got an amazing rose garden."

Evie's hands slid down to my hips, and she leaned back from me in a way that pressed the lower halves of our bodies together. She cocked her head and grinned at me. "You would have brought me flowers, though, wouldn't you?"

I nodded. "Sure. Of course. I am, after all, the sweetest man."

"Because I've been depressed and grouchy."

"There's always a reason why people are grouchy," I said. "Nobody wants to be grouchy and depressed."

"And you've had to put up with me."

"It requires no effort to put up with you," I said.

Both Evie and I, for our own reasons, agreed that we needed to get away from the house and the city and the telephone, so that afternoon we put Henry in the car and drove out to Bolton Flats in Harvard. The Flats are many hundreds of acres of fields and woods bordered along one side by the Still River. The Commonwealth has set this acreage aside for pheasant hunting. For six weeks in the fall they stock it with pen-raised birds, and hunters with shotguns and English setters swarm the place hoping to shoot some of them. For the rest of the year, it's pretty much abandoned.

Bolton Flats is one of the Commonwealth's so-called Wildlife Management Areas, a deliciously ironic euphemism for a place where the wildlife are born and raised in chicken-wire pens and their so-called management involves men and women wearing blaze orange vests trying to kill them.

Evie and I held hands and walked along the rutted roadways, inhaling the country air of a perfect June afternoon, and since it was not October or November, we had the whole place to ourselves. Henry's bird-hunting genes kicked in the minute he leaped out of the car, and he snarfed and snuffled the thick corners where, according to the ancient wisdom imbedded in his DNA, he suspected a pheasant might be hiding. He found no pheasants, but he did point a mourning dove, flush dozens of warblers and red-winged blackbirds, and chase some squirrels.

By the time we'd completed a big circle and made our way back to the car, Henry was panting and mud-soaked and smiling, and Evie and I had that healthy stretched-out feeling in our legs.

On the way home, we listened to NPR and picked up some takeout pad thai and hot-and-sour soup at a Thai place in Lexington.

When we got home, I checked the answering machine. No message from Robert Lancaster, or Dalt or the Judge, either. Okay by me. They knew how to reach me if they needed me. If they didn't try to reach me, it meant they didn't think they needed me. They probably didn't. I'd given the three of them all the advice I had.

We warmed our soup and pad thai in the microwave and took it out onto the patio with bottles of Long Trail ale.

When we were done eating, Evie took the dishes into the house. She was gone for a long time. When she came back. Her eyes looked puffy. I wondered if she'd been crying again.

She came over, sat on my lap, and snuggled against me.

"Did you talk to Ed?" I said.

She nodded.

"Any news?"

She shook her head. "He sounded . . . brave. He tried to cheer me up. It was scary. It's like he's resigned, like he expects to die, like he's trying to . . . to prepare me for it. They've got tests they want to do. It sounds to me like they want to do exploratory surgery, although they didn't tell him that. He doesn't really know anything. Nobody's telling him anything. Just the usual platitudes and evasions. He expects them to tell him that he's going to die."

"What're you going to do?"

I felt her shake her head against my chest. "I don't know. What he's doing, I guess. Wait and see. I can't think of anything else."

"Bring him to Boston," I said. "Best hospitals, best labs, best doctors in the world. You know people. Pull some strings. He could stay with us."

Evie was quiet for a long time. Then she said, "He'd never do that."

We spent Sunday morning drinking coffee, eating donuts, and swapping sections of the *Globe*. In the afternoon we watched the Sox beat the Yankees. When the game was over, I grilled some chicken and cut it up into a big salad with Bibb lettuce and black olives and red peppers and avocado and sliced shiitake mushrooms with a balsamic vinigarette dressing. We ate on the picnic table with a botttle of Chardonnay and a warm baguette of French bread. Henry took up an alert position at the end of the table where he could keep an eye on both of us in case we decided to sneak a morsel to him, which, of course, we both did. Henry loved grilled chicken, but he didn't sneer at olives or mushrooms, either.

After we ate, Evie went in and called her father again. She was dry-eyed when she came back out. She said he sounded about the same. There was no news.

I'd had no news from Dalton or Robert or Adrienne Lancaster, either, and I managed to remain dry-eyed about it.

I spent a frustrating Monday in the Concord district court. Judge Kolb was in one of his notorious crappy moods, so instead of okaying the divorce settlement that Barbara Cooper and I had spent three months hammering out for our respective clients, he sent us out to the lobby to rework our alimony and child-support calculations relative to our property-settlement calculations. Most judges rubber-stamped whatever the adversarial lawyers managed to agree upon. Not Judge Otto Kolb. He thought he knew more and was wiser than any lawyer, which is usually a slippery slope for a judge. But Kolb had been on the bench for almost thirty years, and he showed no signs of slipping down any slopes. He dismissed all criticism, debate, and doubt with Machiavelli's prescription for the prince: "It is better to be feared than loved."

Nobody loved Judge Kolb.

After supper that evening, Evie kissed my cheek and said she was going to take a hot bath and go to bed, maybe read for a while and try to get some sleep for a change. I asked her if she wanted me to wash her back, and she said No thanks, which was disappointing on several levels.

So I spent the evening nursing a bottle of beer and catching up on my e-mail and trying to imagine how Evie would handle it if—when—her father died. It was strictly selfish thinking. I was really wondering how our relationship would handle it.

I watched the eleven o'clock news, then let Henry out, put together the coffee for the morning, and let Henry back in. Then he and I went upstairs. He slipped into the bedroom and curled up on the rug at the foot of the bed. I undressed in the bathroom, brushed my teeth, padded barefoot into the bedroom, and slid in between the sheets next to Evie.

I lay there on my back staring up at the ceiling. I thought about Judge Adrienne Lancaster. I wondered what she planned to do with the unsettling information I'd given her on Saturday.

Beside me, Evie murmured something, rolled onto her side, flopped her arm across my chest, and hooked her leg over my hip. She was wearing her usual sleeping outfit—one of my T-shirts. When she stood up, it would hang down over her hips. Now it had ridden up to her waist. She wiggled herself against me. Her hair smelled soapy.

She moved her pelvis against my hip. The palm of her hand began sliding down over my belly.

"Honey," I whispered, "are you awake?"

"Mm," she said. "You're here."

"I certainly am."

She wiggled herself against me. "My big guy."

"Right now I guess I am."

Her hand continued its travels. "Umm," she said. "My goodness. So you are. I'm glad you're here."

"Me, too."

She moved her face close to mine. Her tongue made a wet circle on the side of my throat. "Show me," she said.

When my eyes popped open, the night was purple-black outside the bedroom window. The illuminated face of the digital clock on the table beside the bed read 3:52.

It took me a minute to realize that Evie was not beside me. Nor was Henry snoozing on his dog bed.

Then I became aware of muffled voices echoing from somewhere in the house. I slid out of bed, pulled on my boxers and a T-shirt, and padded downstairs.

I followed the voices into the living room. The only light came from the television, which was playing some old black-and-white movie. The sound was turned so low I couldn't understand what the actors were saying.

Evie was sitting sideways in the corner of the sofa hugging her legs. Her chin was propped up on her knees, and her T-shirt was bunched up around her hips. She held a half-smoked cigarette in her fingers. The smoke twisted up in the flickering blue television light.

Henry was curled up on the floor in front of the sofa. He looked up at me without lifting his head.

It took Evie a minute to realize I was standing there. "I couldn't sleep," she said.

"Can I get you something?"

"Like what?"

"Glass of milk? Shot of bourbon? Aspirin?"

"No, thank you. Nothing. I'm all set." She took a long drag on her cigarette. "Go back to bed."

"I'll stay with you if you like."

"No," she said. "Please." She returned her gaze to the television.

I nodded and went back upstairs.

EIGHT

Tuesday morning I met with clients, and I spent the afternoon doing what lawyers mainly do, except on television,
where they're either arguing life-and-death cases in front of
packed courtrooms or drinking martinis and eating braised
squab with mayors and senators and mobsters in the most expensive restaurants in the city: I caught up on my paperwork.

We lawyers do spend a lot of time on the phone and at conference tables—and occasionally even in courtrooms—blustering,
arguing, threatening, pontificating, and cajoling. But what really
counts in the law business is what we write. Behind every rich
lawyer is a clerk or a junior partner who loves research and knows
how to write.

In my little one-lawyer office, it was just Julie and I.

So after lunch I set a big mug of coffee on the corner of my
desk blotter, draped my suit jacket over the back of my chair,
loosened my necktie, rolled my shirt cuffs up to my elbows,
and slogged through the big pile of papers that Julie insisted she
had to get faxed or mailed first thing the next morning at the
latest.

There were a few checks to sign and some boilerplate documents that required only my signature, but mostly they were drafts of briefs, and letters to clients and to other lawyers, and motions for submission to courts, in which every word and mark of punctuation and paragraph break could determine who won and who lost, and would be scrutinized for slipups and loopholes by their recipients, and therefore needed to be scrutinized by me.

I wrote the rough drafts. Julie double-checked the citations, plugged in the footnotes, polished the prose, and attended to all the small but crucial details that make the difference between clarity and confusion. Julie knew her commas. You couldn't get a dangling modifier past her, and she was a master of the gerund. She was a semicolon expert and a conjunction wizard, and she was world-class when it came to prepositions and participial phrases. If Julie put a document on my desk, I knew it was already perfect.

But the name that appeared at the top and got signed at the bottom was mine, and anyway, Julie would quit on the spot if she thought I didn't parse her compositions as carefully as she had composed them. So I did. I contemplated her colons and pondered her pronouns.

It was boring. It was painful. It was how I spent a large percentage of my professional life. By comparison, having three months' worth of hard negotiations negated by one of Judge Otto Kolb's quick sneers was fun.

A little after four o'clock, my telephone console buzzed. I picked up the phone and hit the button, and Julie said, "How's it going?"

"Great," I said. "Haven't had so much fun since I slammed the car door on my fingers."

"That's nice," she said. "Can you talk to Mr. Lancaster? He's on line two."

"Got it," I said. I hit the blinking button and said, "Dalt? What's up? Everything all right?"

"No," he said. "Everything is not all right. We gotta talk."

"Sure. Okay. Fire away."

"Not on the phone. Can you come over?"

"You at the restaurant?"

"Yes."

"I'll be done here in about an hour," I said. "I guess I can be there around five-thirty. How's that?"

"Good," he said. "Thanks. See you then."

It took me about half an hour to walk from my office in Copley Square to Dalt's restaurant, the Boston Scrod, in the Faneuil Hall Marketplace, which was also called, for reasons I never understood, the Quincy Market. The Scrod was right around the corner from the venerable Durgin Park restaurant, famous for its platter-sized slabs of prime rib and its surly South Boston waitresses. Evie and I had eaten at the Scrod a few times, and we liked it. The restaurant on the second floor claimed that it served nothing but fresh catch-of-the-day seafood. The entire first floor was a three-sided horseshoe-shaped oyster bar. The Scrod was famous for its extensive oyster menu. Oysters from Nova Scotia and Maine, Long Island and Nantucket, British Columbia and Bristol Bay. Before I went there, I had no idea that oysters came in so many sizes, shapes, textures, and tastes. All, as my friend J. W. Jackson would say, were delish. You could also get an excellent Bloody Mary at the bar, as well as dozens of New England microbrewed beers and ales.

The Scrod was popular with the locals, always a good sign. Dalt seemed to be doing a good job managing it.

At five-thirty on this sunny Tuesday afternoon in June, the brick plaza outside the restaurant was thronged with tourists from Iowa snapping digital photographs, businessfolk from the financial district just getting out of work, and street performers looking for handouts and applause. I weaved my way among them, went inside, climbed the stairs, and knocked on the door to Dalton Lancaster's office.

His muffled voice called, "Come on in," so in I went.

The door opened into a room that reminded me of my recent visit to Paulie Russo's office in another restaurant, except Dalt's was a little smaller than Russo's, with more expensive furniture, and it was occupied only by Dalt Lancaster. Not a thug in sight.

He was on the phone. When I closed the door behind me, he looked up, nodded quickly, and turned his head away. From where I stood inside the doorway, I couldn't see the bruised and beaten side of Dalt's face, the left side. I figured he'd turned away from me so that I couldn't overhear what he was saying into the telephone. So I made a point of not listening.

Dalt could've been renting his office by the week. Its only decoration was a large authentic-looking sepia-toned map hanging on the wall beside the desk. It showed colonial Boston back in the day when Back Bay was still under water. On one wall, a floor-to-ceiling window looked down on the Faneuil Hall plaza. A pair of oak file cabinets and a freestanding steel-and-glass bookcase stood against one wall. The shelves were packed with three-ring binders and stacks of manila folders and magazines. A few small framed photos were lined up on one of the shelves. The big desk and the chairs and the side table were steel and glass and black leather. A computer and a printer and a telephone console sat on the desk. The carpet was a red-and-blue

Oriental. It was the office of a man who'd had many other offices, considered them workplaces, understood that all workplaces were temporary, and let somebody else furnish and decorate them.

After a minute, Dalt mumbled something into the phone, hung up, turned, and smiled quickly at me, as if he hadn't noticed me come in. "Brady," he said. "Thanks for coming. Have a seat."

Now I saw that the left side of his face had turned a sickly greenish yellow. It was a week-old bruise, and it was the same color as Robert's. Father and son with their matching black eyes.

I pulled an armless leather chair up to Dalt's desk and sat down. "How's it feeling?" I touched my own left cheekbone.

He waved his hand in the air, dismissing the importance of how he felt. He leaned forward and frowned at me. "What the hell did you say to my mother?"

"You invited me over here to yell at me?"

He blew out a breath. "I'm sorry. I'm not yelling. I'm upset."

"You asked me to handle your problems," I said, "so that's what I did. You don't have any right to be upset when I do what you ask me to do."

"Well," he said, "whatever you did to handle my problems, my mother the judge is furious with me."

"I don't doubt it."

"What did you say about me?"

"You?" I said. "I didn't say anything about you. Your mother's pretty sharp, you know. She didn't need me to say anything. You understand what this is all about, don't you?"

"I do now," he said. "She called me this morning, said that because of me she had to recuse herself from an important case—something involving the Russo family, I assume—and not only

71

that, but instead of doing it quietly the way she normally would do something like that, she had to announce it at a press conference, which she did at three this afternoon, in time for the rush-hour news cycle. She said it was embarrassing and humiliating not to be able to give any reason or answer any questions, and she was holding me personally responsible, whatever that means. Probably cutting me out of her will, not that the old witch is ever going to die."

"What did you say to her?" I said.

He spread his hands. "What could I say? That I had no idea why those goons beat me up? That I was innocent and misunderstood? That I was still her good little boy?"

I smiled. "That's all pretty much true, isn't it?"

"I told her I was sorry. One way or the other, it's my fault, right?"

"No man is an island," I said.

"You know, don't you?"

"Don't push it," I said. "Judge Lancaster did what she had to do, and you can't blame her for not liking it. Now let's hope that takes care of it."

"I'd be comforted if you could tell me why I got beat up."

"Just their way of putting the screws to your mother, I guess," I said.

He shook his head. "There's got to be more to it than that."

"I've told you everything I can tell you," I said. "Be comforted by the prospect of not getting beat up again."

"That's what I thought," he said. "There is something else."

"Come on, Dalt. Leave it be."

He was shaking his head. "See, what I don't get is, why would Paulie Russo want her off some case? Does he seriously think another judge is going to give him a break?"

"It doesn't matter," I said. "Now it'll be that other judge's problem." I stood up. "Come on. Buy me half a dozen oysters and a Bloody Mary."

"I don't have to buy them," he said. "It's my restaurant."

When I stepped outside I had to pause for a moment to let my eyes adjust to the brightness of the afternoon sun on the Quincy Market plaza. Then I started along the sidewalk, weaving my way through the crowds, heading home. Up ahead a circle of people had gathered, their faces upturned, watching a man in a clown suit. He was weaving back and forth above them, balancing himself on a unicycle, one of the Quincy Market sidewalk performers.

I went over to check out his act.

He had a patter of jokes that I couldn't hear very well in the noise of the plaza, but they made those who could hear him laugh. He managed simultaneously to talk and balance on his unicycle and juggle six balls—a golf ball, a baseball, a softball, a soccer ball, a basketball, and a beach ball, all in the air at once—and while I watched, he somehow managed to unwrap a cigar, stuff it into his mouth, strike a match, and get it lighted without dropping any of the balls.

His audience applauded loudly at this feat, and I did, too, and that's when strong hands clamped down on both of my elbows. I tried to twist away, but the grips on my elbows tightened and held me there.

There were two of them, one holding each elbow. They were standing behind my shoulders so that I couldn't see them, but it wasn't much of a mystery who they were.

"What do you want?" I said.

"You fucked up with the judge," the guy behind my right shoulder said. "Paulie ain't happy."

"That's tough shit," I said.

The fingers on my left elbow moved and poked and probed, then suddenly jabbed at a soft place and dug into my funny bone. It felt like I'd stuck a finger in an electrical socket, and my arm went numb.

"Ow," I said. "Jesus."

None of the people in the crowd around me seemed to notice. They were laughing at something the clown on the unicycle had said.

"So now it's about the money," hissed the voice in my ear. "Understand?"

"Let go of me." I twisted and turned my head around and caught a quick glimpse of the man standing behind my left shoulder. As I'd assumed, he was one of the goons who'd grabbed me a few days earlier in my parking garage and dragged me to Paulie Russo's office. This was the one with the shiny pink mole beside his nose. I supposed the goon holding my other elbow was the short bald one.

The one with the mole squeezed my elbow harder. I turned my head away from him, and he relaxed his grip.

"It's on you," he growled.

"Fuck you," I said. "And tell Paulie Russo he can go fuck himself, too."

He chuckled, and then there came a sudden, searing pain in my lower back just above my hipbone. It felt like I'd been stabbed, or shot, or branded. The pain zinged through my body and left me instantly dizzy and nauseated. Then the life went out of my legs, and I stumbled, toppled forward, fell against somebody who was standing in front of me, and crashed onto the pavement.

As I lay there, the goon bent close to my ear and said, "Just get it done, Mr. Lawyer." Then he was gone.

A moment later I was aware of somebody squatting beside me. "You okay, mister?" It was a kid's voice.

I think I was groaning.

"Hey," said the boy. His voice was louder, more urgent. "Hey. Somebody help. Something's wrong with this guy. A heart attack or something."

"No heart attack," I mumbled.

I sensed that a crowd of people had circled around me. When I opened my eyes and tried to look at them, their faces were blurry and spinning.

I reached around and gingerly touched the place behind my hip where it hurt. When I pulled my hand back and looked at it, I saw no blood. That eliminated knives and bullets, at least.

I sat there with my head between my knees and my eyes squeezed shut, breathing deeply against the pain.

A minute later somebody else was kneeling beside me. Her face was bent close to mine. "I'm a police officer." It was a woman's voice. "Are you all right, sir?" She put her hand on my forehead. "What happened? Can you talk to me?"

I nodded. "I think I'm okay," I said.

She put her arm around my shoulders. My lower back throbbed. Every beat of my pulse sent a dart of pain up my spine. It felt as if somebody had pounded a red-hot railroad spike into me and was twisting it around.

I looked at the cop. She was young and African American, and concern showed in her solemn dark eyes.

"You want me to call an ambulance?" she said.

"No," I said. "Thanks. Really. I'm okay. I just got a sudden pain here." I patted my back. "Hurt like a bastard. It's a little better now."

"This ever happen before?"

I shook my head.

"Ever had kidney stones?" she said.

"No. You think that could be it?"

"I never had 'em, either," she said, "but I saw my uncle have an attack once, and what you describe sounds like what happened to him. Poor guy was thrashing around, cursing and moaning. You'd've thought he was dying. Said it was the worst thing ever happened to him. Maybe we should get you to an emergency room."

"I'm feeling better," I said. "Really." I pushed myself to my feet, wavered for a minute, then found my balance.

She stood up beside me and put her hand on my arm. "Sure you're okay?"

I nodded.

"I've got to take your name, sir," she said. She had a notebook in her hand.

"Can't we just forget it?"

"I have to make a report," she said. "Just let me write down your name and address."

I told her my name and gave her my office address.

She wrote in her notebook, then closed it and put it in her pants pocket. "You sure you're going to be all right?" she said.

I nodded.

"You start peeing blood, get to a hospital."

"I will. Thanks."

"Or another attack like this."

"Right," I said.

She patted my arm. "All right, sir. You take care of yourself."

"I appreciate your help," I said.

She cocked her head and looked at me, and I guessed she thought I was lying about something. Then she shrugged and smiled and wandered away.

I *was* lying, of course. I didn't want to tell her that Paulie

Russo's thug had kidney-punched me, his way of making sure I didn't forget him. Not that it was likely.

I guessed I'd be hurting for a few days, at least, even if I got lucky and didn't start pissing blood.

I started to walk home, but I didn't get very far before I realized that my back hurt way too much. So I took a cab.

NINE

The taxi dropped me off at my front door on Mt. Vernon Street at quarter of seven. When I went into the house, Henry did not come bounding out to greet me, which meant he was in the backyard, and that meant that Evie was already home.

I walked through the house and out onto the back deck. Evie was sprawled in one of our wooden chairs. She was wearing a pair of cutoff jeans and a T-shirt. A cardboard pack of Marlboro reds, a green plastic lighter, and a glass ashtray sat on the arm of the chair. She was balancing a beer bottle on her bare belly, and her face was tilted up to the sky. Her eyes were closed. I guessed she was napping.

Henry was lying beside her with his chin on his paws. He was looking at me, trying to decide whether it was worth the effort to get to his feet and come over just for a kind word and a scratch behind the ears.

He decided to wait for me to go to him.

I stood there for a minute. I didn't want to wake up Evie. She'd been sleeping badly lately, and I figured a little nap would be good for her.

But then she turned her head and looked at me.

"Hi, babe," I said.

She gave me a strained smile. "Hi, Brady."

When Evie called me Brady instead of honey or big guy or Studman, it meant something was bothering her.

I went down to her. She tilted up her cheek—not her mouth—for a kiss, which I gave her. Then I sat in the chair beside her.

"Somebody drive you home?" she said.

"Huh? Why?"

"I heard a car door slam. Then you were here."

"I thought you were sleeping."

"Not really," she said.

"I took a taxi."

"How come?"

"I did something to my back. It kinda hurts to walk."

It was a lie, and lying to Evie reminded me of how I'd lied—or at least withheld the truth, which amounted to the same thing—to Dalt Lancaster and to his mother the judge, and how Robert had been lying to everybody.

Telling the truth was overrated. Sometimes the lie was better.

"Sorry about your back," Evie said.

"It'll be fine," I said. "You okay?"

She held up her beer bottle. "Empty."

I took it from her, went into the house, and snagged two bottles of Samuel Adams lager from the refrigerator. I popped their caps, took them out back, gave one to Evie, and sat in the chair beside her. I had to wiggle around to find a position that didn't make my kidneys scream.

Evie lit a Marlboro. "I don't want you to argue with me," she said. "I don't want your advice. I don't want any philosophy or psychology or wisdom. Okay?"

I looked at her. "What is it, honey?"

"I told my father I was going out there to be with him. I've booked a flight for tomorrow afternoon. A one-way ticket. I don't know when I'll be coming home." She blinked. "He didn't even argue with me."

"He's getting worse, then?" I said.

She turned to look at me. "It's sweet," she said, "that you want to know about him, that you're not focusing on me going out there. It makes me feel better. It makes me think maybe I'm not totally crazy after all. That's why I love you."

I reached for her hand. She gave it to me. I held on to it. "Tell me about Ed."

She gave my hand a squeeze, then let go. "They want to take some blood and do ultrasound and CT scans and MRIs and a bunch of other tests he doesn't explain very clearly. They might want to do exploratory surgery."

"Do they have a suspicion of what's wrong?"

She shrugged. "They probably do. But they're not telling him. Or else he's not telling me. I can't tell which. He says they just give him double-talk he can't understand. I don't know. Maybe he just doesn't want to tell me what they're saying. Either way, it's not good. His symptoms are scary and ominous. So I'm going. To get some answers. And to . . . to be with him."

"Sure," I said. "You should."

"I don't know how long it will be."

I figured she meant that she'd stay with him until he died. "What can I do?" I said.

"Nothing," she said. "That would be best. Just let me do what I need to do. Don't expect anything out of me, okay? Please. Make it easy for me."

"I could go with you."

She snapped her head around. "See? That's what I'm talking about. Saying that makes it hard for me. That makes me have to say, 'No, I don't want you to come with me.' You see what I mean?"

"Sure," I said. "Okay. I understand."

"Do you?"

I shrugged. "I love you. Whatever you want, whether I understand or not."

She lit another cigarette. "I did ask him."

"What?"

"To come here. To our hospitals and doctors. He said no."

"I'm sorry."

"I told him we could have the best in the world. He could stay right here with us. The old poop, he just wants to be close to his stupid houseboat."

"They have great doctors in San Francisco, too," I said.

"Sure," she said. "I know."

"You're doing the right thing," I said. "It's good that you're going to be with him."

"You can drive me to the airport," she said. "Would you do that?"

"I'll do whatever you want me to do," I said. "And I won't do whatever you tell me not to do."

"I know," she said.

She puffed on her cigarette. I watched her, the comfortable, delicate way she held it down near the tips of her fingers, the way she blew the smoke out of the side of her mouth. It made me remember smoking.

After a few minutes, she said, "You can't expect me to call you every night."

"I'll try not to expect anything," I said. "I would like to know how Ed is doing, though. And how you're doing."

"I'll call when I can," she said. "I just don't want you to expect it and count on it and be disappointed when I don't. I don't need that kind of responsibility."

"I understand. I don't want you to feel obliged to me."

"And I don't want you to call me."

"I'll want to," I said. "It will be hard."

"I know. Do you understand?"

"It doesn't matter. I understand what you're asking me. So that's what I'll do."

"I've thought about it a lot," she said. "I just need to be with him. I don't want to have thoughts about not being with him. I don't want to resent him. I don't want to think about you. I don't want to miss you, or our house, or Henry, or my friends, or my job, or the people at work. I don't want to be conflicted any more than I already am. I just want to try to focus on my daddy."

"Okay," I said.

"Do you understand?"

"Sure."

When our beer bottles were empty, I took them inside. I made supper for Henry and some tunafish sandwiches for me and Evie. I brought them out back with a bag of Cape Cod potato chips and fresh bottles of beer, and we ate while the sky darkened and shadows seeped into our garden.

Sometime after we'd finished eating, Evie said, "I will miss you."

"It's better if you don't," I said.

"I'll try not to. But I know I will."

A few minutes later, she said, "You'll be all right, won't you?"

"Don't worry about me," I said. "I lived alone for a long time, and I did fine, and I didn't even have Henry back then."

After Evie went upstairs to get ready for bed, I called my office and left a message for Julie, just telling her I'd hurt my back and wouldn't be in the office on Wednesday. I was glad I'd gotten all of our paperwork cleaned up. Julie could always reschedule meetings, but paperwork waited for no man.

When I went upstairs and crawled into our bed, Evie said, "I don't want to make love tonight. I'm sorry. I just want you to hold me. Will you hold me?"

"Sure," I said. "I'd love to hold you."

She rolled onto her side with her back to me. Then she reached around and touched the back of my leg, urging me to snuggle up to her.

I kissed her shoulder and held her.

A minute later, she said, "Is your back all right?"

"Oh, sure," I said. "It's nothing."

"I am so selfish."

"Stop it," I said.

"I wasn't even thinking about your back."

"Neither was I," I said.

It took me a long time to fall asleep. When I woke up, the morning sun was angling in around the edges of the bedroom curtains. Evie was not beside me, and Henry was not curled up on his bed in the corner.

I pulled on a pair of jeans and a T-shirt. My lower back was tender to the touch, but when I started down the stairs I found that my kidney punch was little more than an old ache.

I poured myself a mug of coffee, went to the back door, and looked out through the screen into the backyard.

Evie was sitting at the picnic table. She was wearing gray sweatpants and a blue tank top. Her long auburn hair was stuffed

84

under a Red Sox cap. She wore it backwards. It made her look like a high school kid. Innocent and sexy.

Roger Horowitz, wearing his usual Columbo-style rumpled brown suit and looking like a homicide detective, which was what he happened to be, was sitting across from her. His elbows were on the table, and he was holding a coffee mug in both hands. He sat motionless, watching Evie over the rim of his mug.

She was looking down at her hands, talking to him in a soft murmuring voice. She kept rotating her coffee mug on the tabletop.

I didn't want to interrupt them, so I stood there inside the screen door. After a minute, Horowitz put down his mug, reached across the table, and knuckled a tear from Evie's cheek.

She looked up at him and smiled. I saw that her eyes were glittery.

I banged on the screen door as if I'd just gotten there, then shouldered it open and went outside. Evie and Horowitz looked up. Henry, who'd been lying under the table, lifted his head, yawned, got to his feet, and walked stiff-legged to me.

I reached down and scratched his forehead, then went over to the table. I kissed the back of Evie's neck and held out my hand to Horowitz.

He shook it. "How's the back?"

I looked at Evie. She shrugged.

"It's okay," I said. "Better. Thanks."

"Pulled a muscle or something, huh?" he said.

I nodded, sat beside Evie, and took a sip of coffee. "Am I interrupting something?"

Horowitz gave me a crooked smile and a small shake of his head.

"We were just talking," said Evie.

"She told you," I said to Horowitz. "About Ed."

"It's a bitch," he said.

Evie stood up. "I bet you boys have important things to talk about," she said. "I've got to get packed." She went around the table, leaned down, and gave Horowitz a kiss on the cheek. "Thank you," she said softly. "Give my love to Alyse."

He looked up at her. "You take care, kiddo."

Evie smiled and nodded and went into the house.

When the screen door snapped shut behind her, I turned to Horowitz. "I don't know what she sees in you."

"That makes us even," he said. "I don't know what she sees in you, either."

"You shouldn't've come here," I said. "It always upsets her."

"She talks, I listen," he said. "I think it helps to talk. Poor kid. I feel bad for her."

"I didn't mean that," I said. "I know she likes to talk to you. Unlike everybody else, Evie harbors the delusion that you're a sensitive and caring person. It's just that whenever you come here, it's because you need me for something, and she knows it, and it makes her nervous, you being a homicide detective and all."

"For the record," he said, "I never need you. I get by just swell without you. Anyway, as far as I know, we don't have any homicide to talk about." He narrowed his eyes at me. "Do we?"

"I don't think so."

"So who's punching you in the kidneys, then?"

I looked at him. "How the hell did you hear about that?"

He smiled. "So it *was* a kidney punch."

I nodded. "Is that how that cop reported it?"

"She surmised it. Her point was, you refused medical treatment, and she was covering her ass for not calling the EMTs anyway, in case you subsequently keeled over and died."

"Do you read all the police reports?"

"The magic of computers, Coyne," he said. "I scan 'em. Part of the job. You never know when something, apparently random, might connect the dots with some other random thing. Your name jumped out at me. Not that I give a shit about you, but I do happen to care about Evie. So I just thought I'd find out what the hell's going on with you."

"That's good detective work," I said, "and I appreciate your interest, even if it's on Evie's behalf, not mine. But a kidney punch is hardly a homicide."

"I like to solve homicide cases," he said, "but I like to prevent them even better."

"I'm in no danger, Roger."

"So this was just some random kidney punch, then? Delivered with a smile by some stranger? No message behind it?"

I shrugged. "Don't push me, please."

"Ah," he said. "More of your client-privilege bullshit, right?"

I waved the subject away with the back of my hand.

Horowitz narrowed his eyes at me. "Evie said something was going on with you, she didn't know what, so I promised her I'd keep an eye on you while she's gone, whether you like it or not."

"You're a good friend," I said. "But don't worry about me."

He looked at me for a minute, then shrugged. "When she gets back, you can take us all out to dinner. You, Evie, me, and Alyse. Someplace expensive."

"She's leaving this afternoon. I don't know when she'll be back. She bought a one-way ticket."

"It's a bitch, all right." Horowitz nodded, then drained his coffee mug and stood up. "I gotta get to work."

I stood up and held out my hand. "Thanks."

He gave my hand his usual limp shake. "You feel like talking, give me a call."

"I'm not going to tell you anything," I said.

We pulled up in front of the curbside check-in at the Northwest Airlines terminal at Logan Airport around two-thirty that afternoon. Evie's flight was scheduled to take off at four-twenty. She was changing planes in Detroit and would land in San Francisco around nine-thirty. She'd reserved a rental car from Avis to get her from the airport to Ed Banyon's houseboat in Sausalito.

I popped the trunk, and we got out of the car. I went around, hefted her two bags from the trunk, and set them on the curb. One was a medium-sized duffel. The other was a carry-on. I was comforted by the fact that Evie had left most of her clothes in her bedroom closet back home. It reassured me that she'd be back.

We'd brought Henry in the car so he could say good-bye. Evie opened the back door, leaned in, and gave him a hug. "You take good care of Brady," she said to him.

He licked her face.

Then she straightened up, shut the door, and turned to me. "Well," she said.

I nodded. "Well."

"I'll call when I land."

"I'd appreciate it."

She came to me and put both of her arms around my neck. "Take care of yourself, okay?" she said.

"Sure. I'll be fine."

She hugged herself hard against me for a moment, then pulled back. "I've got to do this, Brady."

"I know."

"I wish I could tell you . . ." She looked at me and shook her head.

"Don't worry about it, babe. You don't need to say anything. Give my best to Ed. I hope everything turns out to be fine."

"Right," she said. "Okay." She stepped forward, put a hand on my arm, went up on her tiptoes, and kissed me quickly on the mouth. Then she stepped back. "Go now. Please. Just get in the car and drive away."

"Sure," I said.

I went around and slid in behind the wheel. Henry poked his nose against my neck from the backseat. I reached over my shoulder and patted his head. "You can sit up front, if you want," I said.

He hopped into the passenger seat and stood there pressing his nose against the windshield.

"Sit," I told him. "You're smudging the window."

He sat.

I turned on the ignition, shifted into first gear, and pulled away from the curb.

When I looked in the rearview mirror, I saw that Evie was lugging her two bags to the curbside check-in kiosk.

TEN

When Henry and I got home from the airport and went inside, a hole opened up in my chest. Evie wasn't here, and she wouldn't be. Not tonight. Not for a while. Not for a very long time, maybe.

I couldn't help thinking: Maybe not ever.

I found a bottle of Long Trail ale in the refrigerator and took the portable kitchen phone out back. I sprawled in an Adirondack chair. Henry collapsed on the patio bricks beside me.

I called Doc Adams in Concord and got his voice mail. I guessed that he and Mary were at their place in Brewster on the Cape, sailing and digging clams and surf casting for stripers and bluefish. I didn't bother leaving a message.

Charlie McDevitt wasn't home, either. When his voice mail clicked on, I said, "It's me, your wayward fishing partner. Wondering if you're up for a long-overdue excursion to the Swift or the Deerfield this weekend, Saturday or Sunday, either day, see if we can catch a trout. I'll meet you at that Italian place near the Concord rotary. You name the time. Give me a call."

I couldn't think of anybody besides Doc or Charlie whose

company I'd prefer over my own for a day on a trout river. J. W. Jackson was on Martha's Vineyard, a long drive and a ferry ride away, and there weren't any trout on the Vineyard anyway. If Doc or Charlie didn't get back to me, I'd go by myself. I didn't want to spend the whole weekend hanging around the house. Henry was excellent company. But he wasn't Evie.

I found some leftover Italian sausages in a plastic bag in the refrigerator. They reminded me of the evening—when was it? less than a week ago?—when I'd cooked them on the gas grill out on the back deck. While I'd been performing that manly job, Evie had leaned against the railing to keep me company, sipping beer and looking sexy. She'd been wearing a pair of high-cut running shorts and a cropped tank top, and she said she was thinking of getting a tattoo here—she tugged down the waistband of her shorts and touched a spot on her hip—or maybe here, lifting her shirt and circling the tip of her finger on the side of her left breast. She had in mind either a daisy or a ladybug. Something colorful, but small and discreet and intimate that only she and I would know about. What did I think?

The memory of her long golden legs and her flat belly and the way her throat worked when she tilted her head back to drink beer from the bottle and her teasing smile when she touched her body was indelible. We ate the sausages in buns with sauerkraut and chopped onions and mustard and beer, and after we finished, she grabbed my hand and pulled me upstairs, and I touched all of the potential tattoo places on her body with my fingers and my tongue.

I chopped up the sausages, opened a can of baked beans, dumped them in a pot, added the sausages, and got the beans bubbling on the stove. I ate from the pot at the picnic table out back accompanied by half a loaf of not-quite-stale French bread and another bottle of ale. I slipped frequent bites of sausage and hunks of bread to Henry, and when I was done, I put the pot down for him to lick.

I kept checking my watch. Evie's plane was supposed to land at nine-thirty California time, which was half past midnight in Boston.

I took the dishes into the kitchen, brewed myself some coffee, made Henry's supper, and took a mug of coffee and the portable TV out back. Henry and I watched the Red Sox lose a close one, and then I found an old Steve McQueen movie that was already in progress, which was okay because I'd seen it a few times.

All Steve McQueen movies are old, come to think of it.

The movie ended at eleven. I watched the news, then switched over to ESPN, profoundly aware of the fact that I was just waiting for time to pass.

Charlie McDevitt had not returned my call. I figured he was away for the weekend, too. He would have called if he'd gotten my message.

At midnight Henry and I went upstairs. I crawled into my empty bed, and when I patted it beside me, Henry hopped up and curled himself into a ball against my hip. He began snoring instantly. I read *Moby-Dick*. Normally I could count on Melville's overwrought prose and multipage paragraphs of excruciatingly detailed whaling lore to put me to sleep.

But not tonight. I kept glancing at the clock on the bedside table. When twelve-thirty came and went, I began to play out scenarios. Maybe her flight had been delayed. Maybe she missed her connection in Detroit. Maybe San Francisco was fogged in and her flight had been diverted to Los Angeles. Maybe she forgot that she'd promised to call me. Maybe she was just so preoccupied with her father that she wasn't even thinking about me.

Maybe terrorists . . .

The phone jarred me awake, and I grabbed it on the first ring.

"Your little birdie has landed," said Evie.

"Ah, yes," I said in my W. C. Fields voice. "My little chickadee." I looked at the clock. It was twenty after one.

"I woke you up. I'm sorry."

"I wasn't really sleeping. Everything okay? Good flight?"

"Sure," she said. "Uneventful. A little late getting out of Detroit. I'm in the baggage area. I can barely hear you. There's about ten thousand people here, and every one of them is yelling in their cell phones. I'm yelling, aren't I? Are you okay?"

"I'm good," I said. "Yes, you're kind of yelling."

"How's dear old Henry?"

"He's right here on the bed with me. He says he misses you."

"Give him a hug for me."

"I will."

"One for you, too, okay?"

"Okay. Absolutely. You, too. From me."

"Okay, here we go," she said. "The bags are coming out. I gotta go. Be good. Love you."

"I love you, too. My best to Ed. Keep in touch, okay?"

But she was gone.

Julie had packed Thursday and Friday with meetings and conferences, the price I paid for taking a day off. But I didn't mind. It helped me divert my mind from Evie's absence.

She didn't call Thursday night. I had all I could do to keep myself from calling her.

On Friday afternoon I called Robert Lancaster's cell phone. I'd given him until Friday to address his problem with his family. If he failed to do that—and I had no faith that he would do

94

it, despite his promise—I'd have to decide what my responsibility was.

Robert's phone rang five or six times, and then came his voice mail. "It's Robert. I can't talk now. Leave a message and I'll get back to you."

After the recorded instructions and the final beep, I said, "It's Brady Coyne. I was just wondering how everything's going. It's Friday, and I thought maybe you'd gotten together with your family by now and put all your cards on the table, so to speak. I hope so. If there's anything I can do, don't hesitate to ask, okay? Give me a call anyway, please. Any time. I'm worried about you. I'll have my cell phone with me." I recited my number, said good-bye, and hung up.

Evie didn't call that night. Two or three times in the evening I dialed half of her cell phone number before disconnecting. She'd told me she wouldn't be calling me every day, and I'd promised I wouldn't call her. I'd have to get used to it.

I planned to go fishing on Saturday, but when I woke up, it was raining, so I stayed home. People who don't fish seem to believe that stormy weather makes for good trout fishing, but they are wrong. The best time to go trout fishing is actually when it's most comfortable for the fisherman. Early morning and late afternoon during the hot summer months, midday during the cold months, and all day in the temperate months of May and June. Storms bring with them changes in the barometric pressure that often suppress the activity of aquatic life, both the trout and the insects they eat.

Anyway, I didn't feel like getting wet. Sunday would be better.

I tried Doc Adams and Charlie McDevitt again, and again they didn't answer their phones.

I spent the afternoon feeling sorry for myself. The game

at Fenway Park got rained out, so I didn't even have that for entertainment. I tied some flies, paid some bills, read half of an Elmore Leonard novel, drank some beer.

Around suppertime I called Dalt Lancaster at his restaurant. He said he was busy and couldn't really talk. I asked him if everything was all right, and he said that except for the fact that his mother wasn't speaking to him, everthing was fine. Nothing was new.

He didn't mention Robert, which meant that Robert had not convened a family council to tell them about his gambling problem. And that meant that I'd have to do it. Paulie Russo was not a patient or forgiving man.

I thought about going out for supper—I hadn't been to Skeeter's for a long time, and he made the best burgers in the city—but it was still raining, so I settled for a microwaved bean burrito and a bottle of beer at my kitchen table.

My cell phone chirped just as I was swallowing my last bite of burrito. I looked at the screen. It was an unfamiliar number. Not Evie's. I flipped it open and said, "Hello?"

"Is this Mr. Coyne?" A woman's voice. I didn't recognize it.

"Yes," I said. "Who's this?"

"Rebecca Quinlan. Becca. Remember me? I was with Robert Lancaster? At the Dunkin' Donuts last week?"

"Yes, of course," I said. "Is anything wrong?"

"I don't know," she said. "I thought maybe you could tell me."

"Robert, you mean."

"Well, yes. It's just, I don't know where he is. He's not answering his cell. He cut his classes yesterday. We were supposed to hang out today, but he didn't show up, and—"

"Becca," I said, "suppose I buy you a cup of coffee."

"You mean now?"

"Yes. As soon as I can get there. How about that same Dunkin'?"

"I was right, wasn't I?" she said. "Something *is* wrong."

"I don't know," I said. "Maybe we can figure it out. Give me fifteen or twenty minutes."

By the time I retrieved my car from the garage at the end of Charles Street, drove the rain-slick city streets through Kenmore Square, found a place to park, and walked into the Dunkin' Donuts on Commonwealth Avenue, it was closer to half an hour.

Becca Quinlan was sitting by herself in a booth against the wall. She was frowning at a book that lay open on the table and absentmindedly twirling a strand of blond hair with her forefinger. A Red Sox baseball cap sat on the table beside her book, and a backpack lay on the floor beside her.

I went over and said, "Hi, Becca."

She looked up. "Oh, hi."

"How do you like your coffee?"

She waved her hand. "I don't really drink coffee. You go ahead."

"I don't need it." I slid in across from her. "Let's talk."

"This is stupid, isn't it?" she said.

"I don't see why," I said. "You're worried about Robert. You must care for him. It's not stupid to worry about the people you care about."

"No," she said, "but I mean, it's not like he's required to account for himself all the time. It's just . . . it's Saturday, you know? We always do stuff on Saturday. And it's been like three days since I even talked to him. We always hang out."

"So why me?" I said.

She frowned. "Huh?"

97

"Why did you call me?"

"Who was I s'pose to call?"

I shrugged.

"I mean, he doesn't get along with his father, he hates his stepfather, his mother is kind of useless, and anyway, I've never met any of them. At least I met you. Robert told me he trusted you. You're a lawyer. He said he had a long talk with you the other night after you told me and Ozzie to go away. He said you gave him good advice. He respects you and trusts you, so I thought . . . I don't know. I guess it's dumb. I just thought you could tell me that he's okay. I found your number on a card in his room."

"You went to his room looking for him?"

She nodded. "His roommates let me in. He's got an apartment in Brighton, you know. I'm in a dorm right near here. They didn't know where he was, either, and I didn't find any, like, clues. Except your business card. So I called you."

"How has Robert seemed to you lately?" I said.

She blinked at me. "Well, he got beat up, you know."

I nodded. "Did he say who did it?"

She shook her head. "He didn't want to talk about it. I wondered if it was Ozzie. Him and his buddies."

"Your ex-boyfriend?"

"I felt so bad, Mr. Coyne. It wasn't Robert who, like, stole me from Ozzie. It was me. I just didn't want to be with Ozzie."

"Why not?"

"He didn't make me happy. Oh, he never did anything bad. He was always sweet with me. It's just, Ozzie's dark, you know?"

"Dark," I said.

"He seems like he's angry all the time. Mad at the world. Just an unhappy person. I don't need that. I'm depressed enough all by myself."

"And Robert's different?"

"Oh, sure. Robert's cute and nice and fun and, you know, deep. The opposite of Ozzie."

"But Ozzie and Robert are friends."

"That's how I met Robert. He's Ozzie's friend. We all hung out together. We still do."

"So did you talk to Ozzie when you got worried about Robert?"

"Oh, sure. He said he hasn't seen Robert for a couple days, and he told me it wasn't him who beat him up, and . . . I'm worried, Mr. Coyne. That's all. I thought maybe you knew something that would make me feel better."

"You believe Ozzie?"

She smiled. "He's a terrible liar. That was one thing I always liked about Ozzie. A couple times he tried to lie to me about something, and he couldn't look me in the eye, and I'd say, 'Don't lie to me, Ozzie.' And he'd say, 'I'm sorry. I hate to lie to you.'"

"Did Robert ever mention money problems to you?"

She shook her head. "Is that what's going on with him? Because he hasn't been himself. Like the other day when he met with you? He was a wreck. He's usually carefree and fun. But not lately."

"Since when? Can you pinpoint it?"

She nodded. "Actually, I can. It happened all at once. It was one particular night week before last. Tuesday, I think. I was with him when he got a call from his father. He wouldn't tell me what it was about, but after that he's been all broody and paranoid. And then he had this meeting with you. I mean, a lawyer? So, see, I know something's going on, and now when I can't find him for three days, you can understand why I'd be worried." She arched her eyebrows at me. "You gonna make me feel better, I hope?"

99

Mentioning Paulie Russo wasn't likely to make Becca feel better, so I didn't. "There are dozens of explanations," I said. "The fact that Robert didn't tell you or me what he's up to doesn't mean something happened to him."

She blew out a breath, then nodded. "I guess you're right. I'd like to think he tells me everything. But it's not like we're married or something."

I smiled. "Married people have secrets from each other, too, you know."

"Oh, believe me, I know that." She rolled her eyes. "Just take my parents, for example."

"I'll make a deal with you," I said. "If I hear from Robert before you do, I'll call you. You do the same. Okay?"

"Okay, Mr. Coyne. You got a deal."

"You've got my number," I said.

She nodded, then reached down into her backpack, dug out a pen, found a scrap of paper, and wrote her number on it. "That's my cell," she said. "I always have it with me."

"Try not to worry," I said. "It'll work out."

"I know," she said. "Thanks. I feel better."

Not me, I thought. *I feel worse.*

ELEVEN

When I woke up Sunday morning, Henry was licking my face and birdsong and sunshine were pouring through my open bedroom window. It was the kind of cheerful June morning that makes it impossible to think gloomy thoughts. Evie was in California doing exactly what she should be doing, and the Lancaster family were perfectly capable of working out their problems, and I was going fishing.

I fried some bacon and eggs, made some toast, poured a tall glass of orange juice, and ate my fisherman's breakfast out on my picnic table. It would keep me going all day. Then I loaded my trout-fishing gear and my dog into my car and drove out to the Swift River where it exits the Quabbin Reservoir in Belchertown. The fly-fishing-only mile at the outflow of the dam was mobbed as usual, so I followed the dirt road downstream for a mile or so and found some empty water.

Henry was an experienced and competent fishing dog. While I waded in the river, he prowled the banks, always close enough to come to the water's edge if I whistled.

Now and then I took a break and sat on a boulder or a fallen log beside the river, and Henry came over and lay down beside me. We watched the water for rising trout while my thoughts flipped back to Evie. I wasn't used to this.

I'd lived alone for many years. Being alone had never bothered me. I liked solitude.

I guessed I could get used to it again, but right then it didn't feel like solitude. It felt like loneliness.

It would've been worse without Henry.

I quit around four in the afternoon and got home a little after six. I stowed my gear, then checked my voice mail for messages. Maybe Evie had called.

I had three messages. According to the little digital window on the phone, all were from the same "unknown caller." I didn't recognize the phone number.

The first call had come at 11:16 that morning, about two hours after I'd left to go fishing. "Brady, it's Dalt. I'm home. I need to talk to you. It's really important. Please get back to me right away."

The second one came at 12:27. "Oh, fuck," Dalt said. "You're still not there. Call me, dammit."

The third call came at 4:42. "It's me again," he said. "Now we're at my mother's house. I've got my cell with me, or you can call her house phone. First chance you get. This is really urgent. We need you." He recited both numbers.

I wrote down the numbers and dialed the one for Dalt's cell phone.

He answered on the first ring. "Brady? That you?"

"It's me," I said. "Sorry I wasn't here. What's up?"

"They've got Robert."

"*What?* What do you mean?"

"He's—they kidnapped him. I got a—"

"Who?" I said. "Who kidnapped him? Is it—?"

102

"I don't know," he said. "Listen. They put a CD in my Sunday *Globe* this morning. And a cell phone, too, and . . . Brady, listen. You've got to see this. I need you here. You're involved. I'm here at my mother's. Can you come?"

"What do you mean, I'm involved?"

"You'll see. Just come. You know where she lives, right?"

"I do. Okay. I'm on my way."

Henry was sitting there on the kitchen floor watching me expectantly. I gave him his supper, told him I'd be back, got in my car, and headed for Belmont.

Two cars were parked in the circular driveway in front of Judge Lancaster's house on Belmont Hill. I left mine behind them, went up onto the porch, and rang the bell, and a minute later Mike Warner opened the door.

"Hey, Brady," he said. "Thanks for coming." He stuck out his hand to me.

I shook it. "I didn't expect to see you here."

He shrugged. "Dalt called us. Kimmie—my wife—she's Jess's sister, you know, not to mention her best friend. This is a family thing. We're just all holding hands here waiting for you." He stepped away from the door. "Come on in. Dalt's a mess, and everybody else isn't much better."

I followed Warner into the judge's living room. Dalt and his wife, Jessica, and a woman I didn't recognize were sitting side by side on one of the two sofas, Jess in the middle. Three empty highball glasses were on the coffee table in front of them. They all looked up at me.

I shook hands with Dalt and said hello to Jess.

"This is Kimmie," said Jess. "My sister. Mike's wife."

Kimmie and Jess, I noticed, were holding hands. You could see the resemblance. They were both attractive women—well-defined cheekbones, wide-spaced blue eyes, generous mouths.

Kimmie was a little older and a little blonder and a little heavier than Jess.

"Nice to meet you," I said to Kimmie, "despite the circumstances."

Seated in a wingback chair beside the sofa was a pretty dark-haired woman. I recognized Teresa, Dalt's former wife. Robert's mother. I hadn't seen her since the divorce twelve years earlier. She hadn't changed much. She reminded me of the young Sophia Loren. I went over and held my hand out to her. "Teresa," I said. "I'm Brady Coyne."

She looked up at me, then took my hand. Her dark eyes glistened, but she managed a small smile. "I know," she said. "I remember you from the divorce."

"How are you doing?"

She shrugged and shook her head. "Not that good."

Judge Adrienne Lancaster was standing by the front window, peering out through the curtains as if she were expecting somebody. She was wearing baggy blue jeans and a sweatshirt and sneakers, as if she'd just come in from pruning her roses. She turned, scowled at me, and nodded once. "Attorney Coyne," she said. "Good of you to come."

I nodded. "Hello, Judge."

"Dalton," she said, "pour Mr. Coyne a glass of port." The judge, I saw, was holding a wineglass in her hand.

I held up my hand. "No thanks. I want to hear about what's happened to Robert."

Dalt straightened up. On the coffee table in front of him, a compact disc in its plastic case and a cell phone were sitting beside a laptop computer. He picked up the CD and held it out to me. "I found this stuck in the Metro section of the *Globe* this morning when I fetched it from my front steps," he said. "This, too." He handed the cell phone to me. "This is yours."

"What do you mean, mine?" I said.

"It's all on the disc."

I looked at the CD. On the plastic case someone had used a black indelible pen to print the words: WATCH ME NOW. NO COPS. The disc inside the case had no markings on it. It was the kind you could burn in a computer.

The cell phone was a cheap flip-open Motorola model. I flipped it open. The little screen was blank. I snapped it shut. "Okay," I said, "I want to see what's on this disc."

"I'll do it," said Mike Warner.

I handed the disc to him, then sat in a wing chair beside the sofa.

Judge Lancaster stayed where she was across the room, gazing out the window and sipping from her wineglass.

Warner opened the laptop, slid in the disc, and poked a couple of keys. A few seconds later Robert Lancaster's head and shoulders appeared. He was squinting into a harsh artificial light that cast sharp shadows in the rest of the room. You could see the old yellowish bruises around his left eye. There was a new cut on the right side of his face, a jagged, scabbed-over gash, and the swollen redness of a fresh bruise on his cheekbone.

A tiny microphone with a wire running from it was clipped to his shirt pocket. He looked into the camera for an instant, then his eyes dropped. "I am reading this to you," he said. "They have written it, and if I don't read it word for word they say they will kill me. I am reading it so that you can see that I am alive." His voice was a monotone, and he read slowly, pronouncing each word separately, as if he were afraid of inflecting something incorrectly.

Robert paused, and the camera pulled back so that his entire body could be seen. He was sitting in a wooden armchair. He wore a dirty white T-shirt and a pair of rumpled blue jeans. Several bands of silver-gray duct tape encircled his chest, binding him to the back of the chair. His ankles were taped to the chair legs, and his wrists were taped together. His feet were bare. He was holding a sheet of paper in his hands.

"I am fine," he read. "They are treating me well. I am comfortable. They promise not to hurt me if you follow their instructions." He looked at the camera for a moment, then his eyes went back to the paper he was holding. "They want two hundred and fifty thousand dollars in used twenty- and fifty- and hundred-dollar bills. They will give details at another time. They expect my grandmother to get it. It is now Sunday. They will give you until Tuesday at six o'clock to get the money. If you don't have it by then, they will know you are not cooperating, and they will kill me."

Robert paused, swallowed, licked his lips. He looked young and frightened. "If you don't do everything they say, exactly the way they say it, they promise they will kill me. I believe them. If you involve the police, they will kill me. They will know if you involve the police. Please. Don't talk to the police."

He lifted his eyes from the paper and peered into the camera as if he wanted to speak from his own heart. I read fear, embarrassment, and apology in his dark eyes. After a few seconds, he looked back at the paper he was reading from. "The cell phone is for Brady Coyne. He should turn it on at six on Tuesday and have it with him at all times after that. He is the only one they will talk to." Robert looked up at the camera again, blinked a couple of times, then looked down at the paper in his hands. "Don't contact any police. Do exactly as they say. Please. Just get the money. If you don't, they will kill me." He raised his head and looked at something, or somebody, to the side of the camera that was recording him. He arched his eyebrows, then nodded.

Then the screen went blank.

"Play it again," I said.

Mike Warner hit a few keys, and the recording played again. I listened for sounds other than Robert's voice and heard none. I tried to distinguish features of the background behind him, but all I saw was dark shadows and indistinct shapes.

An expert at that sort of thing might be able to isolate a sound that I couldn't hear, or he might zoom in on some shape in the background, enlarge and clarify it, and turn it into a clue. But my ears and eyes noticed nothing that might help me figure out where Robert was or who had hit him on the cheek and taped him to a chair and threatened his life.

When it was over, I said, "You've got to go to the police."

Teresa shook her head. "No. They'll know. You heard what he said. They'll kill him."

"I agree," said Dalt. "We've got to do it their way."

"They always say that," I said. "That's because they know that if we bring in the authorities, they won't get away with it."

Dalt shook his head. "We can't take the chance. We've got to do what they say."

"It's your decision," I said. "But I don't agree with it. Our odds of getting Robert back are better if we bring in the professionals. The FBI are trained to handle this sort of thing. Let me call them."

"No," he said. "It's not worth the risk."

"I agree with Brady," said Mike Warner. "We should let the pros handle it. It's the only way."

From the other side of the room, Judge Adrienne Lancaster said, "No." She came over and looked down at us. "No police. No FBI. My son is right, for once. The police are incompetent, and the FBI are worse. I think it's apparent that these people who have my grandson are quite competent. I will get the money. We will pay them. We'll do it their way." She fixed me with her famous glare. "Are you on board, Mr. Coyne?"

I shrugged. "I've registered my opinion. I'll do whatever you want."

"You have no obligation, of course."

"I said I'd do it."

"Aren't you afraid they'll kill you?" said the judge.

"I'm afraid they'll kill Robert," I said.

She nodded. "Okay, then. You must do exactly what these—these criminals tell you to do. We will all do as we're told. When we get Robert back, then we'll go after the bastards. Agreed?" She looked around the room.

Dalt and Jess and Kimmie and Mike all nodded.

"Teresa?" said Adrienne. "What about you?"

Teresa was crying. She looked up at her former mother-in-law. "I don't know. I guess so. Whatever you think. I just want my boy back."

"Nobody will breathe a word of this to anybody," said the judge.

Everybody nodded.

"Robert is not missing," she said. "Nothing has happened." She looked straight at Dalt. "This is a family matter. We will all keep it in the family. Right, Dalton?"

"Yes, Mother," Dalt said. "Right."

"Teresa?"

Teresa mumbled "Yes."

"Jessica? Michael? Kimberly?"

They all nodded.

She arched her eyebrows at me.

"Of course," I said.

"All right, good," the judge said. "Now I need to talk to Attorney Coyne privately." She jerked her head at me. "This way, please."

108

TWELVE

I got up and followed Judge Lancaster down a hallway and into a large book-lined office.

She sat behind a big oak desk. "Close that door behind you, please."

I shut the door, then sat in a leather chair across from her. The judge's office featured dark woodwork, oxblood leather furniture, glass-fronted built-in bookcases, a fieldstone fireplace, and paintings of clipper ships and pointing dogs. The room was utterly masculine, and I guessed that it had previously been the domain of Frederick Billings Lancaster, Adrienne's husband and Dalt's father, when he was alive.

But Judge Adrienne Lancaster did not seem at all out of place in this office.

"I recused myself from that case," she said. "As you suggested. I announced it at a press conference. I refused to give a reason. It was humiliating and unprofessional, but I did it on your advice."

"I hoped that would take care of this situation," I said.

"You were wrong."

"Evidently," I said. "I'm sorry."

"It's clear that this—this kidnapping—is related to that. I need to know what you know."

"Dalt and Jess are my clients," I said. "You aren't."

"My grandson has been kidnapped, Attorney Coyne. I am putting up a quarter of a million dollars to get him back. I have a right to know."

I thought for a minute, then nodded. "You're right." I hesitated. "Robert has a gambling problem, Judge. He got in over his head."

"Like father, like son," she said.

I shrugged.

"The Russo family?"

I nodded. "I talked with Paulie Russo. He led me to believe that he'd let it go if you, um, took it into consideration."

"That case," she said.

"They sucked him in," I said, "because they knew he was your grandson. They figured having him indebted to them was a way of influencing you."

Judge Lancaster looked at me with narrowed eyes. "But you suggested I recuse myself. You didn't suggest I allow myself to be influenced. They wanted me on the case. They had leverage. They expected me to be influenced."

"I couldn't ask you to do that."

She looked at me for a minute, then nodded. "No, of course you couldn't. So now they've decided to go after my money."

"I think you're making a mistake," I said, "not going to the police."

"Yes," she said. "You already said that. Thank you. We'll see whether it was a mistake or not. Meanwhile, I'm comfortable taking responsibility for that decision."

"Well," I said, "it is your money."

Her head snapped around. She fixed me with that famous Lancaster glare. "It is," she said, "isn't it? And it's my grandson, too."

"So it is," I said. "Okay. I'll follow the kidnappers' instructions. I'll do whatever I can to get Robert back."

"Thank you." She pointed her elegant finger at me. "So why you, Attorney Coyne?"

"What do you mean?"

"Why do you suppose they chose to involve you, to designate you to be the intermediary in all of this?"

"I guess," I said, "they just figured that Dalt would be too, um, emotional, and that you . . ."

"I am too old," said the judge.

"Maybe Robert told them," I said. "Maybe they asked him who he trusted to handle it, understanding that screwing it up would mean they'd kill him."

The judge nodded. "I suppose that makes sense. So don't screw it up, Attorney Coyne."

"I'll try not to."

"I know you'll do it right." She smiled. "My other question is, how did they arrive at the number two hundred and fifty thousand? Does Robert owe them that much, for heaven's sake?"

"I don't know what he owes them," I said. "He mentioned fifty thousand to me, but I had the feeling he didn't really know. A quarter of a million makes it worth their effort, a reward commensurate with the risk." I shrugged. "It's a nice round number."

She smiled. "It used to be a fortune."

"Maybe they just figured it's what you could come up with in a couple of days," I said.

"In fact," she said, "that's exactly what it is. I can get two hundred and fifty thousand in a day. Half a million would take a week."

"Well, lucky you," I said.

"Lucky Robert, too. Lucky all of us. I will have it tomorrow afternoon. How shall we handle it? They said they would be dealing with you."

"Call me when you have the money," I said. "I'll pick it up. Then when they call to arrange the exchange, I'll be ready to go."

She had her head cocked and was peering at me. After a moment, she nodded. "I know why they chose you."

"Why?"

"Because I trust you," she said. "They must know that. I tend not to trust people. I know I have the reputation of not trusting anybody, and it's not far off. But I have no qualms about handing over a big pile of my cash to you, and I find myself believing that if anybody can do this the right way and get my only grandson back, it's you." She shook her head. "Can you explain that, Attorney Coyne?"

"Nope," I said.

She smiled. "Neither can I." She looked at me for a long moment, then said, "You must think I'm some kind of coldhearted old witch, not to be wailing and gnashing my teeth about this."

I shrugged. "Wailing and teeth-gnashing aren't all that helpful."

"I love my grandson, you know."

"I never doubted it," I said. "Somebody has to take charge."

She stood up and went to a sideboard, where two decanters and some wineglasses sat on a silver tray. "Now that we've got all that settled," she said, "will you join me in a drop of port?"

I nodded. "Why not."

We sipped some smoky old port while the judge told me about a case she had recently heard that involved a class-action lawsuit against a Boston investment company, and about fifteen minutes later we went back out to the living room. Dalt and Jess and Teresa and Kimmie Warner were still sitting there. Mike was in the kitchen. I picked up the kidnappers' CD from the coffee table, patted my pocket to make sure the Motorola cell phone was there, and said, "I'm going home now. Anybody wants to talk to me, you all have my numbers."

I leaned down and exchanged air kisses with the women. When I held out my hand to Dalt, he said, "I'll walk you out."

Mike Warner came out of the kitchen. "You leaving?" he said. "I just put on some coffee. It'll be ready in a minute."

"No," I said. "Thanks."

He held out his hand. "Well, good luck. I hope, if there's anything I can do . . ."

I nodded.

"Dalt's not just my brother-in-law," he said. "He's my best friend. Robert's like a son to me. This whole thing is unbelievable."

"We'll do our best," I said.

The judge was standing in the foyer near the door. She held out her hand. "Attorney Coyne," she said, "we do appreciate your efforts." Her hand was dry and bony, but her handshake was strong.

"We'll be talking, Judge," I said.

"Bet your ass we will," she said.

Dalt and I went outside and walked over to my car. "I don't understand," he said.

"What?"

"Any of it. Why those thugs beat me up. Why they've kidnapped my son. It is them, right?"

"I assume so," I said. "Did Robert contact you anytime in the past few days?"

He shook his head. "Last time I talked to him was that night at the hospital. Why?"

"He promised me he would."

"What for?"

"Look," I said, "he didn't want you to know, but I made him promise to tell you. To tell all of you. Since he didn't, I guess I should." I hesitated. "He's got a gambling problem. He's into the Russo family for a lot of money. They set him up."

"Jesus," said Dalt. "You saying those goons beat me up because my son owes them money?"

"Something like that. They hoped to influence your mother. She had a case involving them. That's why they fronted Robert the money. That was their leverage. When she recused herself, they lost their leverage, and then I guess they figured all they could do was go after the money."

"It's my fault," said Dalt. "I wish they'd kidnapped me."

"Your fault?"

"Sure. Robert got it from me."

"You think it's genetic?"

"I don't know. It seems like it, doesn't it? Some strand on the Lancaster DNA? I taught Robert and Jimmy—that's my nephew, Mike and Kimmie's boy—how to play poker. This was after I quit the casinos. We played for matchsticks and pennies, that's all. I just figured every boy should know how to play poker. It's like throwing and catching and kissing girls. But both of those boys were really into it. They played against each other all the time, taught their friends, organized games."

"Robert told me about what happened to Jimmy," I said.

He shook his head. "Maybe I should blame myself for what happened to him, too. An awful, terrible thing. Kimmie's never been the same. It just clobbered Mike. You've got sons, Brady. You can imagine."

"I really can't," I said. "It's unimaginable."

"It's been almost six years since Jimmy went missing," Dalt said. "They still jump whenever the phone rings."

"All kids learn how to gamble sometime or other," I said. "You can't blame yourself."

"Easier said than done." He shrugged. "So now it's Robert. You think they'll kill him?"

"Sometimes they do," I said, "sometimes they don't."

Dalt shook his head. "Thanks for sugarcoating it. Makes me feel a lot better."

"If you don't want the answer, don't ask the question."

"Sure." He smiled quickly. "We're doing the right thing, giving them the money, aren't we?"

"I don't know."

He shook his head. "Why didn't he come to me? He should've come to me. I would have helped him. That's what fathers are for."

"You'll have to ask him when you see him," I said.

"If they kill my son," Dalt said, "I don't know what I'll do."

THIRTEEN

I got home from Judge Lancaster's house a little after ten-thirty. Henry was glad to see me, and I was glad to see him. He filled the house with his happiness and made the hole Evie had left behind feel smaller.

I let him out into the yard, then checked the phone for messages.

There were none.

Ten-thirty was only seven-thirty in California. I imagined Evie and her father sitting on the deck of his houseboat watching the sun go down, drinking margaritas, getting reacquainted with each other. They'd talk about old times, and they'd have some laughs, I hoped, retelling family stories, conjuring up happy memories from Evie's childhood. They'd avoid the subject of Ed's illness. He'd feel better with her there to keep him company. She was doing the right thing.

I wondered if Evie would talk about me and our life together, or if Ed would ask.

I realized I hadn't eaten anything since half a granola bar—

Henry got the other half—and a bottle of water in the car on the way home from the Swift River. I found some leftover chicken in the refrigerator, another memento of an earlier dinner with Evie. I sliced it up and made a sandwich, and after I let Henry in and rewarded him with a slice of chicken, I took my sandwich and a can of Coke into my office.

I slipped the kidnappers' CD into my computer and watched it again. This time I wasn't interested in the message, which was pretty straightforward. Instead, I tried to pay attention to the medium. I studied Robert's face and body language, and I listened to the syntax and vocabulary of the speech that had been written for him.

I couldn't read much from Robert's appearance. He had those old yellow bruises around his eye, and he had that new cut on his cheekbone, but he seemed pretty composed and calm for a young man who'd found himself wrapped in duct tape and being held hostage. He didn't blink excessively, nor did he lick his lips or stumble over the words he read. I saw no sweat on his brow or upper lip. His hands and chin didn't tremble. If Robert Lancaster was frightened for his life, he was doing a good job of controlling it.

He had a good poker face. Hard to read.

The words he read were bland and simple and precise. The absence of contractions made it sound a little stilted and contrived, and it struck me that whoever wrote it was trying hard to preclude misinterpretations.

I guessed it was Paulie who wrote Robert's speech. In spite of the dese-and-dem language Paulie affected for the benefit of the goons who worked for him, I happened to know that he had graduated from Lawrence Academy and been accepted at Boston College. It was a great disappointment for Vincent Russo when his only son decided to go to work in the family business rather than attend college.

I played the disc again. It occurred to me that Robert might have been Morse-coding us a message with his fingers or eyes, or that he'd tried some other method of secretly communicating with us. If he had, I failed to catch on.

I was ejecting the disc when the phone beside my computer rang.

My heart bloomed in my chest. Evie.

I snatched up the phone and said, "Yes? Hi."

"Well, hi yourself." It was Charlie McDevitt.

"Oh," I said.

"Well, I'm sorry," he said. "Clearly I am a disappointment. You pissed that I didn't go fishing with you?"

"You're never a disappointment," I said, "and I'm not pissed. I had a grand time today fishing all by myself. Landed five nice rainbows. One went about seventeen inches. Henry came along and didn't argue politics or baseball with me. When the phone rang, I thought you were Evie."

"Easy to tell us apart," said Charlie. "Her hair's longer than mine."

"She's in California," I said. "I was kind of expecting her to call."

"It's only me," he said. "You called, remember? I just got your message. We were in Connecticut for the week, only got back a few minutes ago." He hesitated. "Is everything okay? With you and Evie, I mean?"

"Oh, sure. Her father's sick, so she went out there to stay with him for a while."

"I'm hearing something else in your voice, old friend."

"I miss her," I said. "It's empty around here without her, that's all. I'm not sure when she'll be back." I hesitated. "I've got a peculiar question for you."

"Wouldn't surprise me," he said. "You're a peculiar person. What is it?"

Charlie had been my law school roommate back in New Haven. He joined the U.S. Department of Justice when he graduated, and he'd been an attorney in the Boston office for most of his career. We'd been best friends all that time. There had been a couple of occasions when he didn't mind bending some bureaucratic regulations to dig up information that I needed. I'd done him a few favors, too. That, we told each other, was what friends were for.

"I was just wondering," I said, "what the FBI's solve rate is on kidnapping cases."

"Kidnapping, huh?" he said. "Where'd that come from?"

"Just idle curiosity."

"Idle? Jesus, Brady. I hope to hell—"

"Don't worry about it," I said.

I heard him blow out a breath. "Okay," he said. "If by solve rate you mean how often do they catch the bad guys, it's pretty good. I don't have a statistic for you, but it's way over fifty percent. Sixty or seventy, I'd say. On the other hand, most of these cases are amateur hour. Mr. Magoo could solve them."

"Thinking about the, um, nonamateur cases," I said, "do you have any idea how frequently the hostage is released or rescued unharmed?"

"Listen," he said, "the Feebs are better at that sort of thing than anybody. They've got the technology and the training and the experience. That's all you need to know. And you should tell me what the hell is going on."

"I wish I could."

"Well, shit," he said. "If I'd gone fishing with you—"

"I wouldn't even have raised the subject," I said. "That wasn't why I called you. I wanted to go fishing, just like I said, and anyway, this afternoon I didn't know what I know now."

"I'm still sorry I wasn't with you," he said. "It would've been fun. You caught five rainbows, huh?"

"Rising fish, all of them," I said. "They ate a little deerhair beetle imitation. Henry was with me. He was quite impressed with my skill."

"Your dog's never seen me in action is why. So, listen. About this kidnapping."

"I didn't say anything about any kidnapping," I said.

"Okay. So you didn't. Be careful, will you?"

"Always."

"Tell Evie hi for me when you talk to her."

"I sure will."

"You've got my cell phone number," he said. "Don't hesitate to use it."

"Next time I want to go fishing," I said.

"Any time," he said.

Melville had no problem putting me to sleep that night, and it wasn't until I woke up Monday morning in an empty bed that I realized Evie had never called.

I called Julie at the office a little after nine. She reluctantly confirmed what I thought I remembered—that my first appointment of the day wasn't until eleven. I told her that's when I'd be there, and before she could launch her predictable speech about my responsibilities to my clients and the necessity of accruing billable hours and all the paperwork we had to do, I said, "I've

121

got something important that can't wait. Gotta go right now. Thanks." And I hung up.

Henry was sitting there watching me. "You stay here and guard the house," I told him. "Don't forget to bark at that shifty UPS guy if he tries to leave a parcel on the front porch."

Henry lay down and dropped his chin onto his paws.

I squatted beside him and scratched that magic place on his forehead. "I know you miss Evie," I said to him. "I do, too. Looks like it's going to be just us two bachelors for a while, so we'll have to make the best of it. Okay?"

He rolled his eyes and looked up at me without lifting his head. Then he sighed and closed them. Henry would handle the situation in his own way. He'd sleep through it.

I put the kidnappers' CD in one jacket pocket and their cell phone in another one, made sure Henry's water dish was full, gave him a new rawhide bone for company, and left the house.

I picked up a dozen donuts at the bakery on Newbury Street—six glazed, six jelly-filled—and walked into Gordon Cahill's PI office on Exeter Street around quarter of ten.

His wife had designed the space. It was open and airy, with bright abstract paintings and big potted plants and modern furniture. The areas were defined with movable partitions rather than walls, so I could see Gordie's office space from the doorway.

When I stepped inside, he looked up and frowned. He was on the phone. Then he noticed the donut box in my hand, and he smiled and pointed to the chair across from his desk.

I put the donuts on his desk. Then I went over to the coffee urn in the corner, poured myself a mugful, and arched my eyebrows at him. He waved his hand over the mug on his desk and shook his head, still talking on the telephone.

I went over and sat across from him.

After a minute, he hung up. "Hey," he said. He reached his hand across his desk.

I shook it. "Hey."

He tapped the donut box. "Jelly? Glazed?"

"Both," I said.

"Oh-oh," he said. "Whaddya want?"

I took a twenty-dollar bill out of my wallet and put it on his desk blotter.

He pushed it back at me. "You can't pay me," he said. "I owe you my life. I'm not taking your money."

A couple of years earlier I'd hired Gordie, who was the best private investigator in Boston, to do some snooping for a case I was working on. The situation exploded on us in ways I never expected, and Gordie nearly died. I managed to rescue him and get him to a hospital, but his leg was permanently damaged.

Before that, he'd loved the fieldwork. Tailing people. Staking them out. Skulking around taking pictures through a telephoto lens.

Now he hobbled around on a crutch and did all his detecting from his desk.

He kept focusing on the fact that I'd saved his life.

I kept reminding him that if it hadn't been for me, his life wouldn't have been jeopardized in the first place.

"Let's not argue about that again," I said. "I am hiring you to ensure your confidentiality."

"You don't need to pay me for that. My word is my bond. Not to mention, you can always bribe me with donuts." He opened the box, leaned over, took a sniff, then plucked out a glazed donut. He took a big bite. "Mmm," he said with his mouth full. "Take one."

I reached into the box and picked a jelly-filled. "Keep the to-ken money, Gordie," I said. "Let's make it legal this time."

"Legal, huh? Cops involved in this?"

"No," I said. "Not yet, anyway." I took the CD and the cell phone from my pockets and put them on his desk. "Take a look at the disc. You'll see what I'm talking about."

He opened the plastic case and popped out the CD. He looked at both sides of it, then slid it into his desktop computer. I went around, stood behind him, and watched over his shoulder.

When it ended, we watched it again.

I went back and sat in the chair across from him.

We both ate another donut.

"Judge Adrienne Lancaster, huh?" he said.

I nodded.

"Okay. Now I understand the twenty bucks. My lips are sealed. So who's the kid with the beat-up face doing the talking?"

"His name's Robert Lancaster," I said. "The judge's grandson. His father and mother—and now, by extension, Judge Lancaster herself—are my clients."

"And you're sharing this with me . . . why?"

"Because you're the best investigator I know, and you're a technical wizard, and you've got state-of-the-art detecting equipment. Not to mention, I trust you. Since the cops aren't involved, that leaves me. So I'm wondering if you can figure out where this video was made. And anything else you might notice."

"Find where it was made, find your hostage, huh?"

I shrugged. "I just figure knowledge is power, and right now I'm feeling pretty powerless."

"Ignorance being weakness," he said.

I nodded.

"How much time do you have this morning?"

"I've got to be at the office by eleven."

Gordie looked at his wristwatch. "I'll have to get back to you, then," he said. "You want me to do this right, it'll take a little while."

"Today?"

"Oh, sure. I'll call you sometime this afternoon."

I stuffed the rest of my donut into my mouth, took a sip of coffee, and stood up. "I'll make sure Julie puts you through regardless of what's going on." I reached my hand across his desk. "Thanks."

Gordie grabbed my hand. Instead of letting go, he said, "You know Arnie Coblitz?"

"Coblitz?" I shook my head. "Don't think so."

"Arnie's a lawyer like you," he said. "Partner with a firm on State Street. Month or so ago, his cousin from Czechoslovakia, a young woman named Sofia, came to Boston, visiting the states for the first time. She yearned to see the West—she used to watch old American westerns on Czech TV—so Arnie took her out to Yellowstone Park. You've been there."

"I have," I said. "Wonderful trout fishing. But—"

Gordie kept his grip on my hand. "So Arnie and Sofia are in the park hiking through the woods, and they get attacked by a pair of grizzly bears, a big male and a medium-sized female. The female goes after Arnie, who runs like hell and manages to climb a tree. When he looks down, to his horror, he sees the male bear devouring his Czechoslovakian cousin. Pretty soon, there's nothing left of Sofia but one of her shoes, and the two bears go wandering away. So—"

I tugged at my hand until Gordie let go. "I know what you're doing," I said, "and I don't have time for it."

Gordie placed his hand on his chest. "You wound me deeply," he said. "This is something Arnie Coblitz, your fellow barrister, told me just the other day. I assumed you'd be interested, inasmuch as you're a lawyer, too, and you've also been to Yellowstone."

"Fine," I said. "Go ahead. Speed it up, though, will you?"

"So, okay," Gordie said. "After the bears go away, Arnie climbs down the tree, hikes back to his rental car, and drives to the nearest ranger station. He tells the two rangers that his Czechoslovakian cousin just got eaten by this enormous male grizzly. So the rangers grab their high-power bear rifles, and they tell Arnie to get into the truck with them, and Arnie shows them where it happened. Poor Sofia's shoe is still there. So the rangers start creeping through the woods, with Arnie right behind them, and pretty soon one of the rangers stops and whispers, 'There they are,' and he raises his rifle and shoots the female bear. 'Hey,' says the other ranger, 'you shot the wrong bear. This guy said it was the big male who ate his cousin.' And the first ranger looks at his partner and shakes his head and says, 'And you believe some lawyer when he tells you the Czech is in the male?' "

I tried not to smile. "Damn you, Cahill," I said. "You did it again."

"Bad, huh?"

"Awful," I said.

He grinned. "Thank you."

I got the hell out of there.

FOURTEEN

It was a little after three that afternoon, and I had just ushered my last scheduled appointment of the day out of my office when Julie buzzed me. "Mr. Cahill on line two," she said. "You want to tell me why a private investigator is calling you?"

"Nope," I said.

I pressed the blinking light on my telephone console and said, "What've you got for me?"

"You still mad?" said Gordie.

"Why, because you inflicted another one of your horrible puns on me?"

"I didn't think that one was so bad."

"Only in comparison to all your others," I said. "So tell me what you learned."

"Come on over and I'll show you."

"No more donuts for you today."

"That's okay," he said. "I still got a couple left from this morning."

"I'm on my way," I said.

I grabbed my jacket from the back of my chair and went out to our reception area.

Julie was frowning at her computer monitor. She looked up, glanced meaningfully at her watch, and frowned at me. "Are we leaving already?"

"I am. You may, too."

She waved at her computer. "I, for one, have not finished my day's work yet."

I put both hands on the edge of her desk and leaned toward her. "I can't talk about it yet," I said. "All I can say right now is, it concerns one of our clients. You know I'll fill you in when I can. Okay?"

She shrugged. "If you say so."

Ten minutes later I walked into Gordon Cahill's office. He was at his desk talking to a strikingly pretty African American woman. I thought I might have recognized her from one of the Boston television news programs.

I sat in the reception area and thumbed through a recent issue of *Gray's Sporting Journal* until the woman stood up, shook Gordie's hand, and came toward the door.

She smiled at me, and I smiled back at her. Seeing her up close, I guessed I didn't recognize her after all.

Gordie waved his hand. "Come on over."

I went over to his desk.

"Pull that chair around so you can look at this with me," he said.

I did that and sat beside him. "So what can you tell me?" I said.

"I'm not sure what you expected."

"I have no expectations," I said.

"Let's look at it, then." He poked some keys, and Robert's face filled the computer screen. He began to speak, and after a minute Gordie paused it. "Look here," he said. He touched the screen with the eraser end of a pencil. "He's got an old black eye plus this new wound on his cheek."

"I know about the black eye," I said. "Happened a couple weeks ago."

"Well this one here"—Gordie pointed at the cut on Robert's cheekbone with the pencil—"is only a day or two old, I'd say. That's a new scab, and see how around it it's still red?"

"That's good observing," I said.

"I was going to observe further," he said, "not knowing this young man, that he seems quite comfortable, given the words he's reading and the duct tape on his ankles, wrists, and chest."

"Comfortable?"

"Unstressed. At ease. In control. You know him, right?"

"Not that well."

"Could he be drugged or something?"

"I don't know. See, when I saw it, I just thought he was dealing with it. Stoic. Tough."

"Is he stoic and tough?"

I shrugged. "I don't know him well enough to say. He's just a college kid. He plays a lot of poker. Knows how to bluff."

"Maybe that's what he's doing," said Gordie. "Playing it close to the vest. He's not sweating. Nothing that looks like nerves. Nothing in his voice that would suggest he was anxious or worried or afraid for his life."

"I noticed that, too," I said. "I looked at this disc with other people who know him. None of them seemed to think he was acting out of character." I looked at Gordie. "What are you thinking?"

"Thinking?" He shook his head. "Nothing. No interpretations or hypotheses, if that's what you mean. I'm just observing."

I shrugged. "Okay. Good."

"Anyway," said Gordie, "that's one of the things I was observing. A kidnapping victim, his life apparently in dire jeopardy, how he's holding up. Pretty good, it looks like. So, let me . . ." He played the tape until the camera pulled back to show how Robert was taped to a chair. "Take a look here," said Gordie. He paused the image, then manipulated the mouse and zoomed into the upper-right quadrant behind Robert's left shoulder. "See? This looks like a bedsheet. Pale blue. You can see the creases and folds. They hung it behind him so that you wouldn't see any details of the room."

"Interpret that for me," I said.

"Obviously," he said, "they're either very professional and thorough, or else they think somebody might recognize the room they're in."

"Or both," I said.

"Right," said Gordie. "Most likely both. Anyway, here's the interesting thing." He pointed with his pencil. "See that?"

I looked. "I'm sorry. What am I looking at?"

"See this lighter-colored section here?" He moved the pencil in circles over the hanging blue sheet.

"Yes," I said. "Now I do. What about it?"

"There's light coming in from behind. It looks to me like there's a window there."

"I see what you mean," I said. "How does that help us?"

"Hell," said Gordie, "I don't know. Maybe it doesn't. You're the one with all the information. You're going to have to figure that out."

I was looking at the bright spot. "It looks sort of roundish," I said. "This patch of light."

"With some space between the sheet and the wall," he said, "the shape would be distorted. But I'd guess it's a window with daylight coming in, and it looks like it's smaller and higher up on the wall than your regular house window. He could be in a basement. This could be one of those little cellar windows up near the ceiling."

I nodded. "This is good, Gordie. I'm not sure how it helps, but maybe it will. It would be an even bigger help, of course, if you could give me the address or GPS location."

"Yeah, sorry," he said. "Anyway, that's all I noticed on the visual part of the recording. This kid's affect, the blue sheet, and that patch of light. I don't have the equipment to isolate and amplify sounds. That might be worth doing, you know."

"Who can do that?"

"State police. FBI." He cocked his head at me. "I know I'm not supposed to know anything, or ask any questions." He arched his eyebrows.

I shook my head.

"The family refuses to go to the cops, huh?"

"Right."

"So it's you?"

I nodded. "It's just me."

He looked at me for a minute, then shrugged. "As far as the audio is concerned," he said, "I think I'm hearing something. It's frustrating not to have the equipment."

"Play it for me."

"I can slow it down to half speed and fool around with the bass and treble, just like you can do on your hi-fi. Pretty low-tech, but better than nothing. Listen." He fast-forwarded it for a few seconds, then paused it. "It's coming up here." He played it at normal speed. "Hear that?"

"I don't know what I'm supposed to hear except his voice," I said.

"Ignore that. Listen for background noises." He backed it up and played it again, and I detected a faint, rhythmical sound. It seemed to rise and fall over the space of about thirty seconds.

"Okay," I said. "I think I hear what you're hearing. But I don't recognize it."

"Me, neither," said Gordie. "Let's amplify it."

He reversed it again, made some adjustments, then played it at half speed. Robert's voice deepened so that it sounded hollow and echoey. The rhythmical sound came through more clearly. It was a kind of soft thumping noise, as if somebody were slapping his hand on a table.

"What do you make of it?" I said.

He shook his head. "Beats the hell out of me. Like I said—"

"I know. Better equipment. I can't go to the cops."

"Talk to your clients," he said. "It's stupid not to bring in the pros."

"I'll try again. So was there anything else?"

"One thing," he said. "Pretty obvious. I bet you noticed it, too."

"What's that?"

"No tape over the kid's eyes."

I nodded. "That's not good."

"No. It means they don't care if he sees them."

"They could be wearing masks," I said.

"Let's hope," said Gordie.

"Right," I said. "Anything else about the disc?"

"Nope. That's it. What do you want for a dozen donuts?"

"Don't forget," I said, "I also had to listen to your dumb pun. That's a stiff price to pay. What can you tell me about that cell phone?"

It was sitting on Gordie's desk. He picked it up and bounced it in his palm. "You got yourself a brand-new, bottom-of-the-line, prepaid Motorola cellular telephone," he said. "You can get these babies online from a hundred places from here to Tokyo, or from any Wal-Mart or Circuit City. Cost you about fifty bucks."

"Meaning you can't trace where it was purchased?"

"If there's a way," he said, "I don't know it, and it would probably take weeks of legwork anyway. There's no serial number or anything like that on it to distinguish it from all the others just like it. Whatever might've been programmed into it has been erased. I couldn't even figure out its phone number."

"The phone's a dead end, then."

"Well, again . . ." He looked at me and flapped his hands.

"Right," I said. "Take it to the cops."

He gave me the phone, then ejected the disc from his computer, put it in its plastic case, and handed it to me, too. "If there's anything else I can do," he said.

I put the phone and the disc into my pockets. "I know," I said. "I appreciate it."

"Just don't forget the donuts."

I turned to leave. Then I went back to his desk.

He looked up at me. "You disappointed I didn't have another story for you?"

"God, no," I said. "You remember on the disc how Robert was all taped up? Wrists, ankles, around his chest?"

"Sure."

"Could a person do that to himself?"

"Interesting." He frowned. "Hmm . . ." He gazed up at the ceiling. "I'm trying to visualize it," he muttered. Then he looked at me and shook his head. "I don't see how. The ankles wouldn't be a problem, and maybe if you used your mouth you could tape your wrists together . . . although once you taped your mouth, you couldn't do that, and if you taped your wrists first, you couldn't very well tape your mouth. Anyway, that tape around his chest went around the back of the chair and it was right up snug in his armpits. Human arms don't bend that way." He shook his head. "Nope. You'd have to be Houdini or something. Why? You think—?"

"I don't think anything," I said. "Just trying to get my head outside the box."

"Always a good plan," Gordie said. "Listen, speaking of Houdini and boxes, did I ever tell you—"

"I gotta go," I said.

FIFTEEN

When I got home, I scraped the frost off a supermarket pepperoni-and-onion pizza I found in the freezer and heated it in the oven. I ate it with a can of Coke at the kitchen table while I watched the evening news. Without Evie to share it with, I realized that I had no desire to make any kind of ceremony out of cooking or eating. Food was fuel for the machine.

I was remembering how to live alone again.

Henry sat beside me, alert and grateful for the occasional pizza crust that I gave him. For Henry, food was joy.

The phone rang at seven-thirty.

"It's Adrienne Lancaster," she said in that raspy voice of hers, as if I might be expecting phone calls from other women named Adrienne. "I have it."

"The money?"

"Yes. A quarter of a million dollars. Used twenties, fifties, and hundreds. It's making me nervous. Please come and collect it."

"I'm on my way," I said.

I'd left my car in a residents-only space on the street in front of the house. Henry came with me. We pulled into the judge's driveway around eight-fifteen. There were no other cars parked there.

I cracked the windows so Henry could stick out his nose and sniff the evening air. I told him to be patient, I wouldn't be gone long. Then I went up to the front porch and rang the bell.

A minute later the judge opened the door. "Come in, please," she said.

I went in and followed her into the living room.

"Can I get you something?" she said.

I shook my head. "I think this is a mistake."

"I know you do."

"You're going to lose your money, and you won't get Robert back."

She shrugged. "The money is unimportant."

"It's not too late," I said. "Let's bring the police into it. I can make a call, and—"

"No. Absolutely not." She was wearing blue slacks and low heels and a white blouse. Gold earrings and a gold necklace. I guessed it was the same outfit she'd worn under her judge's robes that day. She combed her fingers through her steel gray hair, blew out a breath, and gestured at a chair. "Sit down, Attorney Coyne. Please."

I sat, and she took the sofa.

"I'm fully aware that this could be a mistake," she said.

"It *is* a mistake."

"Either way could be a mistake," she said. "We won't know until it's over. I've thought about it, believe me, and I have concluded that we'd all feel worse if refusing to do it their way resulted in . . ." She shook her head, then turned and glared at me. "If you've changed your mind and have decided you don't want to play the role that these people have assigned to you, Attorney Coyne, you'd better tell me right now."

136

"If I back out," I said, "will you bring in the police?"

"If you back out," she said, "Robert is dead, police or no police."

"I didn't come here to tell you I was backing out," I said. "I'm just not optimistic about how it's going to end."

She nodded. "Neither am I." She slumped back on the sofa and gazed up at the ceiling. "I love my grandson, Mr. Coyne. I love my son, too, in spite of his weaknesses. I love them more than I love my money." She moved her head so that she was looking at me. "No, I'm not optimistic, either. Involving the police wouldn't make me feel better about it, though."

"I guess we'll do it their way, then," I said.

"Thank you." She pushed herself to her feet and left the room. She was back a minute later with a red Nike gym bag in her hand. She plopped it onto the coffee table in front of me. "It's all here," she said.

I unzipped the bag. It was nearly full of paper currency in decks about an inch thick bound by rubber bands. I picked up one of the decks and riffled through it with my thumb. Twenty-dollar bills. Some were crispy and new, some were soft and old.

I emptied the bag onto the coffee table.

"You'll find fifty-five stacks of bills there," said Adrienne. "Two hundred and fifty thousand dollars, one hundred bills per stack. Twenty-five stacks of twenties, twenty stacks of fifties, and ten of hundreds. I called four banks this morning, and this afternoon they had the money ready for me. According to them, most of those bills have been in circulation."

"How did you handle it?" I said.

"Handle what?"

"Collecting all that currency. The banks. What did you tell them?"

"I didn't handle anything," she said. "I simply filled out

137

withdrawal slips, told them what I wanted, and reminded them that I'd called earlier to be sure they would have the currency on hand. They verified that my accounts would cover it, and they gave it to me."

"No questions?"

She smiled. "I am a judge. I can be quite imperious."

"Yes," I said. "I've noticed that." I put the decks of bills back into the gym bag and zipped it up. "Now we wait to hear from them."

"They said they'd call at six tomorrow," she said.

"Not exactly," I said. "They said I should turn their cell phone on at six. Who knows when they'll call."

"But you'll be ready."

I hefted the gym bag. "I'll be ready."

"And you will keep me informed."

"As you keep reminding me," I said, "it's your money."

Around midnight I was trying to keep my eyes open so I could finish one of Melville's riveting dissertations on whale blubber when the phone rang.

It was Evie. "Hey," she said. "You wanna get married?"

I smiled. "Sure."

"My daddy says we should get married. Make an honest man out of you, he says. You being a lawyer."

"I don't think I'm dishonest," I said.

"You're a lawyer," she said. "Sly. My sly lawyer."

"You're pretty drunk, huh?" I said.

"Wine. A lovely Syrah from the Cline vineyard. Cline Syrah, Syrah. What will be, will be." She was singing to the tune of "Que Sera, Sera." "Not to mention some sacred weed, also from California's Sonoma Valley. Daddy loves Sonoma weed. So do I.

Vastly superior to Napa weed. I love Brady, too. Weed and Brady."

"I'm flattered," I said, "even to be mentioned in the same breath as Sonoma weed."

"They grow grapes and cannibis," she said. "The Sonoma Valley. Bet you didn't know that."

"All the important food groups."

She said nothing for a minute. "Are you mad at me?"

"Of course not. I miss you. Henry and I are here in bed reading *Moby-Dick*. Missing you. Henry sends his love. I'm glad you called."

"Dear Henry," she said. "And good old sober old unstoned old Brady. Curled up in my bed."

"So how are you, honey?"

"Outta my skull, baby. Whew."

"Aside from that."

"Oh, gosh." She paused. "Oh, jeez, Brady." And then I heard that she was crying, and I realized that she'd been crying the whole time. "My daddy is scared. Do you see? He's not supposed to be scared. I can be scared. I'm his little girl. He's supposed to be fearless. But he's not. So I don't know how to feel. I'm just my daddy's little girl. I can't be fearless for both of us. I can't even be fearless for me."

"What can I do, honey?"

"Are you fearless?"

"Yes, I am," I said. "I will be fearless for all three of us. You go ahead, be scared. It's okay."

She was quiet for a minute. Then she said, "It doesn't really work that way."

"I know." I hesitated. "Is there any news?"

"We go to the hospital Wednesday. Then there will be news, I bet."

"I'll be thinking of you," I said. "You and Ed."

"You better," she said.

"Call me, okay?"

"Mmm." She was quiet. I could hear her breathing. Then she said, "Love you."

"Love you, too."

"I really don't want to get married, you know," she said.

"I know."

"I was just kidding."

"I knew that."

Mike Warner called me at my office around noon on Tuesday. "Today's the day, right?"

"I guess so," I said. "I'll turn on their cell phone at six. Then we'll see."

"Adrienne got the money?"

"She did. I have it."

"A quarter of a million, huh?"

"Yep."

"Well," said Warner, "if there's anything I can do, you know?"

"I can't think of anything."

"You're going to have to deliver that money," he said. "I could go with you."

"They said just me," I said. "We better do it their way."

"Dalt's my best friend. I feel like I should be doing something."

"I understand that," I said. "But this is how they want it."

"Not that I don't trust you," he said, "but I think it's a mistake. Not bringing in the police, I mean."

"So do I," I said.

"I lost my son," he said. "Now this."

I couldn't think of anything to say to him.

I left the office early that afternoon. I fed Henry and made myself a ham-and-cheese sandwich, which I took out to the patio and washed down with a Coke.

I brought the kidnappers' cell phone out with me, and at six o'clock I turned it on.

It sat there on the picnic table. Darkness began to seep into my backyard, and the phone didn't ring.

I might have dozed, because the ring seemed to come from far away. I groped for the kidnappers' phone, put it to my ear, and said, "Yes?"

When the phone rang again, I realized the sound was coming through the screen door from the kitchen. I jumped up, jogged into the house, and grabbed the kitchen phone as it was ringing again.

"Yes," I said. "Hello."

"You're all out of breath." It was Dalt. "I'm sorry I made you run. I just called because—"

"I haven't heard from them yet," I said.

"Oh."

"When I have any news," I said, "I'll let you know. Are you home?"

"I'm at my mother's. She said she got the money. I'm . . . this isn't easy. Waiting, I mean. Doing nothing but waiting."

"I know," I said. "Look. Try not to worry. I'm going to do what they tell me to do. We'll get Robert back."

"I shouldn't have called," he said. "It sounds like I don't trust you. That's not it. It's just . . . there's nothing for me to do."

"I know," I said. "It's hard. Did Adrienne want to speak to me?"

Dalt said something I didn't understand, then he said, "No. She says you and she have nothing further to discuss. I don't think she means it quite the way it sounds."

After I hung up with Dalt, I went back outside and watched the sky darken and the stars pop out. The kidnappers' cell phone did not ring.

Around nine-thirty I put the phone in my shirt pocket, snapped my fingers at Henry, and went into the house. I took the phone to the bathroom with me. It was in my pocket when I went into the living room to watch the end of the Red Sox game, and after the game ended I brought it with me when I went to the kitchen to brew a pot of coffee.

At half past midnight I'd started on my third mug of coffee, figuring it was going to be a long, late night, when the kidnappers' cell phone rang.

I pressed the on button and said, "Brady Coyne."

"Do exactly as I say," said a voice. It was muffled and hollow. He was doing something to disguise it, and he was succeeding. Maybe it was Paulie, but if it was, I didn't recognize his voice. He spoke very slowly, pausing after each word. "Robert Lancaster's life depends on you."

"Let me speak to him."

"You have the money?"

"I want to talk to Robert."

"You are going to need two large black heavy-duty plastic trash bags. I hope you have them."

"What if I don't?"

"That would be tragic."

"I have trash bags," I said.

"Get them."

142

"I've got to hear Robert's voice."

"You will. Do as you are told. Keep the phone with you while you get those bags and the money. Tell me when you have them."

"Okay." I tucked the phone into my shirt pocket and headed for my den. I'd put the red gym bag in the closet. I brought it to the kitchen table. Then I pulled two trash bags out of the box we keep under the kitchen sink.

I took the phone out of my pocket. "I have the bags and the money."

"The bills are bound in stacks?"

"Yes."

"Two hundred and fifty thousand dollars."

"Yes."

"In stacks of one hundred bills."

"That's how banks do it, yes."

"Take the bands off the stacks," said the voice, "and dump it all into one of those bags. When you have done that, tie the top of the bag and put it inside the other bag. Tie the top of that bag the same way. Do it now."

I opened the gym bag and dumped the stacks of money onto the table. Then I held a trash bag open, and one by one I removed the bands from the stacks of currency and dropped the bills into the bag. I tied the top, stuffed it inside the second bag, and tied the top of that one. All those loose bills nearly filled the bag, although when I hefted it, it was lighter than I'd expected. More air than money.

I left the double-bagged two hundred and fifty thousand dollars on the floor and picked up the phone. "All right," I said. "That's done."

"Take it to your car," said the voice. "Be sure to bring the phone. It is Robert Lancaster's lifeline. Keep it turned on. Put the bag on the passenger seat. Then get behind the wheel and start the car. I want to hear you starting the car. Then I will give you your next instruction."

"When will I talk to Robert?"

"Go to your car now."

I put the phone in my shirt pocket, slung the trash bag over my shoulder, and headed for the front door.

Henry scurried ahead of me and sat beside the door. He looked at me with his ears cocked.

"You can't come," I said to him.

The voice in the telephone said something I couldn't understand. I took it from my pocket and said, "I didn't hear what you said. The phone was in my pocket."

"Who is with you?"

"Nobody."

"I heard you speak to somebody."

"It's just my dog," I said. "I told him he couldn't come with me. He's disappointed."

"Leave him there. Go to your car."

"That's what I'm doing," I said.

"If there is anybody with you," said the voice, "if you do not do this exactly as I tell you, Robert Lancaster will die and it will be your fault."

"I hear you," I said, and then I realized that he was using the telephone as a listening device, a bug, as well as a way of communicating with me. Whatever I did, he'd know, as long as the phone line was open and I kept it with me.

I'd parked my car in front of the house. I unlocked it with the remote, opened the passenger-side door, and put the trash bag on the seat. Then I went around to the other side, got behind the wheel, started the ignition, and put the phone to my ear. "Did you hear that?" I said.

"Yes. On your phone you will see a button you can press for volume."

I looked at the phone. "I see it."

"Maximize your volume, please."

I pressed the button several times and a kind of bar graph grew taller on the little screen. "Okay," I said. "How's that?"

"It's for your hearing, not ours," said the voice.

"All right," I said. "Your voice is loud and clear."

In fact, I had been listening closely to the voice. I hoped I might pick up speech patterns, dialect, word choices, pronunciation. I assumed it was Paulie Russo or one of his henchmen, but so far, at least, I hadn't been able to detect anything in the voice on the phone to help me identify him.

"I want you to drive safely," he said. "You carry valuable cargo. You will drive with the phone on the console beside you. You will be able to hear my instructions. Try it now."

I put the phone on the console. "Okay," I said.

"Can you hear me?"

"I hear you," I said.

"Very good, Mr. Coyne. Now let us begin. You are parked on Mt. Vernon Street, directly in front of your house. I want you to get onto Route 93 heading north. You will narrate your journey for me. Tell me each landmark as you pass it, each turn you take, each street sign you pass. Do you understand?"

"I understand," I said.

"Do not exceed the speed limit. Do nothing to draw attention to yourself or your automobile."

"I've got to speak to Robert," I said.

"You will," he said. "Now get started."

SIXTEEN

I negotiated the rotaries, blinking yellow lights, and one-way streets from Beacon Hill to the Zakim Bridge, dumpy old Boston's splendid anachronism of modernistic design, with its illuminated struts and cables and its elegant lines. I narrated every turn and street sign into the cell phone on the console. Now and then, the voice on the other end said, "Yes," or, "Good." Just letting me know that he was there, paying attention.

I crossed the bridge and headed north on Route 93. By now it was after one o'clock on this Wednesday morning in June. Traffic was light. Mostly delivery trucks and taxis. The commercial establishments I could see from the highway, the restaurants and used-car lots and factories and warehouses, appeared to be closed. The empty parking lots in Medford and Somerville were lit by yellow floodlights on tall poles. The office buildings in Stoneham shone lights from their eaves. Their windows were darkened.

I wondered where I was going, of course, but I knew there was no way I could guess. The voice on the cell phone would direct me to someplace the kidnappers had chosen because they believed it was ideally suited for their purposes. It was unlikely that our rendezvous had any connection to where the kidnappers lived or had their headquarters, or where they were holding Robert hostage.

In Woburn, the voice on the cell phone said, "Take Route 95 north. You will see the sign in about one minute."

"I know the exit," I said, and when I came to it, I took it.

A few minutes later, in Peabody, Route 95 took a jog to the left—north, paralleling the coast—and became a wide divided highway cutting through woods and fields, suburban developments, and farmland and fairgrounds, from Lynnfield to Danvers to Topsfield, heading toward the New Hampshire border, thence into Maine.

The more distance I put between myself and Boston, the thinner the traffic grew. I kept my speedometer needle on 65. Now and then a ten-wheeler went slamming past me. Otherwise I had the highway to myself.

Somewhere around Boxford I became aware of headlights behind me, and I realized that they'd been there for a while, hanging a couple of hundred yards back, moving in my lane at my speed.

"Are you following me?" I said to the cell phone on the console.

"You are doing well," said the voice.

"I've got to speak to Robert."

"Soon, Mr. Coyne."

"I need an assurance that he is all right."

"I assure you," said the voice. "He is all right."

"Fuck you," I said.

The voice chuckled.

If they had chosen the Massachusetts North Shore or coastal New Hampshire because they thought that taking me out of

148

the city where I lived and worked would disorient and confuse me, they were mistaken. I knew these areas quite well. I'd spent a lot of time in and around the old port cities of Newburyport in Massachusetts and Portsmouth in New Hampshire. I'd driven the back roads, and I'd fished in the rivers and their estuaries, and I'd eaten in the restaurants. I had friends and clients who lived and worked in those cities and their suburbs.

Of course, for all I knew, I might drive all night and end up in Canada.

I passed the Newburyport exit, then crossed the bridge that spanned the Merrimack River.

"Mr. Coyne," said the voice suddenly.

"I'm here," I said.

"You will take the next exit," he said. "When you come to the end of the ramp, bear right."

I did as I was told. A minute after I turned onto the road, I saw the headlights come down the ramp behind me. The signs didn't make it clear, but I figured I was in Salisbury, which I knew was the next town north of Newburyport.

As I approached the first intersection at the traffic lights, which by day was a busy commercial area with a boat dealer on the left and a Jeep dealer on the right and a strip mall straight ahead, I saw the headlights coming up behind me.

"Go right at the lights," said the voice.

I put on my turn signal. The light was green. I turned right, and then the headlights behind me also turned.

I was on a winding two-lane country road. There was no traffic except me and the car behind me, which remained about fifty yards back.

"Ahead of you," said the voice, "the road bends to the left and you will come to an iron bridge. You will stop halfway across the bridge. Do you understand?"

149

"Of course I understand," I said.

"Pull your hand brake. Leave your motor running and your lights on."

"Yep."

A few minutes later I drove onto the iron bridge. I'd crossed this bridge many times. It was, I knew, a couple of miles east of the Route 95 bridge I'd just driven over. This one also spanned the Merrimack River, which separated Salisbury from Newburyport here, just a few miles upstream from the river's estuary at Plum Island.

I stopped halfway across and pulled on my emergency brake. The headlights in my rearview mirror stopped on the road just before the bridge.

"Get out of the car," said the voice. "Bring the phone with you."

"Where's Robert?" I said. "I want to see him."

"One thing at a time. Do what I say."

"Let me speak to him, at least."

"This is not a negotiation, Mr. Coyne. Get out of your car now."

"Without Robert, you don't get the money."

"I think you will agree," said the voice, "that you are in no position to submit ultimatums."

"Ultimata," I said. "Plural. From the Latin. It's a neuter noun."

"In one minute," said the voice, "if you continue to fuck around, you will hear a gunshot. Do you understand?"

"Okay," I said. "Sure. I understand."

I got out of my car and stood there on the bridge. The river gurgled beneath me. Here the Merrimack was a tidal river. The water below me was black, and judging by its sound, the tide was ebbing, and the river was emptying into the sea. The old iron bridge felt electric. It was vibrating under my feet from the power of the flowing water around its supports and abutments.

The night air was cool on my face. It smelled damp and salty. My car and I were illuminated in the high beams of the car at the end of the bridge behind me. When I looked back at it, all I could see were the blinding headlights.

"Go around to the passenger side," said the voice, "and take out the bag of money. Hold it up so we can see it."

I did that.

"Now," said the voice, "drop it off the upstream side of the bridge."

"What?"

"You heard me. Drop it over the railing. Do it now."

I went to the railing and looked down. Then I heard the soft burbling of a marine engine in low gear, just holding its place in the river currents, and I could see the glow of its lights under the bridge.

I knew that once I let go of the money, I'd have no bargaining power. On the other hand, I hadn't had any bargaining power from the beginning. It had always been a matter of trust.

I assumed it was Paulie Russo who was calling the shots, although I'd been scrupulous not to hint at that to the voice on the phone. I sensed that it would be dangerous to suggest that I knew who had kidnapped Robert Lancaster. I guessed, in fact, that despite his efforts to disguise his voice, it was Paulie himself who'd been giving me my instructions from the car that had followed me all the way from Boston. Paulie was smart. He was capable of planning this elaborate scheme. He knew the word "ultimatum."

I had no choice but to assume that Paulie would keep his word. I believed that if I disobeyed him, he'd kill Robert. Paulie Russo had killed plenty of people. He did it easily.

I was not confident that he'd return Robert unharmed even if I did what I was told. But like Vincent, his father, Paulie claimed to be a man of honor. Maybe that would translate into sparing Robert's life if I continued to do everything he said. I had to hope so.

I didn't see that I had any choice.

I lifted the bag of money over the rail and let go.

The black bag disappeared into the darkness, and instantly a spotlight went on from under the bridge.

I listened for the splash the bag would make when it hit the water, but the swish of the river currents around the bridge abutments and the burble of the boat's engine beneath me muffled the sound.

The boat's spotlight was panning across the surface of the water.

I put the phone back to my ear. "Okay?"

"Good," said the voice. "Well done."

"Now," I said, "I assume you will give me Robert Lancaster. That was our deal."

"Now," he said, "you will continue to do what I say." A note of impatience, the first kind of emotion I'd detected since he first spoke to me, had crept into his voice. It sounded dangerous.

The spotlight continued to pan the water under the bridge below me. Then the pitch of the boat engine grew suddenly louder. It had shifted gears and was, I assumed, moving to pick up the floating trash bag of money.

"Now what?" I said into the phone.

"Now you wait for my next instruction."

I waited for two or three minutes. Then the voice said, "Okay."

I said, "Okay what?"

"We have recovered the bag," he said. "It appears to be as we agreed. Now you will turn around and drive home."

"What about Robert?"

"Assuming that bag contains exactly what it is supposed to contain, and assuming you do not do anything foolish, you will be hearing from us."

"When?"

"Within twenty-four hours."

"Let me hear his voice, at least."

"That is not possible," he said. "From here on, Robert Lancaster's life depends on you. Do you understand?"

"Of course I understand."

"Good." He paused. "One last thing."

"What?"

"Throw your phone off the bridge."

"Are you—?"

"Do it now, Mr. Coyne. Unless you want to hear a gunshot. Then go home."

I threw the cell phone over the bridge rail into the darkness. Then I climbed into my car, put it in gear, and drove away.

The headlights followed me back over the dark, narrow roads to the southbound ramp onto Route 95, and they stayed about a hundred yards behind me as I turned onto the highway, heading back to Boston. According to the digital clock on my dashboard, it was twenty minutes after two in the morning.

My first, dreadful thought was that I had signed Robert Lancaster's death certificate. I tried to analyze it coldly, and that was still my conclusion. Robert's captors had their money. It would be easier and safer for them to kill him than to let him go. If Robert were freed, they knew, we would go to the police, and Robert would be able to tell them things that would very likely enable them to track down his kidnappers.

If they did release him, that's what I'd insist we do. Which is why I doubted that they'd do it.

As I drove along the empty highway, I kept going over it in my mind. What did I do wrong? I'd dumped a trash bag containing Judge Adrienne Lancaster's quarter of a million dollars off a bridge, and I didn't have her grandson. Surely I'd blown it about as badly as the situation could possibly be blown. But what could I have done differently?

I reconstructed the entire sequence of events step by step, thinking of the options I'd had at each point, the choices I could have made, the roads I didn't take.

I could have disobeyed Dalt and Adrienne and gone to the state police or the FBI. In retrospect, I probably should have. Otherwise, I couldn't isolate my mistake. Maybe I should have been more insistent with them, although at the time I wasn't sure they were wrong. In any case, it would have been an ethical, if not pragmatic, mistake to disobey them. Robert was Dalt's son. The quarter of a million dollars was the judge's.

As much as I tried to blame myself, I kept concluding that I'd done nothing wrong. It was the kidnappers who'd done everything right. They'd left no clues about their identity. From the beginning, they'd made it impossible to anticipate their next move.

I wouldn't have thought that Paulie Russo was capable of designing such a sophisticated plan and executing it with such flawless precision. Presenting his demands via a recording by the kidnap victim himself reading a script on an untraceable compact disc was clever. Communicating with me, their chosen go-between, on a prepaid cell phone made it impossible to trace their call. And then, when the drop was completed, having me dump the phone precluded tracing whatever evidence of their call the phone might've stored in its memory.

Picking up the ransom money in a boat at two in the morning guaranteed their easy getaway. Who could have anticipated that they'd do that?

All the way home I kept thinking about it and analyzing it, and I always came to the same conclusion. So far, at least, they'd committed the perfect crime.

It should have made me feel a little better. But it didn't. They had their money, and they still had Robert, and I was not an inch closer to recovering him than I'd been yesterday.

Twenty-four hours, he said.

What did that mean?

I had no faith that it meant we'd have Robert back in a day.

Most likely it meant that they hoped I'd do nothing for twenty-four hours but wait patiently and hopefully while they put time and space between themselves and me and Robert Lancaster.

I wondered if I'd hear from them again.

The headlights followed me back to the city, over the bridge and down the ramp and around the rotaries all the way to Charles Street, where they pulled to the curb and stopped with their high beams on as I turned onto Mt. Vernon Street. I wondered if they'd watch my house for the rest of the night. I found the idea unnerving.

I wasn't particularly frightened, though. They had no reason to do me any harm. I'd done everything their way, and I knew nothing.

Not that they needed a reason for what they did.

For the first time since she'd left, I was glad that Evie was on the other coast. I would certainly have been frightened for her if she'd been home.

I parked in front of my house, locked the car, and went in. Henry was waiting inside the doorway. He stretched and yawned and wagged his stubby little tail. I scooched down so he could lap my face, and I hugged him against me. I told him he was a perfect pal and a paragon of patience.

He was unimpressed with my alliteration. He shook himself and headed for the kitchen.

I let him out the back door, then found a can of Coke in the refrigerator. I popped the tab and took a long swig.

I noticed that the red message button on the kitchen phone was blinking. I dialed voice mail and was told that I had five messages.

The first had come at 1:16. It was Dalt. "Where the hell are you?" he said. "I thought I'd hear from you by now. Call me, will you? I'm here at my mother's. I don't know if I can stand this much longer. I'm kinda going nuts."

The second call came fifteen minutes later. "Hey. It's your sweetie." Evie, in her unbearably sexy telephone voice. "It's late there, isn't it? I figured you wouldn't mind if I woke you up. You okay?" She hesitated. "Hey. You gonna pick up the phone? No? Hm. Well, it's just, I'm thinking of you, that's all." She paused. "You're not going to pick up, I guess. Okay. Well, sleep tight. Love you."

The next three messages were all from Dalt. The last one came at three-thirty. It was now ten of four. "Brady," he said, "for Christ's sake call me. It doesn't matter what time it is. Don't worry about waking me up. Believe me, I'm awake. What the hell is going on, anyway?" There was a silence. Then he said, "Are you okay?"

I sat down at the table with the phone in my hand. I didn't want to talk to Dalt. But I had to.

He picked up in the middle of the first ring. "Brady?"

"It's me."

"Oh, jeez. I'm a wreck." I heard him blow out a breath. "So . . . ?"

"I don't have Robert," I said.

"What? Jesus. What happened?"

"I'm sorry," I said. "They—the kidnappers—they said we'd hear from them within twenty-four hours."

"Oh." He paused. "Well, that makes sense, doesn't it?"

"It's not what I expected."

He was quiet for a minute. Then he said, "So what happened? What went wrong?"

"I gave them their money. I did exactly what they said. Nothing went wrong. They just . . . they didn't release Robert."

"Is he all right?"

"I don't know. I just got back. I'm waiting to hear from them."

"But I thought . . ."

"There was no way of knowing how they would play it," I said. "I'm hoping that once they count the money, they'll release him."

"Within twenty-four hours."

"Yes."

"Do you think they will?"

"I don't know, Dalt. I'm sorry, man. I wish I could be more confident for you. I honestly have no idea what they're going to do."

"Twenty-four hours," he said. "They're just buying time."

"It's very possible."

"Maybe we should have listened to you," he said. "We should have gone to the police like you said."

"We don't know that," I said. "Who knows how that would have played out. No sense in second-guessing ourselves now."

"If we don't get him back . . ."

"Don't blame yourself," I said. "You didn't do this. You're not the criminal here."

He laughed quickly. "Easy for you to say."

"Don't beat yourself up," I said. "What's done is done. We've just got to take it from here. Let's wait and see how it works out. We'll have to give them their twenty-four hours. They said I'd be hearing from them, and so far they've done everything they said they'd do."

"Sure," he said. "You're right." He said nothing for a minute. Then he said, "So meanwhile, what am I supposed to do?"

"Try to get some sleep, I guess," I said. "Is Adrienne there? I'd like to talk to her."

"She took a pill and went to bed around midnight. Said she had to be in court in the morning."

"Well," I said, "she's keeping busy. It's a good idea."

"You don't think for one minute I'm going to go to the restaurant today, smile at the customers, count the oysters, do you?"

"I guess not," I said. "Call in sick and go to bed. I promise I'll be in touch as soon as I know anything."

"Maybe I'll take one of my mother's pills." He hesitated. "Hey, Brady?"

"What, Dalt?"

"Thank you."

"I didn't do a very good job."

"You did the best you could," he said.

"Have you talked to Teresa?"

He blew out a breath. "I should, shouldn't I."

"I'm sure she's as anxious as you are."

158

"You're right. Of course she is. It's just . . . we don't talk much, you know?"

"You want me to call her?"

"No," he said. "I should do it."

"You're right," I said. "You should."

SEVENTEEN

I heard a little yip at the back door. I opened it and let Henry in. He glared at me, then padded down the hallway to my den.

"What?" I said. "You think I forgot about you?"

He kept going.

It was a little after four in the morning. I'd been up all night, and between the pot of coffee I'd drunk before driving to the bridge over the Merrimack River and the adrenaline that was still crackling in my brain, it didn't look like I'd get to sleep anytime soon.

The sun would rise in less than two hours. That would make it an official all-nighter.

I hadn't pulled an all-nighter since law school, unless you wanted to count midnight-to-dawn striped-bass fishing adventures with J. W. Jackson on Martha's Vineyard. J. W. and I had done that a few times. In the summer on the right kind of tide, your best chance of catching a big striper happens in the dark.

I loaded up the electric coffeemaker, switched it on, and went into the den to reconcile with Henry.

He was curled on his bed in the corner with his back to me and his nose touching his stubby tail. When I went over to him, he rolled up his eyes, looked back at me, then closed them.

I knelt beside him. "Hey," I said. "Look at me."

He opened his eyes again.

"I'm sorry, okay?" I scratched his forehead. "I was gone for a long time. It was nighttime, and you thought I'd never be back. Even though I always come back, I know that's how you think. You miss Evie, huh?"

Henry was searching my eyes, the way dogs do. They know that the words men speak are less trustworthy than what comes through their eyes.

"I miss her, too," I said.

Henry sighed and rolled onto his back with his legs sticking up in the air. This was his way of saying, "Oh, okay. Despite all your shortcomings, I still love you. You may rub my belly."

I sat on the floor and rubbed his belly.

It was the darkest time of the night and Evie was not snoozing upstairs. The house felt empty and hollow, and so did I.

The shrill of a siren dragged me up from the dark pit of a dreamless sleep. I was lying on the daybed in my den. Henry was curled up beside me with his back pressed against my hip.

The siren blasted again, and I identified it as the ringing of the telephone on my desk.

I opened my eyes. Pewter gray light filtered in from the window and fuzzed the shadows in the room. Soon the sun would rise.

I looked at the wall clock. It was 5:47.

I pushed myself to my feet, went over to my desk, and picked up the phone. I cleared my throat and said, "Yes?"

"Mr. Coyne?" It was the same voice, disguised and echoey.

"Yes," I said again.

"One moment."

I waited.

Then: "Brady?" It was Robert. His voice sounded scratchy and shaky.

"Robert," I said. "It's good to hear your voice, man. Are you all right?"

"I'm okay. They—"

"All right, Mr. Coyne," said the other voice. "You'll be hearing from us."

"Wait," I said. "Listen—"

But then there was a click, and we were disconnected.

I hit the redial button.

Nothing happened. All I got was a dial tone.

I pressed the message button on the phone and looked at the little display screen. "Unknown caller," it said.

I expected no less. They were probably using a prepaid cell phone, too.

Well, anyway, Robert was alive, at least. That was good news.

The question was, how much longer did he have?

I called Dalt at his mother's house. It rang several times before his sleepy voice mumbled, "H'lo?"

"It's Brady," I said. "I wanted you to know that I just talked with Robert."

"Oh, my God," he said. "He's all right?"

"He sounded fine," I said, exaggerating a bit. "We're going to get him back."

"Good," he said. "That's good news. Thanks, man."

"Go back to sleep."

"Took a pill." He yawned into the phone. "All set. G'night."

I knew that I wouldn't be able to get to sleep again, so I

poured myself a mug of coffee, and Henry and I went out to the backyard and watched the sun come up.

I sipped my coffee while the finches and sparrows and nuthatches came flitting and flocking at the feeders and worst-case scenarios came darting and swirling in my brain.

I went back into the house a little after seven, fed Henry his breakfast, and refilled my coffee mug. When Henry finished eating—he's perpetually starved, poor dog, and it never takes him more than a few minutes to inhale his breakfast—we went back outside, where I tried to persuade my muddled, overtired brain to do some linear thinking for a change, without much luck.

At eight I called my office voice mail and told Julie that I wouldn't be coming to the office and she should reschedule whatever she had lined up for me today.

A little while later I remembered that Evie had called. It wouldn't yet be six in the morning at Ed Banyon's houseboat in Sausalito. Too early to call her.

It was Wednesday. Today Evie was taking her father to the hospital. By tomorrow, presumably, they would know his fate.

Another mug of coffee later I took a shower, got dressed, ate an English muffin with peanut butter, drank a glass of orange juice, said good-bye to Henry, and got into my car. I drove through the Boston streets to the North End, where I turned onto Salem Street, then onto the side street, and cut into the back alley where Paulie Russo had his office.

I parked my car beside the Dumpster, climbed up onto the loading platform, and banged on the door.

I waited a few minutes, than pounded on it again, harder, with the side of my fist.

No one opened it. I heard no movement behind it.

I moved out to the end of the loading platform and looked

up. There were two windows on the brick wall over the door. I figured those windows opened to Paulie Russo's second-floor office.

"Hey, Paulie," I yelled up at the windows. "I want to talk with you. Let me in. I'm not going away until we talk."

A few minutes later the door opened. The goon with the mole on his face, the one who had punched me in the kidneys on the plaza outside the Boston Scrod, was standing there. He jerked his chin at me, gesturing for me to enter. "Awright," he said in his growly voice. "Come on. Mr. Russo says it's okay."

I went over to the door. Mole-face stepped aside and held the door open, and I walked past him into the storeroom.

The door closed behind us, and then the flat of his hand pushed between my shoulder blades and slammed me against the wall. If I hadn't managed to get my hands out in front of me, my nose would have been mashed.

"Don't fuckin' move," he said, and he patted me down.

When his hands slid up along the insides of my legs, I had to stifle an overpowering impulse to turn around and kick him in the balls. I owed him that.

"Okay," he said. "Go on up."

I climbed the steep flight of stairs. Mole-face came along right behind me.

When we got to the top, he knocked on the door with one knuckle.

"Yeah, come in." Paulie's voice from inside.

The goon opened the door and stood back.

I went in.

Paulie was seated behind his desk. When he saw me, he stood up, came around, and held out his hand to me. "A surprise, Mr. Coyne. You want some espresso?"

I ignored his hand. "No."

165

He shrugged. "I didn't expect to see you."

"You didn't?"

He frowned. "Not unless you had some money with you I didn't."

I narrowed my eyes at him. "Paulie," I said, "I didn't get much sleep last night, as you know, and I'm pretty grouchy, so don't bullshit me, okay?"

He shook his head. "I don't know what the fuck you're talking about, Mr. Coyne."

I jerked my head back at the thug with the mole, who was standing there with his back against the door. "I want to talk, you and me, just the two of us."

Paulie looked at me for a minute, then nodded. He lifted his eyes to his goon. "You frisk him?"

" 'Course," said Mole-face.

"You sure he ain't wired?"

The thug pushed himself away from the wall and came over to where I was standing. He hooked his forefinger inside the top of my shirt and yanked it down. Buttons went flying, and my chest was bared. He pulled my shirt open and turned me so I was facing Paulie.

"Okay?" he said.

"Good," said Paulie. "Now get outta here and close the fuckin' door behind you."

After Mole-face left and the door closed, Paulie went back behind his desk and sat down. "Sorry about your shirt," he said. He picked up a tiny cup, lifted it to his lips with his pinkie finger curled, took a noisy sip, then put it down. "Come on, Mr. Coyne. Have a cup. Excellent espresso."

I shook my head. "No, thank you."

He waved at a chair. "Have a seat, at least."

I sat in the chair.

"Okay, Mr. Coyne." He put his elbows on his desk and leaned toward me. "Here we are. The two of us. Just you and me, man to man. No witnesses. No wires. No threats. No bullshit, right? So what the fuck do you want?"

"For one thing," I said, "I want you to stop ordering that thug of yours"—I jerked my head toward the door where the guy with the mole had just exited—"to accost me in public places and punch me in the kidneys. It hurt like hell. Knocked me down with all those people there. It was embarrassing, and anyway, it's the opposite of a good way to persuade me to cooperate. Makes me stubborn and crabby."

"Huh?" He frowned. "Kidney punch?"

I nodded.

"You saying Louie did that to you?"

"If that's the name of that guy who just let me in, yeah. Him."

Paulie narrowed his eyes at me. "No bullshit?"

"Ah, come off it, Paulie."

"He wasn't supposed to do that, Mr. Coyne. What can I say? I apologize for him. It ain't right, and I'll take care of it. It won't happen again." He cocked his head and looked at me. "That's not why you're here, though, I bet."

"Come on, Paulie. You're still with the bullshit. You know why I'm here. Let's get this thing taken care of."

"Fine by me," he said. "You got money for me, we're all set."

"Me?" I said. "No. You've got your money. Now I want Robert Lancaster."

Russo was shaking his head. "You're making riddles, Mr. Coyne. The judge, she took herself off our case, and that fuckin' kid, Lancaster, there, he owes me about fifty K, him or his old man, I don't care which, and they ain't paid me, and if you didn't come here to take care of that, I don't know why we're even talking."

"You trying to tell me you didn't kidnap him?"

"Kidnap who? The fuck you talking about?"

"Robert Lancaster."

Paulie laughed. "Jesus Christ. You telling me somebody kidnapped the kid?"

"I've done everything your way," I said. "Now it's your turn. Let the boy go."

Paulie Russo was shaking his head and looking hard into my eyes.

"So far," I said, "no police, just like you said. I would've brought them in, but Robert's father and mother and grandmother all said no, do it exactly the way he says. We'll pay the money, they said. All they want is to get their boy back. Okay, fine. You got all the money you asked for, and you said twenty-four hours. So I just want you to know that if I don't have him back in good health by midnight tonight, I'm bringing the FBI into it."

Russo was silent for a long minute. Then he said, "That's what you came here to tell me? You came to my office this morning to threaten me with the FBI because somebody kidnapped Robert Lancaster?"

"And you want me to believe that it's not you?"

"Yeah." He nodded. "I'm fuckin' telling you it's not me."

"I thought you had some honor, Paulie. I'm disappointed that we can't discuss this truthfully, just the two of us, man to man, and arrive at an agreement."

"We are discussing it man to man," he said. "So, okay. Man to man, I'm telling you. I don't know where that kid is, and I just want my fuckin' money."

I raised both of my hands and showed him my palms. "Fine," I said. "Play it that way. I've told you what I wanted to tell you. You've got till midnight. If I don't have him back by

168

then, you might as well kill him, because the feds are going to be all over you either way." I stood up and went to the door.

"Mr. Coyne," he said, "wait a minute."

I stopped and turned around.

Paulie came over to me. He put his hand on my arm.

I looked at it.

He took away his hand. "What've I got to do to convince you?" he said.

"There's nothing you can say," I said. "I don't believe you. You're a criminal. You lie. You have no honor. You're nothing like your father. I'm very disappointed." I turned the knob and pushed the door open.

"You're wrong about that," said Paulie.

"Return Robert Lancaster unharmed," I said. "Then I'll believe you."

Louie, the thug with the mole, was standing there outside the door. I brushed past him and went down the stairs and out onto the landing platform, where one of Paulie Russo's other goons was standing with his hands clasped behind his back looking up at the sky.

He turned his head and nodded to me.

I ignored him.

I got into my car, backed out of the alley, and headed home.

It hadn't gone as well as I'd hoped it would. I figured I'd probably done more harm than good.

When I got home, I tried to call Evie's cell phone and got her voice mail. I guessed that by now she was in the hospital with her father, where cell phones are supposed to be turned off.

"It's me, babe," I said after the beep. "I'm really sorry I missed your call last night. I'd love to talk with you. My thoughts are with you and Ed today. Please call when you can and tell me how things are going. I miss you. Henry sends his love. So do I."

Then I went into my office, collapsed on my daybed, and fell into a dark, disturbing sleep.

The ringing of my telephone woke me up in the middle of a confusing dream. By the time I realized where I was and groped my way over to my desk, the ringing had stopped. The digital display on the telephone showed Dalt and Jess Lancaster's home phone number, and the message light was blinking.

It was ten minutes of five. I'd slept the afternoon away, and I felt worse than before I went to sleep. My thoughts were jumbled and fuzzy, still mixed up with disturbing dream images that I couldn't pin down, and I had a hangover-type throbbing headache behind my eyes.

I dialed my password for my voice mail. One message. "Brady, it's Dalt. What's going on? We haven't heard from you all day. I'm having horrible thoughts. Please call me."

I bumbled out to the kitchen and made a fresh pot of coffee. Then I went into the bathroom, took off my T-shirt, filled the sink with cold water, and immersed my face in it. I splashed water on my chest. I wet my fingers and combed them through my hair. I held a wet washcloth against my eyes.

After a few minutes of that, I felt a little better.

When I got back to the kitchen, the coffee was ready. I poured myself a mugful and grabbed the portable kitchen phone, and Henry and I went out to the patio.

I drank half of the mug of coffee before I called Dalt.

"I tried to call you a few minutes ago," he said. "I'm going crazy here. We all are."

"I understand," I said. "Of course you are. You've got to hang in there. I don't have any news. I would've told you. Far as

I know, Robert's all right. We'll be hearing from the people who have him."

"Every minute that goes by . . ."

"I know what you're feeling. So listen. I was going to call you anyway. I want to have a meeting of the minds. You, me, Jess, Teresa, and Adrienne."

"Sure," he said. "The minds. Ha. Okay." He hesitated. "You got an agenda?"

"I want you all to know what I know," I said. "I don't want to have to repeat myself, and I want to be sure everybody hears it exactly the same way. And I also want all of you to know what each of you knows. No secrets, no misperceptions, no nuances. Then we can try to identify our options and decide together how we want to proceed."

"No secrets, huh?"

"This is no time for secrets, Dalt."

He was quiet for a minute. Then he said, "You're talking about going to the police, huh?"

"That's one option," I said. "We need to reconsider it, think about it seriously. Plus, I want to clear the air, make sure we're all on the same page."

Dalt paused. Then he said, "Well, yeah, okay. You're right. We should do that."

"You set it up," I said. "Make it happen. Be sure Teresa's there. This is her son we're talking about. Make it seven o'clock at my house."

He hesitated. "I've never actually been to your house."

"Mt. Vernon Street," I said. "It's the next left off Charles after Pinckney. Just before you get to Beacon."

"I know where Mt. Vernon is," said Dalt.

"I'm halfway up the hill on the right. Number 77. My green

BMW will be parked right in front, and I'll leave the porch light on."

"Maybe it would be easier to do it at my house, or my mother's. Driving into the city, parking . . ."

"Residents-only parking on my street after six o'clock," I said. "There will be plenty of spaces at seven. Or are you worried about getting a ticket?"

He laughed quickly.

"My house," I said, "because I don't want to be away from my telephone."

"For when they call again," he said.

"For *if* they call again."

EIGHTEEN

Around quarter of seven, even though it hadn't begun to grow dark outside, I turned on the porch light, and Henry and I went out and sat on the front steps. I brought a can of Coke. I still hadn't recovered from my all-nighter. My body craved caffeine.

About five minutes later a new-looking sand-colored Nissan Murano came creeping up the hill. It stopped in front, and I saw that the driver was Teresa, Robert's mother. I remembered that her husband was a Nissan dealer. She rolled down the window on the passenger side and leaned over to peer at me.

I lifted my hand. "This is the right place," I said.

She pulled up in front of my car, parked there, got out, and came up the brick-paved path. She was wearing blue jeans and sandals and an orange jersey. The jeans fit her snugly. She looked good.

She lifted her hand and tried out a smile, which didn't quite make it. "Hello," she said.

I said hello. Teresa sat on the steps beside Henry, who was sitting beside me.

She let Henry sniff her hand. "I hope you're going to tell me what's going on," she said.

"I want to wait till the rest of them get here," I said. "I'd rather tell everybody at the same time. Did Dalt call you?"

"He said you gave them the money," she said. "He said you talked to Robert afterward. I said thank you for keeping me informed. That was about it. Dalton and I don't have long conversations."

"That's really all the news there is," I said. "Can I get you a Coke?"

"I'd love a Coke," said Teresa.

I stood up, then looked down at her. "I don't know your married name."

She shrugged as if it hardly mattered. "Samborski," she said. "My husband is Adolph. Everyone calls him Sam."

"He couldn't make it tonight, huh?"

Teresa gazed out at the street. "He works a lot," she said.

I went inside, fetched another Coke, and brought it out to Teresa Samborski, and about ten minutes later a big boat of a silver Chrysler nosed into the parking space behind my little green BMW. Dalt got out from behind the wheel. Jess climbed out of the passenger side, then opened the back door and held it for Adrienne.

The three of them stood on the sidewalk and looked around. The judge wore dark tailored slacks and a matching jacket over a white silk blouse. She looked stern and strong, pretty much like a judge. The Chrysler, I guessed, was hers.

"This way," I called to them, and waved them up.

The three of them came up the path. Dalt and Jess were holding hands. Teresa and I stood up. Henry held his ground until everybody patted his head.

Then we all went inside.

The four of them took seats in my living room, Dalt and Jess side by side on the sofa, Teresa in one of the easy chairs, and Adrienne in the rocker. I offered coffee and Cokes. Dalt and Jess asked for coffee, milk, no sugar. Adrienne said she didn't want anything. Teresa already had her Coke.

I fetched the two mugs of coffee, then sat on one of the side chairs and looked at the four of them. "I want to tell you everything that's happened so far," I said. "We need to figure out what to do. Okay?"

They nodded.

Adrienne said, "What I want to know—"

"Let's do it my way," I said.

"But—"

"This isn't your courtroom," I said. "I'm in charge here."

Her smile contained neither warmth nor humor. "Of course, Attorney Coyne."

"Friday a week ago," I said, "I had coffee with Robert. That's when he told me that he'd piled up a big gambling debt with the Russo family. Robert's debt was why you got beat up, Dalt. Russo was holding you responsible for your son. So Robert promised me that he'd talk with you"—I waved my hand, taking in all of them—"his family, clear the air, and work out something." I raised my eyebrows at Dalt.

He shook his head. "I never heard from him. Last time I talked to Robert was that night at the hospital."

"That's what I thought," I said. "So on Saturday, Robert's girlfriend, a girl named Becca Quinlan, a student at BU, called me. She was worried about Robert, hadn't seen him for a few days. She'd gone to his apartment. His roommates hadn't seen him, either. I met with her and we talked. She told me that she and Robert hadn't been together very long. There's an ex-boyfriend named Ozzie who's a friend of Robert's. Anyway, on

Sunday morning in the *Globe* on your doorstep, you found that cell phone and the CD that we looked at. I want to look at it again."

I stuck the disc into the DVD player on my living-room television. Robert's duct-taped image appeared. The four of them watched as Robert read his appeal, and I watched their faces.

Dalt was clenching his jaw.

Jess sat beside him staring at the screen.

Teresa blinked at the tears that brimmed her eyes.

Adrienne scowled.

The whole thing lasted about three minutes.

"I showed this disc to a friend of mine," I said when it was over. "He pointed out that a bedsheet is draped behind Robert, most likely to make it impossible for us to draw any conclusions about the room he's in. But my friend did notice a light source behind the sheet. He guessed from its location high up on the wall and its apparent size that it might be a basement window. He also was able to tinker with the audio so that we could hear half a minute or so of some kind of rhythmic slapping sound in the background. Neither he nor I could identify the sound." I paused. "I'm telling you this because the disc was designed by the kidnappers to contain no clues, and they did a pretty good job. But there may be clues in it nevertheless, and I aim to look into them further."

"They're keeping him in a basement, then?" said Teresa.

"It's likely," I said.

"Otherwise," said Dalt, "we don't have a clue."

"That's about right," I said. "So to continue our chronology, on Monday Adrienne got the money in the exact numbers and denominations they asked for. I picked it up from her that evening. The kidnappers called on the cell phone they left for me a little after midnight Tuesday, which was last night. This morning, actually. They told me to take the bands off the money and dump all the bills into a plastic trash bag, then to put that bag into another bag and tie the tops. They kept me on the phone and told me to begin driving. They gave me directions along the way. They followed behind me so they could see where I was and what I was doing. I figure they probably were watching me all the time, starting from when I got into my car, but I didn't notice them right away, which means they were pretty good at it. They directed me over some back roads and told me to drop the bag of money off a bridge into the Merrimack River in Salisbury, which I did. They had a boat under the bridge to pick it up. They also told me to throw their cell phone into the river, and I did that, too. Then they followed me all the way home."

"What about Robert?" said Adrienne.

"I asked to speak to him, of course," I said. "Repeatedly. I asked when he would be released. I threatened not to give them their money until they delivered Robert, or at least let me talk to him. They refused. They only said that I would be hearing from them. I thought about disobeying them, but I decided I'd better do what they said. As a result, they have the money, and we don't have Robert. I've been second-guessing myself all night."

"You talked to one of them on the phone," said Dalt. "You didn't recognize his voice?"

I shook my head. "He disguised it. He—or she, for all I know it was a woman—he spoke precisely. I didn't notice anything about his speech. No accent. No quirks at all in his language or diction that I could tell."

Dalt started to say something.

I held up my hand. "Let me finish. A little while after I got back home this morning my house phone rang. It was him. The

177

same disguised voice that had been giving me instructions. He put Robert on the phone, and we had a very brief conversation. He said he was okay."

"That was when?" said Adrienne.

"Around quarter of six."

"You're sure it was him?"

I nodded. "It was Robert."

"That was over twelve hours ago," she said.

"So by now he might be dead," said Dalt. "Right? I mean, maybe that's why they called. So we'd relax and give them time to—"

"We don't know anything like that." I drained my can of Coke. "Those are the facts of it. I've been thinking about how they planned it out, and I can't find a flaw in their scheme or in their execution of it. I might have screwed the whole thing up, but if I did, I can't think of anything I'd do differently if I had to do it over." I hesitated. "Except for one thing. We should have gone to the police the minute we got that CD."

I looked at Adrienne. She looked steadily back at me.

"Of course," I said, "I could've just disobeyed them. I might have saved Adrienne a quarter of a million dollars, but I don't see how I would have saved Robert's life."

"We should have gone to the police," said Teresa. "I should have spoken up before." She looked at me. "You said that's what we should do, Brady. I agreed with you, but I was too intimidated to say anything."

"You had your chance," said Dalt. "You can't sit there now and blame us."

Teresa snapped her head around and glared at him. "Don't you think for even one minute—"

"Whoa." I waved my hand. "We can all second-guess ourselves," I said. "I'm very good at that myself. You guys can blame each other, too, if you want, but I don't see what good it'll do. I'd rather focus on trying to figure this out so we can decide how to proceed. Okay?"

I looked at each of them, and all four of them shrugged and nodded and mumbled "Yes" and "Okay."

"Good," I said. "All right. I have assumed from the beginning that the man behind the kidnapping is Paulie Russo."

"It was Russo's mobsters," said Adrienne, "who encouraged Robert to go into debt to them as a way of getting leverage with me." She paused. "When I recused myself from their case, they lost their leverage and decided to go after the money. Isn't that right, Attorney Coyne?"

"That's about right," I said. "But let me finish. This morning I confronted Paulie Russo. He denied knowing anything about the kidnapping or the ransom money."

"Are you saying you believe him?" said Adrienne.

"I don't really know," I said. "He's a terrible man who lies easily and without conscience. But he did seem genuinely surprised when I accused him of kidnapping Robert. I actually think I hurt his feelings."

Nobody said anything. I allowed the silence to hang there.

After a minute, Teresa said, "So now what do we do?"

"That," I said, "is the question."

"All along," said Dalt, "Mike has said we're making a mistake not going to the FBI. Brady, that's what you recommended, too."

"What could they have done?" said Adrienne. "These people had it all figured out. Dropping the money off a bridge to a waiting boat? Clever, if you ask me. Brilliant, really. You think the FBI would have anticipated that?" She shook her head. "I love my money, but now this is all about hoping that Robert is still alive and getting him back. It's not about money. We did

179

what they asked. Now we have to hope that they'll arrange another clever way for us to retrieve him."

"We should be prepared for another ransom demand," I said. They all looked at me.

I shrugged. "It's what I'd do. I'd get greedy. Last night went so smoothly, and it really wasn't that much money. I'd be thinking that we didn't ask for enough. I'd think, *These people will do anything we say.* I'd think we could scheme out another tricky way to drop the money. I'd think we should demand more this time. A million would be a nice round number."

Adrienne was nodding. "They'd know I can get it," she said, "and they'd figure we'd just continue to follow their instructions."

"How could they know you have it?" said Jess. It was the first thing Dalt's wife, Robert's stepmother, had said since they arrived. I guessed she was deferring to the blood relatives.

"They seem to know everything, don't they?" Adrienne smiled at Jess. "It doesn't take much research, dear, to learn that Dalton's father was a very wealthy man, and that what he left to me, unlike what he left to your husband, has been invested well, and that I can convert a large amount of it to cash in a short amount of time. Why else would they have specified on their recording that I would be the source of the payoff? They know. They've done their homework. They are obviously very good at what they do." She paused. "And that's why I say, absolutely no FBI. These people are smarter than the FBI."

"If they're so smart," said Dalt, "what are the odds that they'll release my son?"

"If," said Adrienne, "he's still alive."

"Sure," said Dalt. He gave her a hard look. "Jesus."

I said, "I don't think the question is really about the odds."

Dalt nodded. "Because the odds are bad."

180

"I agree with the judge about one thing," I said. "These people are very slick. Everything they've tried so far has worked perfectly. This has been a great success for them. It's possible that they're confident they can devise a slick way to return Robert to us, too."

"Is that what you think?" said Teresa. "That they'll return him?"

"I don't know," I said. "But it's what we all want, and if you refuse to go to the authorities, we have to play it that way."

Adrienne said, "We must not go to the police."

"We need to decide," I said. "The four of you, you're the ones who have to make this decision. I have my own opinions. But Robert isn't my son or grandson or stepson, and it's not my money we're talking about."

"No police," said Adrienne again.

"Why?" said Dalt. "To protect your reputation?"

Adrienne's head snapped around, and she glared at her son. "How dare you? My reputation is not an issue. I am willing to pay more money, if that's what happens, because it might get my grandson back. This is not about me. I simply believe that these kidnappers are smarter than the police. If you want Robert back, we've got to keep the police out of it."

"I'm not comfortable with that," said Teresa. "I mean, we know who it is, don't we?" He turned to me. "That Russo man? Shouldn't we just tell the police and have them arrest him?"

"We don't know that it's him," I said.

"Well," she said, "who else could it be?"

I shrugged. "That's the question, all right. It's something we all need to think about. Look. Paulie Russo is most likely behind it. He's a seasoned criminal and a smart, greedy man. He's got the motive, not even to mention the means and the opportunity. This morning he swore to me he didn't do it. But that's

181

what he'd say anyway. I'm just saying, we need to remember that it's possible somebody else is behind it."

"Like who?" said Dalt.

I shook my head. "I don't know."

"Brady," said Teresa, "we need your advice."

"I'll do whatever you folks want," I said. "I'll go to the police, or I will not go to the police. I'll deliver some more ransom money. I'll negotiate with Paulie Russo or anybody else. But I'm not going to make this decision for you."

"We'll decide," she said. "Just tell us what you think. We need your opinion. Please."

She looked at Dalt and Jess and Adrienne. Dalt and Jess both nodded. Adrienne shrugged.

"Okay," I said. "Here's what I think. I think that we don't know what we're doing. None of us has ever been through anything like this before. And what have we accomplished up to now? We've given them a pile of money, and we're no closer to getting Robert back. We don't even know if he's still alive. We are amateurs. We're outclassed here." I shrugged. "My advice is, you should call the FBI right now."

Adrienne was shaking her head. "Calling in the FBI or the police is the conventional thing to do. It's what they do in the movies, on TV. Those make-believe agents are heroic and smart and competent. But for one thing, that's probably what these kidnappers expect, and they're prepared for it. Anyway, I know law enforcement bureaucracy. I know how it works in the real world. I've seen the posturing, the politics of it, the image-polishing, the reluctance to make decisions, the fear of making a mistake." She paused and glowered at all of us. "If you turn this over to them, we'll be giving them responsibility. Then when it all goes wrong, you can say, 'Oh, well. It wasn't our fault.' Is that what you want?"

"But listen," said Dalt. "I don't—"

"No," said the judge. "You listen. Let me finish. I, for one, am willing to take responsibility. I don't agree with Brady. I think we should at least hold off for a couple of days before we call in the authorities. Robert's still alive. Let it play out. See if these people call again. See what we can figure out."

Dalt started to say something, but Adrienne held up her hand. "Listen. Calling the FBI is irreversible. Once we call them, we can't change our minds about it. Once they're in, there's no getting them out. We can call them anytime. I just don't think this is the time." She sat back in the rocker and glared at Dalt.

Teresa said, "I'm sorry, Mrs. Lancaster. I do understand what you're saying, but I don't agree. I'm with Brady. We should turn it over to the professionals." She turned her head and looked at Dalt.

Dalt leaned forward. "I actually think my mother makes a good point," he said. "If we wait, we have options. We can change our minds anytime. Assuming Robert is still alive, it's what makes me feel most comfortable. If he's not, well . . ." He looked at me. "So what're we going to do?"

"It's up to you guys," I said. "I'll do whatever you want. I'm just the lawyer here."

Jess touched Dalt's arm. "Whatever you say, I support you."

Dalt gave his wife a quick smile, then turned to Teresa. "You're outvoted."

She looked at him. "You think we should decide what's right by majority rule?"

He smiled. "Hard to believe we stayed married that long."

Teresa smiled back at him. It was a sweet smile that struck me as poisonous. "I'll go along with Mrs. Lancaster," she said. "And you and Jessica. If we're going to vote, it might as well be unanimous."

Dalt looked at her for a minute, then turned to me. "It's decided, then. So now what?"

"I guess that's it for now," I said. "Go home. Try to get some sleep. Let's see what happens. We'll stay in touch. Keep your cell phones with you. Any thoughts or conjectures or questions or brainstorms, let me know. I'll do the same."

"Like what?" Dalt said.

"Like," I said, "see if you can think of anybody besides Paulie Russo who might have kidnapped your son, for one thing."

He nodded. "What are you going to do?"

"Me?" I said. "I'll wait and ponder, just like you. I'll hope that somebody calls. As soon as you leave my house, I'm going to try to make up for a sleepless night."

"Right," he said. "We should all leave and let Brady get to bed. He was up all night trying to help us."

We exchanged cell phone numbers. Then we all moved over to the door. Jess and Teresa both hugged me. Adrienne gave me a bony handshake. Dalt shook my hand, too.

Henry and I went out onto the porch and watched them drive away, Teresa alone in her Nissan Murano and the three Lancasters in Adrienne's big Chrysler.

NINETEEN

After the Chrysler's taillights blinked out of sight up the hill, I sat on the steps beside Henry. The streetlights on Mt. Vernon Street had come on. Where they shone through the trees, they cast wavering shadows on the street and sidewalks. "I think that was a mistake," I said to him. "What do you think?"

He cocked his head and looked at me. I was familiar with that look. He was wondering about food.

"Thanks for your input," I said.

It was another pleasant June evening, and Henry and I sat there savoring the sweet-smelling breeze. I realized that I'd been so intensely involved in the Robert Lancaster situation that Evie had scarcely entered my mind all day.

But now thoughts of Evie came swarming. How weird it felt coming home to an empty house, sleeping in an empty bed, having nobody except Henry to talk to. How alien and unpleasant living alone had become for me even after just a few days, since I began sharing my life with Evie.

Tomorrow she would know her father's fate. I guessed it

was harder for her now, not knowing, than it would be after tomorrow.

I assumed that Ed Banyon's fate would determine Evie's fate, and mine, too. I tried to focus on her and what she was going through, and not on the hole in my own life that she'd left behind.

Get over it, Coyne, I told myself. *It's not about you.*

I hoped she'd call tonight. It would be okay if she woke me up. It would be fine.

I gave Henry's ears a scratch. "Well," I said to him, "I don't know about you, but I'm ready for bed."

He sort of shrugged, then stood up and pressed his nose against the door.

I had my hand on the knob when a voice from behind me said, "Mr. Coyne."

I turned around. A man was standing on the sidewalk at the end of my front walk. He wore sunglasses and a green Celtics sweatshirt with the hood over his head. Black jeans, sneakers.

Beside me, Henry growled deep in his throat.

I touched the top of his head. "Sit," I told him.

Henry sat. I couldn't make him stop growling, though.

"What do you want?" I said to the man.

He held out his hands. He was presenting a rectangular cardboard box as if he were one of the three kings of Orient. It looked like a shoe box, and I suspected it did not contain gold, frankincense, or myrrh.

"This is for you," the guy said.

"What is it?" I said. "Who the hell are you, anyway?"

He bent over and put the box down on the brick pathway leading up to my house. Then he turned and started to walk away.

"Hey," I yelled. "Wait a minute."

He stopped and looked at me from the darkness of the hood that shadowed his face.

"Come back here," I said. "Take the top off that box for me."

He seemed to think about it for a minute. Then he came back to the shoe box, leaned over, and took the top off. He held it up for me to see. "Okay?" he said.

"Thank you," I said.

I was happy that the box hadn't exploded, spewing shrapnel around our neighborhood and killing me and Henry. I figured the guy would have refused to take the top off if that's what was going to happen. "Now," I said, "tell me who I should send a thank-you note to for this gift."

He fitted the top back onto the box, straightened up, and laughed. Then he turned and walked down the sidewalk in the direction of Charles Street.

Henry bounced off the front steps and started toward the shoe box. A growl rumbled in his chest. He moved stiff-legged like a bird dog that had smelled a pheasant hiding in the grass. Henry was, of course, a bird dog. On the other hand, I was pretty sure a pheasant was not hiding in that box.

"Stay," I told him.

He stopped. But he kept growling.

I went to where the box sat on my brick sidewalk. It looked inoffensive. Just a buff-colored shoe box. I used the side of my foot to push it up my front walk to the bottom of the porch steps. Henry remained standing where I'd told him to stay. His growl had turned into a whine.

Under the bright porch light I saw a Nike swoosh logo on the side of the box. I also saw a dark blotch on the bottom corner. A bloodstain, it looked like.

I snapped my fingers at Henry. "Get in the house," I said.

He stood up and came toward me. He stopped at the box, put his nose close to it, and growled.

"In the house," I told him again.

He came up the steps, and we went inside.

I found my cell phone on the kitchen table and two dish towels in a drawer. I told Henry he had to stay inside, then went out to the front porch. I used the towels like oven mitts to lift the top off the Nike shoe box.

At first all I saw was a plastic zip-top storage bag. There were some wet rust-colored stains on the inside of the plastic.

Old blood.

I bent closer to see what was in the bag. It took me a minute to identify what I was looking at. It was a squarish slab of gray skin with some bloody flesh attached to it—part of a man's upper lip with some bristly black hairs sticking out of it and a section of his cheek with a big pink mole on it.

I swallowed back a sudden spasm of nausea.

Hello, Mole-face Louie.

I put the top back onto the box, still handling it with the dish towels.

Then I sat on the front step. I took a few deep breaths to settle my stomach and slow down my heartbeat.

Paulie had used a knife, or maybe heavy shears, to cut out this piece of the man who'd given me that kidney punch. I wondered whether he'd killed Louie first or afterward.

Probably not Paulie himself. Probably one of his goons. Now that I thought about it, the man in the Celtics sweatshirt had looked and sounded familiar.

I poked out Roger Horowitz's cell number on my own. I figured that without a big hunk of his face, Louie would have a hard time staying alive, so I probably had evidence of a homicide in the Nike shoe box.

It rang four times before he answered. "Jesus Christ, Coyne," he snarled. "This better be good."

"It's not good," I said.

"It's eight-thirty on a Wednesday night," he said. "I only got home half an hour ago. Alyse and I just sat down to eat. We haven't eaten together all week. She made a nice pot roast. Carrots, potatoes, onions, biscuits, gravy. Alyse makes the world's best gravy." He blew out an exasperated breath. "So what the hell have you got that you're calling me on my business cell rather than my home phone, which I wouldn't've answered, that's more important than my wife's gravy?"

"That's exactly why I didn't call your home phone," I said. "Because I figured you wouldn't answer. And I'm sorry about the gravy. What I've got is a man's face."

"Yeah," he said. "Last time I looked you did."

"It's in a shoe box," I said. "Somebody else's face. Not mine."

He said nothing for a minute. Then he said, "Okay. I'll bite. Whose face?"

"One of Paulie Russo's thugs. They called him Louie."

"And you have this Louie's face in a shoe box . . . why?"

"Please come and take it away," I said.

"Yeah, yeah," he said. He sounded as if he had stopped listening to me. "Christ," he muttered, and then I heard him say, "Keep it warm in the oven, honey. I gotta go. . . . Well, don't be mad at *me.* You can blame your pal Brady." Then he said, "Hey, Coyne? You still there?"

"I'm here, Roger."

"I suppose you got your fingerprints all over that box."

"No. I handled it with dish towels."

"Henry slobbered on it, though, I bet."

"He did not. I told him not to."

"Right," he said. "Good dog. Okay. Sit tight. Don't let the fuckin' box out of your sight." And he disconnected, as he usually did, without saying good-bye.

I told Henry to sit still and guard the box while I went inside for a can of Coke. Then the two of us sat on the front steps and waited.

Less than fifteen minutes later a dark sedan with a portable red-and-blue light flashing on its dashboard pulled to a stop in front of my house, and a short woman with a long black braid stepped out. It was Lt. Saundra Mendoza, a Boston homicide cop. Mendoza and I were old friends.

She came up the path to where I was sitting on my front steps. She was wearing jeans and a T-shirt and dirty sneakers. She had a big leather bag slung over her shoulder. "Horowitz called me," she said.

I nodded.

"Jurisdiction," she added.

"Right."

In Massachusetts, the city of Boston has its own homicide department. For the rest of the Commonwealth, the state police have jurisdiction over homicides. In the case of Louie with the mole on his face, or what we had of him, and assuming he hadn't survived his face-lift, it was uncertain where he'd been killed and where his face had been lopped off and where the rest of his body might turn up. In cases like this, the city and state cops worked, usually reluctantly, together.

Mendoza looked down at the shoe box. "Looks innocent enough," she said.

I shrugged. "Except for the bloodstain."

She nodded and sat beside me. "You looked inside?"

190

"It's a bloody hunk of face."

"Ha," she said. "What a world, huh?"

"What a world, indeed," I said. "We going to wait for Horowitz?"

"Only way to do it," she said.

"I got some coffee."

She jerked her head at the can of Coke I was holding. "I'd rather have one of those."

I went inside, fetched a Coke for Saundra Mendoza, and brought it out to her.

We sat on the front steps sipping our Cokes. We talked about the Red Sox. I understood that she didn't want to have any conversation about the face in the shoe box until Horowitz arrived. That was all right by me. It gave me a chance to figure out what I could and couldn't tell them.

TWENTY

Roger Horowitz pulled up to the curb on Mt. Vernon Street about twenty minutes later. He got out of his car, gave the door a hard, angry slam, and as he walked toward Mendoza and me, he snapped latex gloves onto his fingers.

He stood there on the pathway looking down at the box. "You opened it, you said?" he said to me.

"Yes. With a dish towel."

"And it didn't blow up, huh?"

"It's not a bomb."

"Yeah," he grumbled. "Sometimes, Boston, Baghdad, you can't tell the fucking difference. Faces in shoe boxes. Christ, anyway." He bent down and picked up the box. "Let's go inside."

We went into the kitchen. Henry, who'd been sulking on the living-room sofa, scrambled down and followed us.

I spread an old newspaper on the kitchen table, and Horowitz put the box on it and lifted off the top with his gloved fingers. He and Mendoza peered inside.

I looked the other way.

After a minute, Horowitz put the top back onto the box. "You got another Coke?" he said.

I went to the refrigerator and took out a Coke for him.

He sat at the kitchen table. Mendoza and I sat, too.

Horowitz looked at Mendoza with his eyebrows arched.

"You go ahead," she said. "I'll interrupt."

They both fished out notebooks.

"Okay, Coyne," said Horowitz. "What can you tell us?"

"Henry and I were sitting on the front steps this evening," I said, "sometime around eight, eight-fifteen, and this man came walking up the street. He was carrying that box. He was wearing dark jeans, dark glasses, and a hooded green sweatshirt with the word 'Celtics' on it. The hood was pulled over his head and I couldn't see his face. He was maybe five-eight or -nine. Heavy build, but not fat. He spoke my name. I think I recognized him, but I wouldn't want to swear to it. He put that box down at the end of my front walk. I asked him to take off the top, and he did. Then he walked away. That's what happened."

"You said you recognized the guy?" said Horowitz.

I nodded. "I'm pretty sure he's one of Paulie Russo's goons. Like Louie here. Or what's left of him."

"Names?"

I shook my head. "I once heard Louie called by name, though I suppose it might not be his real name. I recognize this piece of face because of that big mole there beside where his nose used to be. The other guy, I have no idea."

"Could you pick him out of a lineup or ID him from a mug shot, do you think?"

I shook my head. "I couldn't see his face."

"So, okay," said Horowitz. "The big question—"

"I can't say much," I said.

"Can't? Or won't?"

194

"Can't. Ethically."

"Which," he said, "in my book, means won't. We most likely got a murder here, Coyne, in case you hadn't figured that out. You're obligated—"

"I understand all my obligations," I said. "I've told you what I know about the apparent murder of this guy with the mole on his face."

Horowitz glowered at me. "You know more than that."

I shook my head. "No, I really don't."

He sighed. "At least you must have some idea why Paulie Russo had Louie's face delivered to you in a shoe box."

"I think it's his way of apologizing."

Horowitz snorted. "Apologizing? Russo? To you?"

I nodded. "Louie's the one who gave me that kidney punch the other day. Hurt like hell."

Horowitz turned to Mendoza. "Quincy Market. Coyne fell down, made a big scene. Bystander, figuring he'd had a heart attack or something, summoned an officer. Coyne didn't say anything about Paulie Russo to her."

Mendoza looked at me with her eyebrows raised.

I shrugged.

"Louie did that, huh?" Horowitz said.

I nodded.

"And for that, by way of saying he's sorry, Russo has the guy killed? That what you're saying?"

I shrugged. "Basically, yes. That's how I interpret it."

"Basically," he repeated.

"It's a little more complicated than that."

"Come on, Coyne. Help us out here."

"I'm trying."

"Well, so far it makes no sense."

"There are things I can't tell you," I said.

"Right," he said. "Things between you and some damn client. Confidential things. Like why you got yourself kidney-punched in the first place. That privilege bullshit."

"It's not bullshit."

He waved his hand in the air. "Tell us what you can, willya?"

"I thought Russo was, um, responsible for something that might have happened to one of my clients, and—"

"What client?" said Horowitz.

"—and in connection with that, one of his thugs, the guy with the mole on his face—Louie—gave me that kidney punch. Subsequently I confronted Russo. He said he didn't order Louie to hurt me, apologized for it, and said he wasn't responsible for this, um, other thing. I made it clear I didn't believe him. He said something like 'How can I convince you?' So I think this"—I pointed my chin at the shoe box—"is his way of trying to convince me."

"That's crazy," said Horowitz.

"Of course it is," I said. "Paulie Russo isn't exactly the world's sanest human being."

"You gotta tell us about this other thing with your client," he said.

I shook my head. "No, I don't. At least not now. Not yet. Stop pushing me."

"You've got information about a crime," he said. "You're withholding it."

I didn't say anything.

Horowitz glowered at me.

"Did it occur to you," said Saundra Mendoza, "that this— this piece of a man's body—might be something other than an apology?"

"Like what?"

"Like a warning."

I looked at her. "*The Godfather*? That horse's bloody head in the rich guy's bed?"

She shrugged. "Or a dead fish wrapped in newspaper."

"I'll have to think about that," I said.

Horowitz leaned across the table toward me. "It sounds to me like you've got yourself into some deep shit," he said. "You really don't want to be involved with Paulie Russo."

"I'm not involved with him."

"That ain't what it sounds like."

"I wish I could turn it all over to you," I said. "But I can't."

"We can get a subpoena," he said, "haul you in, and if you refuse to talk, we can prosecute you for withholding information relevant to a police investigation of a felony."

I smiled at him. "I'm scared."

He narrowed his eyes at me. "You should be."

"I've told you everything I know that's relevant to this particular crime," I said. "The alleged crime being, cutting off a piece of a man's face. The man in question hasn't filed a complaint, and you don't have a dead body, or a witness, or any evidence, really, if you're thinking there's been a murder committed. All you've got is a hunk of face in a shoe box. As a law-abiding citizen and an officer of the court, I have done my duty by reporting it and turning over the, um, evidence to you, and I have been additionally helpful by tentatively identifying the owner of this piece of face and suggesting to you that Paulie Russo, our local crime boss, might know something about it. Might have even done it, or had it done. I have further hypothesized a motive, such as it is, as to why this shoe box was presented to me."

"Hypothesized," muttered Horowitz. "Christ. Fuckin' lawyer."

"Means, motive, and opportunity," I said. "What more do you want?"

He looked at Saundra Mendoza. "I got interrupted in the middle of a nice pot roast dinner for this happy horseshit." He sighed. "How do you want to handle it?"

"It's hardly horseshit," I said. "Happy or otherwise."

He glared at me. "I was having dinner with my wife, for Crissake. Look what you've done to my appetite." He turned back to Mendoza. "So what do you think?"

Mendoza shook her head. "Without a body . . ."

"We know there's a fucking body," Horowitz said. "Unless you think there's some guy walking around without his face."

"All I meant," she said, "was that until a body turns up, we can't treat it as a homicide. But, okay. Here we are on Beacon Hill. It's my jurisdiction, for now, at least. I'll get forensics to deal with the box, see if they can lift the prints of the guy who delivered it, maybe get lucky with the plastic bag. I'll get an ID for this Louie guy with the mole, and I'll see if we can conjure up a complaint so we can go after him on the grounds that we want to arrest him. That way, we can put the squeeze on Russo."

Horowitz was nodding. "Sounds good. Keep me in the loop."

She cocked her head and smiled at him. Saundra Mendoza had a great smile. Big brown laughing eyes, wide mouth, white teeth. "You think I want this?"

"Get your name in the paper," he said.

"Yeah," she said. "Just what I need." She fished some latex gloves out of her shoulder bag and pulled them on. Then she stood up and picked up the box. "I better get this to the lab before it goes bad." She started for the front door.

Horowitz and I went with her. I held the door for her, and we went outside. I sat on the porch steps. Horowitz walked Mendoza to her car. She handed the shoe box to him while she unlocked the trunk. He put the box into the trunk, and she slammed it shut.

They stood there on the sidewalk talking for a few minutes. Then Mendoza got into her car and drove away.

Horowitz came back up the front walk and sat on the steps beside me. "I wouldn't mind a beer," he said. "How about you?"

"A beer sounds good." I went inside, snagged two bottles of Long Trail from the refrigerator, popped the caps, and took them out to the porch.

I handed one to Horowitz. He held it up, and we clicked bottles. He took a long swig, then wiped his mouth on the back of his wrist. "So how's Evie doing?" he said.

"I don't know," I said. "She's out there with her father, and we haven't talked much since she left. She was taking him to the hospital today. Tomorrow they should know what they're dealing with, at least."

Horowitz was leaning forward with his forearms on his thighs and his hands dangling between his knees and his beer bottle dangling from his hands. He seemed to be gazing out at the shadowy street in front of my house. After a little silence, he said, "What I meant was, how are you doing?"

"I'm okay."

"Your eyes look like two holes burned in a blanket, you know. I mean, you look like shit."

"Thank you. I haven't been sleeping that well."

"Miss her, huh?"

"Wouldn't you?"

He shrugged, as if it were self-evident.

A soft evening breeze ruffled the maple trees that lined Mt. Vernon Street, and we watched the streetlight shadows dance on the sidewalks.

"She coming back?" said Horowitz.

"Jesus, I hope so. Why would you say that?"

He shook his head.

"What did she say to you?" I said.

"To me?" He smiled quickly. "Not much. She's got some kind of guilt thing with her father. Here's her chance to get rid of it."

"She told you that?"

"Not in so many words," he said. "I inferred it."

"She never said anything like that to me," I said.

"Maybe you just weren't listening."

After Horowitz left, I poured myself some coffee, and Henry and I went out to the backyard. Henry lifted his leg against his favorite azalea bush, and I sat in my favorite Adirondack chair.

I sipped my coffee and thought about that hunk of Louie's face.

A warning, Mendoza had suggested.

I doubted that. It was uncharacteristic of Paulie Russo. Too clever. Too dramatic. And unnecessary. If Paulie had kidnapped Robert Lancaster, as I assumed he did, so far he had no reason to doubt that he'd done it right. He wouldn't be afraid of me. He'd understand that we hadn't called in the FBI because the family didn't want it, and he wouldn't want to rock the boat.

When Paulie Russo wanted to warn or threaten you, he sent his goons to beat you up in a parking lot. When Paulie warned you, he didn't leave much room for interpretation.

I figured Louie's face was just Paulie's way of saying: *Here's proof that I've punished the man who punched you in the kidneys. I didn't kidnap Robert Lancaster, so now we're even.*

It didn't exactly convince me that he hadn't kidnapped Robert

Lancaster. Paulie Russo was an accomplished liar. But it did raise the question: If he didn't do it, who did?

The question seemed hypothetical, but important nevertheless.

I thought about it while Henry finished snuffling around the garden and I finished my coffee, and I came up with no compelling theories.

Tomorrow, I decided, I'd do my best to figure it out.

That night I slept on the daybed in my office. I didn't want to use the bedroom. It felt like an alien place without Evie.

TWENTY-ONE

Henry woke me up the next morning whining to go outside. It was a little after eight. I figured I'd slept for at least nine hours, and I felt like I could've snoozed for another nine if Henry hadn't insisted that I rise and shine.

I let Henry out, plugged in the coffeepot, took a quick shower, and got dressed. Then I poured myself a mug of coffee, grabbed the portable kitchen phone, and joined Henry in the backyard.

The clouds hung thick and low overhead. It smelled like rain. I sipped my coffee and watched the goldfinches and nuthatches and titmice that were swarming the feeders. A hummingbird was dipping his beak into the begonias that Evie had planted back in May, which seemed like a long time ago, and a couple of mourning doves were pecking fallen sunflower seeds off the ground. City wildlife.

It was Thursday. Today, presumably, they'd know what was wrong with Ed Banyon, and how bad it was, and what, if anything, they could do about it.

Evie hadn't called last night. I hadn't called her, either. I hoped she knew I was thinking about her.

Guilt, Horowitz had said. That's why she felt compelled to be with her father. I didn't understand why she'd need guilt to do that. It just seemed like a logical thing for a daughter to do.

I wondered what she'd said to Horowitz that she hadn't said to me.

I called my office at quarter of nine—purposely well before Julie arrived so that I'd be sure she wouldn't answer. I didn't want to talk to her, or argue with her, or defend my decisions to her. It was easier just to leave a message.

"Reschedule everything for today and tomorrow," I said to our office voice mail. "Tell anybody who seems to care that I'm under the weather. Which, actually, I am, more or less, not that it matters. I'm sure I'll be in on Monday all geared up to accrue a mountain of billable hours. After you make the calls, go home, and don't come back till Monday. And I don't want you to argue with me. I'm the boss, don't forget. Aren't I? Have a nice weekend."

I finished my coffee, and Henry and I went inside. I gave him his breakfast and toasted a cinnamon-and-raisin bagel for myself.

Then I went into my office and slid the kidnappers' CD into my computer. I played it through, once again hoping to detect codes or nuances or hidden messages in Robert's words and facial expressions and body language.

Again I detected nothing.

I played it a few more times, focusing on the shadowy room instead of Robert himself and listening to the background noises instead of his voice. It did appear that he was in a cellar with a bedsheet hung behind him to hide details of the interior, as if the kidnappers thought somebody might recognize it, but I suspected the only reason I thought that was because Gordie

Cahill had put the idea into my head. So I was seeing it with expectations and preconceptions.

I could barely hear the soft rhythmic slapping sounds that Gordie had detected. If he hadn't pointed them out, I would never have noticed them. Now, listening for them and trying to block out Robert's voice, I still couldn't figure out what they were. They sounded like somebody slapping a wet towel against his bare leg. I doubted that's what the sounds actually were.

The most ominous detail on the recording was the absence of a blindfold over Robert's eyes. Kidnappers who intended to return their hostage wouldn't want him to be able to identify them.

I thought some more about having Louie's face delivered to me in a shoe box. I still figured it was Paulie Russo's unique way of apologizing for that kidney punch and trying to convince me that he didn't have Robert.

Saundra Mendoza had suggested that it was a warning. Paulie telling me that he wouldn't hesitate to cut off a man's face. Robert's face, for example.

Or mine.

Maybe. But suppose Paulie Russo was telling the truth? Suppose he wasn't the one who'd kidnapped Robert?

Either way, I figured I had a day—two at the most—to figure it out.

I found the cell phone number that Becca Quinlan, Robert's girlfriend, had scribbled on a scrap of paper for me and dialed it. It rang five times before her voice mail invited me to leave a message. Maybe she was in class. Maybe she was still asleep. Or maybe she just didn't want to talk to me.

"Becca," I said after the beep, "it's Brady Coyne. I'd like to talk to you about Robert. Please give me a call." I left my own cell phone number.

We'd see if she returned my call.

Teresa Samborski, Robert's mother, answered on the second ring. When I told her who it was, she said, "Do you have news? What have you heard?"

"No," I said. "No news since last night. I'm sorry." I saw no reason to tell her about Louie's face in a shoe box. "I was wondering if you'd mind if I came out to your house."

"No, I'm here. That would be fine." She hesitated. "Why?"

"I thought we could talk," I said. "And I wanted to look at Robert's room."

"His room?"

"I don't know Robert very well."

She laughed softly. "I guess I don't, either. But what good . . . ?"

"I don't know," I told Teresa. "Maybe between the two of us we can figure something out."

"I'll put on some coffee," she said.

I followed the directions Teresa gave me to her home in Acton. It took almost an hour in the morning traffic to wend my way out of the city to the Route 2 rotary in Concord, where I picked up 2A into Acton.

Teresa Samborski lived in a modest colonial in a little cul-de-sac lined with closely spaced modest colonials that looked like they'd all been built by the same developer at the same time during the housing boom of the eighties. Teresa's was stained brown with red shutters and an attached two-car garage. A basketball hoop and backboard stood on a steel pole beside the driveway. There was no net on the hoop.

I parked behind Teresa's Murano and went to the front porch.

Before I could ring the bell, she opened the door. "Come on in, Mr. Coyne," she said.

"It's Brady," I said.

She was wearing cutoff jeans and a plain white T-shirt. Her feet were bare. She looked too young to have a son Robert's age.

I followed her into the kitchen, and she gestured for me to sit at the table by a window. It overlooked a small backyard that backed up on somebody else's small backyard. There were some empty birdfeeders hanging from a spindly maple tree.

"Coffee?" she said.

"Thank you," I said. "Black, please."

She poured two mugs full and brought them to the table. She sat across from me, took a sip, and looked at me over the rim of her mug. "So?"

"Your husband's not here?"

"He's at work."

"What's his take on this?"

"Sam?" She shrugged. "He has no particular take on it. He's, um, supportive."

"But he's at work."

She looked at me. "What are you trying to say?"

I shook my head. "Nothing."

She gazed out the window. "My husband," she said after a minute, "is a good man. He works hard. He's helping put Robert through school. He's not very good at expressing his feelings. I believe he's concerned about . . . about what's happened." She shrugged.

"How do he and Robert get along?"

"About as you might expect. They keep their distance from each other." She smiled quickly. "They're a couple of guys living in the same house. Sam's not his father. They're polite with each other. Never had an argument or anything. Robert resents him, I'm sure, although he's never said so. Sam tolerates Robert. They

207

don't shoot baskets or rake leaves together, if that's what you mean."

"I didn't mean anything," I said.

"But Sam not being with me during this," she said, "it's noticeable."

"I noticed, sure," I said.

She shook her head. "Don't read anything into it. Running an automobile dealership is a hard business. He works seven days a week."

We sipped our coffee in silence for a minute.

"I never knew he gambled," Teresa said finally.

"I wonder if your husband did."

She turned and looked at me. "What are you trying to say?"

I waved my hand. "I'm not trying to say anything."

"You don't think Sam . . ."

"I just wondered if Robert might have confided in him, asked him for money, maybe."

"No," she said. "Sam would have told me."

"Robert could have sworn him to secrecy."

"They don't have that kind of relationship, Mr. Coyne." She shook her head. "Anyway, I don't see what difference it makes. Those criminals have kidnapped him. It's got nothing to do with my husband. I just want to get my boy back."

I nodded. "You're right. I'm sorry. I guess I was just being nosy. I wonder if you'd mind if I looked at Robert's room."

"Sure. I don't see why not."

"I know he has an apartment now . . ."

"That's just a room he rents with some other kids while he's at school," she said. "He still lives here. He hasn't moved out. He comes home most weekends, and when his summer classes are over, he'll . . ." She gave me a little smile, then stood up. "This way. I'll show you."

TWENTY-TWO

I followed Teresa up the stairs. She pointed to a closed door at the end of the hall. "That's Robert's room," she said. "If you don't mind, I'll wait for you downstairs."

I went into Robert's bedroom and closed the door behind me. A big poster of Tom Brady dominated one wall. Tacked to the back of the door was a poster of Janet Jackson. The single bed was neatly made. A bookcase and a bedside table flanked the bed. A small desk with a computer and a plug-in telephone sat under the room's only window. There was a small closet and a chest of drawers. That was it.

I glanced in the closet and saw nothing but clothes. No boxes of money or marijuana or guns. Not even a stack of old *Penthouse* magazines. The chest held underwear and socks and sweaters. No pill bottles or diaries or homemade videotapes in the drawer of the bedside table.

I sat at Robert's desk and turned on his computer, and when his e-mail server asked for his user name, I typed in ROBERT and BOBBY and LANCASTER and RLANCASTER and

ROBERTL and several other permutations of his name, all of which were rejected.

I rummaged through the desk drawers and found nothing except paper and pencils and paper clips—nothing with anything written on it that resembled a user name or password.

An experienced PI like Gordie Cahill, with a lot of trial and error and persistence and creativity, might be able to deduce Robert's user name and password, depending on how dogged he was and how random and obscure the codes were. I was not dogged.

I went over to the bookcase. It held an ancient set of Hardy Boys adventures, a few Stephen King novels, an old set of World Book encyclopedias, and a whole shelf of science and history and psychology college-level textbooks.

Several small photos in plastic frames were lined up on top of the bookcase. I took them down to look at them.

One showed Robert, wearing a cap and gown, flanked by Dalt and Teresa. High-school graduation, I assumed. Mom and Dad, smiling bravely on an occasion that had reunited them. Robert had an arm around each parent's shoulders. He looked happy.

In another photo, a much younger Robert Lancaster—he looked about ten—was standing with a younger-looking Dalton Lancaster. They both wore hip boots and were standing calf-deep in the water of a fast-moving stream. Robert was grinning and holding a fly rod. Dalt was holding up a net that cradled a trout that couldn't have been more than ten inches long. Robert's very first fly-rod trout, maybe. A milestone for a boy, and a happy father-son moment.

Robert looked older in this photo than he was when his parents were divorced. I was glad to see that he and his father had spent some quality time together after Dalt and Teresa split.

Another photo showed Dalt and Jess with Jess's sister, Kimmie, and Kimmie's husband, Mike Warner. The four of them were sitting at a round outdoor table squinting and grinning into the sun. In the background was a harbor filled with boats rocking at their moorings and seagulls wheeling in the breeze. The two men wore captain's caps at cockeyed angles. The women wore bikini tops. Highball glasses sat on the table in front of them. They all looked a little drunk.

Another photo showed Robert looking a few years younger than in his graduation picture. He and an older-looking boy were standing in the stern of an oceangoing fishing boat. Both of them were holding up good-sized striped bass and grinning like they'd just won the lottery. The seas in the background behind them were gray and choppy, and the horizon was slightly atilt, as if whoever took the picture was standing on a rocking deck.

I'd been fishing in weather like that. Sometimes you had all you could do just to remain standing on the slick deck. Casting in the wind was always a challenge. Seasickness didn't plague me, but it wasn't much fun to watch your partners puke over the transom.

Sometimes a harsh slanting rain and choppy seas would bring the big stripers out to play. That's what I guessed had happened to Robert and his friend on the day this photo was taken. It reminded me of a time a few years earlier when I'd gone out with J. W. Jackson and a Martha's Vineyard boat-owning friend of his. We'd motored over to the Elizabeths on the tail end of a September nor'easter, and we'd found the water churning with mixed schools of big stripers and bluefish.

Remembering that day, and gazing at this photo of Robert and his companion holding up the nice fish that they'd caught on a similar day, I could almost smell the wet salty sea air on my face and feel the deck rocking under my feet and hear the rhythmic slap-slap of the waves against the hull . . .

That's when I got it.

That sound in the background on the kidnappers' CD. I knew I'd heard it somewhere.

Waves slapping against the side of a boat.

When he was trussed up in duct tape reading his plea for the videocam, Robert was in the cabin of a boat.

The light that showed through the bedsheet wasn't a cellar window. It was a porthole.

On the CD, the sound lasted only a minute or so somewhere in the middle of Robert's recitation. That rhythmic slapping wasn't caused by the persistent rolling waves of a storm. I guessed it was the wake of a passing boat.

We would have heard the rumble of the engines if the boat Robert was in had been moving. I figured it was moored, per- haps tied up at a dock, when he was reading and the wake came along.

It was probably the same boat that had been waiting under the bridge for a trash bag full of currency. Maybe I'd been that close to Robert when I delivered the ransom money. Maybe he'd been in the boat that picked it up.

I thought about it for a minute, then sat on Robert's bed, took my cell phone out of my pants pocket, and dialed Charlie McDevitt's number at his office in the federal courthouse in Boston.

When his secretary answered, I said, "Shirley, it's Brady Coyne. I've got a serious emergency here. I need to speak to Charlie right away."

"Why, Mr. Coyne," said Shirley. "How lovely. We haven't heard from you for much too long. I hope you're going to take

Mr. Charlie fishing. He needs to go fishing. He works so hard, don't you know."

"Well, actually—"

"And how are those dear boys of yours?"

"The boys are both well," I said. "Joseph is in his second year at Stanford, and William is rowing boats for fly fishermen in Idaho. One of these days I'll come by the office and show you some pictures. I bet your grandchildren are growing fast. But right now—"

"Like little weeds," she said. "My Colleen had another one in April, a darling boy named Thomas David." She hesitated. "A serious emergency, you say. Oh, dear. Let me interrupt him for you."

I sighed. Shirley was a formidable guardian of Charlie McDevitt's portal. She could go on and on.

A minute later, Charlie said, "I think you just set a new record for getting through to me. Shirley mentioned something about a dire emergency."

"Dire is her word," I said. "It's a better word than mine, which was 'serious.' I hope you can tell me if Vincent and/or Paulie Russo own boats."

"Boats? What—?"

"It would be better if you didn't ask," I said. "I know your people are surveilling the Russo family."

"Sure. We've been watching them for years."

"So do they own boats?"

"Well, yeah," he said. "All those made men own boats. It's an important status symbol among them. But if you want to hang on, I can try to be specific with you. All I gotta do is poke the right keys on my computer here."

I waited for a couple of minutes, and then Charlie said, "Okay. Not sure what you're after, but here's what I got. Vincent owns a forty-nine-foot yacht that he keeps moored down in Boca Raton. That's a lot of boat for a shriveled up old godfather. It's not just a status symbol. It's a serious phallic symbol. Young Paulie's got a cabin cruiser about half that size tied up in a marina in Scituate. He wouldn't dare have a bigger dick than his old man. We keep a close eye on both boats. The magic of GPS. Our eyes in the skies. Beep their electronic reports to our satellites, thence directly to our computers. Our watchers sit in air-conditioned offices eating pizza and tracking hundreds of boats and automobiles and private planes. Be nice to nail one of the Russos transporting bales of weed or crates of AK-47s or something. Actually, though, neither Russo is what you'd call an enthusiastic seaman. They hardly ever go aboard their boats, and when they do, it's for social or business purposes, not for actually sailing o'er the bounding main. We got both boats bugged, too, of course." He hesitated. "This what you were looking for?"

"What about their goombahs and compadres?"

"You mean do they have boats?"

"Well, yes. Or do they use the Russos' boats?"

"It would take some more poking around to tell you who owns what," he said. "But like I said, we always know where the Russo boats are, and if any other persons of general or specific interest connected to the Russos owns a boat, we probably got an eye on it, too."

"Vincent's is in Florida, you said."

"Yes. Boca Raton. They use it for parties. Bimbos in bikinis and politicians in blazers, mostly."

"What about Paulie's boat in Scituate?"

Charlie was quiet for a minute. "You didn't enjoy my clever conceit about status and phallic symbols?"

"I did," I said. "It's not original, but in this case it's particularly apt. But—"

"Maybe this is the place where you tell me what the hell is going on, old buddy."

"Don't worry about it," I said.

"The other day you mention kidnapping," he said, "and today you mention the Russo family, and I'm not supposed to worry?"

"I can't talk about it," I said.

"Yeah," he said, "I figured that out all by myself. Okay, so what do you specifically want to know?"

"I'd like to know where Paulie Russo's boat was Tuesday night, Wednesday morning."

"This past Tuesday, you mean? Day before yesterday?"

"Yes. Can you look that up?"

"Sure. Logged directly into our computers from the GPS. Just gotta find the file. Hang on a sec." A minute later he said, "Okay. Here we go. Paulie's boat was right there at its mooring. Been there since May when they took it out of dry dock and put it in the water, except for one Saturday, Memorial Day weekend, it was, when Paulie took two blond women, neither of them his wife, out for a ride down to Provincetown and back." He hesitated. "Am I helping you at all?"

"Sure," I said. "You always help me. You're telling me Paulie Russo was not out in his boat Tuesday night."

"I don't know where Russo was," said Charlie. "I can only tell you where his boat was. I mean, he could've been out in somebody else's boat. I'm not sure what you're after here."

"Me, neither," I said. "How close do you guys watch Russo's goons?"

"Russo's got a lot of goons working for him, Brady. He's got more helpers than we do, I think. They come and go, you know? Anyway, actually watching them, tailing and surveilling them, is pretty labor intensive. So the answer is, it depends."

215

"I understand."

"I can check and see if we got anything unusual going on Tuesday night, Wednesday morning, if that'd help."

"It would. I'd appreciate it."

"It'll take a while. That stuff, unlike the electronic stuff on the boats and cars, is inputted by hand, and they don't necessarily keep up with it. I'll have to talk to some people, twist a few arms, access some restricted files."

"There's a platter of Marie's deep-fried calamari in it for you."

"Ah, you don't need to do that. But, since you mention it, okay. It's a deal."

"So how long is a while?"

"Don't know if I can do better than a couple of days. That okay?"

"Probably not," I said. "But—"

There was a beep in my telephone.

"Charlie," I said, "I've got a call coming in. I better get it."

"Okay," he said. "You'll be hearing from me."

"I appreciate it, old friend."

"Calamari," he said.

I hit the button on my phone and said, "Yes?"

"This is Adrienne Lancaster," she said. "You were right."

TWENTY-THREE

Wh"hat was I right about?" I asked Judge Lancaster.

"They want more money." She blew out a loud, inju-
dicious breath. "You were right about that. But you were wrong
about the amount. This time they want five hundred thousand."

"Only half a million."

"Yes," she said. "Only."

"What did they say about Robert?"

"I talked to Robert."

"You did? You had a conversation with him?"

"Yes." She paused. "Well, not exactly a conversation. I said I
wanted to speak with my grandson, and they put him on the
phone, and he said hello. I asked if he was all right, and he said
he was okay. Then they took the phone away from him."

"Are you sure it was him?"

"Certainly. I know Robert's voice. He sounded terrible. But
it was he."

"Terrible how?"

"Groggy," she said. "Raspy. I could barely hear him."

"Like he was sick?"

"Yes. Weak. Disoriented."

"Well," I said, "it's a relief just to know he's still alive. So start from the beginning. Tell me everything."

"This was just a few minutes ago. I called you right away. I was in my chambers, at my desk, where I am now. My morning recess. I was eating my yogurt and going over some papers and trying not to think about all of this horror, and my cell phone vibrated. I had it in my pocket so I wouldn't miss any calls, as we agreed. I usually leave it in my purse in my chambers, but this morning I kept it with me in court. So I took it out of my pocket and looked at the screen. The call was coming from Robert's cellular phone. I thought, *Oh, how wonderful. He's calling me. He's all right. They've let him go.* But it wasn't Robert. It was some other voice telling me he needed more money."

"Needed," I said.

"Yes. That was the word he used."

"And he was using Robert's phone."

"Yes. That was smart. These people are clever."

"This other voice," I said. "Did you recognize it?"

"It was all tinny and distorted. It kind of echoed, as if his head were in a trash can or something. Purposefully disguised, it seemed to me. I didn't recognize it."

"What else did he say?"

"He said that if we wanted Robert back it would cost five hundred thousand dollars more. He wants it the same as the other time. Twenties, fifties, hundreds. Used bills. He said they'd be in touch with you sometime tomorrow and you'd better have the money. He said if we contacted the police they'd kill Robert. I said I didn't know how he expected me to get that kind of money on such short notice, he'd need to give me a few days, at least, and he sort of laughed and said no, it had to be tomorrow. I didn't think it would do any good to argue or try to negotiate with him. Then I said I wanted to speak to Robert, and that's when he put him on."

"They're going to call me, huh?" I said.

"That's what the man said."

"But he didn't say when."

"Just tomorrow sometime."

"At which time he expects me to have the money?"

"Yes, I think so."

"Did he say which of my phones he'd use?"

"No," she said, "he didn't, and I didn't think to ask."

"Have you talked to Dalt?"

"Not yet," Adrienne said. "You're the first one I called. I should bring poor Teresa up to date, too."

"You call Dalt," I said. "I'll talk to Teresa. Can you get the money?"

"In one day? I don't see how. If it were a week, maybe even just a few days, I could."

"Well," I said, "you better see what you can do."

"I will." She hesitated. "So when is it going to end?"

"When we get Robert back."

"Or . . ."

"We will," I said. "We'll get him back."

She laughed quickly. "I wish I could be so confident."

Me, too, I thought.

After I disconnected with Adrienne, I sat there in Robert's bedroom trying to get my thoughts organized. He was still alive. It looked like we had one day to get him back. After that, if the judge couldn't come up with half a million dollars in used currency, I had a pretty good idea what would happen.

I picked up one of the photos I'd been looking at when Adrienne called. Jess, her sister Kimmie, Dalt, and Kimmie's husband, Mike Warner, sitting together at an outdoor table looking drunk and happy. All four of them looked four or five years younger. I noticed it in the men more than the women. Their faces were less puffy, and their bodies looked slimmer and solider and more tanned. Mike wore a mustache in the photo. He didn't have one now.

I put that photo down and picked up the one of Robert and his friend on the boat holding their fish. I wondered who'd been behind the camera and whose boat they were on.

The harbor, the captain's caps, the fish, the ocean.

The sound of the wake of a passing boat slapping against a hull. The glow of light shining through a porthole. Robert duct-taped and imprisoned in the cabin of a boat.

The ransom money, tossed off a bridge, then retrieved from the Merrimack River . . . by somebody on a boat.

If not Paulie Russo's boat . . . whose?

Paulie or one of his goons could have borrowed somebody else's boat to retrieve the bag of ransom money under the bridge, of course. Otherwise, I had no brainstorms.

I picked up the photo of Robert and his friend with their fish and the one of the four adults sitting at a table outdoors by a harbor and took them downstairs.

Teresa was unloading the dishwasher in the kitchen. When I walked in, she stood up, wiped her hands on the fronts of her jeans, and gave me a halfhearted smile. "So? Did you learn anything?"

"Judge Lancaster just called me," I said. "She spoke to Robert a short time ago. She heard his voice."

"He's alive, then."

"Yes."

"But they've still got him."

"Yes. But—"

"They're asking for more money, is that it?"

"That's right," I said.

"Just like you said they would," said Teresa.

"Yeah," I said. "I'm a genius." I told her what Adrienne had told me.

"So she's going to get the money?"

"She's going to try," I said, "but that's a lot to raise in twenty-four hours, even for her. She's not sure she can do it."

"If she can't . . ."

"We'll get more time out of them," I said. "They've got to know they're being unreasonable. They want their money. We'll get him back."

Teresa went over and sat at the table. She looked out the window for a minute, then turned to me. "You really think so? You think we'll get him back?"

"I do," I said. I sat down across from her and put the two photos on the table.

She looked at them, then at me. "You took these from his room? How come?"

I pointed at the one showing the four grown-ups sitting at the outdoor table. "Do you have any idea when and where this was taken?"

"Not a clue. You can see that they're all quite a bit younger. I always wondered why Robert framed it and kept it there on his shelf. He doesn't have a photo of Sam anywhere."

"What about this one?" I turned the photo of Robert and his friend with their fish so Teresa could see it better.

She nodded. "That's Robert with his—cousin, I guess you'd call him. Jimmy. Jessica's nephew." She looked at me. "You know what happened to Jimmy?"

I nodded.

"He gambled, too, you know."

"Yes," I said. "I'm sure there's no connection."

"Gambling *is* a connection," she said. "Dalt gambled. It wrecked our marriage." She shrugged. "Robert worshipped Jimmy. He always seemed like a good kid. Jimmy, I mean. He was several years older than Robert, but they got along like brothers. It was tragic, what happened to him. Robert took it very hard."

"When was this photo taken?" I said. "Do you know?"

"I remember it very well," she said. "It was a Saturday in September. Robert had just started high school, and it was Jimmy's first year in college. Robert was thrilled that they were getting together for a day of fishing. He sort of figured that when Jimmy went off to college they wouldn't see much of each other. He got up around four that morning, and Jimmy and his father came and picked him up."

"Jimmy and Mike Warner?"

She nodded. "They were going out on Mike's boat. Up around Gloucester, I think. They had a wonderful day of fishing, even though it was quite stormy."

"Mike has a boat?" I said.

She nodded. "Yes. Robert went out with him and Jimmy several times." She hesitated. "Not since Jimmy disappeared, though."

I touched the two photos. "Do you mind if I borrow these?"

She shrugged. "I don't care. Robert will want them back."

I stood up. "I'll return them, I promise. I've got to get going."

She walked me to the front door and gave me a hug. "Thank you," she said.

"I haven't done anything," I said.

"Keep in touch, okay?"

"I promise," I said.

As I drove back to Boston, three thoughts kept colliding with each other in my brain:

The kidnappers' CD was filmed on a boat.

The bag of ransom money had been picked up in a boat.

Mike Warner owned a boat.

TWENTY-FOUR

I got back home a little after two in the afternoon, driving in a misty spring rain that had started sometime while I was at Teresa Samborski's house in Acton. Henry was pretty happy to see me. I scootched down so he could lap my face for a while, then let him out back.

I checked my phone for messages. None. My thoughts flipped to Evie. It was not yet noontime in California. I assumed she'd call me when she knew something.

Henry yipped from the back porch. He didn't enjoy the rain.

I let him in, gave him a Milk-Bone, then went into my den. I put the two photos I'd taken from Robert's room on my desk and found a magnifying glass in my desk drawer.

I didn't know what I was looking for, but I hoped I'd recognize it if I saw it.

I detected nothing that struck me as significant on the photo of Robert and Jimmy holding up their big striped bass, although when I magnified the fly that was hooked in the corner of Robert's fish's mouth, I could see that it was a chartreuse Lefty's Deceiver. He'd caught it on a fly rod. Good for him.

I turned my attention to the photo of the four adults at the outdoor table. I did it systematically, moving from the bottom, left to right, then back across right to left so that I wouldn't fail to examine every square centimeter of the photo.

I was trying to figure out where this outdoor bar or restaurant was, and I saw what I'd been looking for in the upper-left corner, in the background. It was a banner flying under the American flag from a flagpole on the wharf that angled across the top corner of the photo. In the breeze, the banner was almost completely unfurled and I could read the fuzzy letters on it: CAY.

There was another letter at the end, but the way the tip of the banner was flapping in the wind, all I could detect was the beginning of the curve of that last letter. The left edge of an O, maybe. CAYO.

Or a G or a Q or a C.

I wrote down each possible combination. CAYO. CAYG. CAYQ. CAYC. I stared at the combinations of letters.

Meaningless.

I blinked. Looked away. Looked again.

Then I saw it. YC.

A harbor in the background. Captain's caps on the men, bikini tops on the women. Seagulls. Dozens of moored boats. They were drinking at an outdoor table on a veranda or an open-air porch or a patio.

YC. Yacht Club.

If Dalt and Jessica Lancaster and Mike and Kimmie Warner were having drinks at a yacht club, and if Mike owned a boat, chances were this CAYC was the yacht club where he kept it moored.

I Googled CAYC on my computer, then scrolled down through Mr. Google's seemingly endless list of hits.

The Canadian Association for Young Children.

The County Antrim Yacht Club. I clicked on that one.

County Antrim was in Ireland. Maybe the two couples had this picture taken when they were vacationing in Ireland together.

If so, it didn't help me.

I kept going.

The Corning Area Youth Center.

The Community Alliance for Young Children.

The Cambridgeshire Association of Youth Clubs.

Then . . . *aha*. The Cape Ann Yacht Club.

Cape Ann was a bump of land detached from the mainland by the Annisquam River, a peninsula on the northern tip of the curve of Massachusetts Bay. The artsy seaport village of Rockport and the famous old fishing community of Gloucester were on Cape Ann. So was the town of Essex, home of the best clam shacks in New England, on the north side, and Manchester-by-the-Sea, a pretty seaside village on the southeastern side of the cape.

Cape Ann was less than an hour's drive from Boston, a likely place for somebody living in one of the suburbs to keep a boat moored.

I clicked on this CAYC link. The Cape Ann Yacht Club was located in Essex, about twenty-five or thirty miles south of where the Merrimack River emptied into the sea at Plum Island. In other words, about an hour's boat ride along the coast of the North Shore and up the Merrimack River to where I threw a quarter of a million dollars off the iron bridge.

The CAYC Web site gave its address and the phone numbers for the business office, the marina, and the restaurant.

The question I needed to answer was: Did Mike Warner keep his boat moored there?

227

I knew what Gordie Cahill would do. He called it "social engineering." A delicious euphemism. "Soshing," in the shorthand of PIs, was the art of manipulating people so that they'd divulge information they weren't supposed to divulge. Soshing required lying, or at least exaggerating and fudging and distorting the truth. As long as it wasn't specifically illegal, Gordie said, you did it. You had to do it because everybody else did it. If you didn't, somebody less scrupulous than yourself would, and pretty soon you'd be out of business.

Effective soshing usually involved what they called "pretexting," creating a false pretext to explain who you were and why you needed the information you wanted. You wouldn't impersonate a police officer. That was specifically illegal, and therefore dangerous and stupid pretexting. But there was no law against impersonating a bank officer, or a customer-service representative of the telephone company, or an underwriter from a life insurance company. That was clever and effective pretexting.

Pretexting, like soshing, required lying, or at least serious deception, which PIs like Gordie rationalized the way deceit has been rationalized since long before Machiavelli institutionalized it in *The Prince*: The ends justify the means.

My end was to figure out if Mike Warner's boat had been the setting for the ransom video starring a duct-taped boy named Robert Lancaster, or if Mike's was the boat that had picked up the trash bag containing a quarter of a million dollars from the Merrimack River. Or, most likely, both.

Because I didn't know whom I could trust, I had to accept the likelihood that the means to my end would require some soshing and pretexting and other difficult and uncomfortable deceptions.

I could justify it.

I was a lawyer. We lawyers, of course, were sworn to uphold the law. But lawyers social-engineered and pretexted all the time, especially with each other. We never called it lying. We called it Doing What It Takes to Win.

Laypeople think we lawyers are sleazy and conniving and bloodthirsty. We are the butt of some truly mean-spirited jokes. We tell some pretty nasty lawyer jokes ourselves. We think they're funny, although when nonlawyers tell them they're just mean-spirited.

But we don't believe them. We lawyers have gotten a bad rap. We're misunderstood. We're at least as honorable and lovable as the next guy. Whatever we do, it's because we're committed to our clients. Our work is adversarial. That's how the law in America works. There's a winner and a loser. Our clients want to win. So do we. Winning is our job.

So we do what it takes, within the bounds of the law. Rarely do our clients think we're sleazy or bloodthirsty. When we don't win, in fact, our clients blame us for not being as sleazy and bloodthirsty as we should have been. For lawyers, the clients are the ones whose opinions count.

I sat there at my desk and thought about it for several minutes. Then I took a deep breath, picked up my cell phone, and dialed the number for the marina at the Cape Ann Yacht Club.

A raspy-voiced man answered. "Cape Ann Yacht Club. This is Dave."

"Hey, Dave," I said. "It's Phil calling from Marine Engines over in Beverly? I'm looking at a recall notice here on some engine parts for—hang on—okay, the name is Warner. Michael Warner? My records are showing he's got his boat docked there?"

"Warner?" said Dave. "Sorry. It's not ringing a bell. You want to spell it for me?"

229

I spelled Warner for him.

"I'm looking on my computer," he mumbled. "Hm. Walter, um, Wexler. Nope. We got no Warner. You don't mean Walter, do you?"

"No," I said. "It's Warner. Well, damn. So now what'm I s'pose to do? I gotta get this recall notice to him, you know? There's this whole liability thing."

"You don't have a home or business number for him?"

"Yeah. He's not answering. It says Cape Ann Yacht Club on these papers, man."

"Sorry I can't help you," he said.

"I am screwed," I said. "How could this be wrong? It says right here in black and white. Cape Ann Yacht Club."

Dave was quiet for a minute. Then he said, "Hang on a minute there, Phil. Lemme try something for you."

I hung on for close to five minutes.

"Hey, Phil?" he said when he came back on the line. "You still there?"

"Still here," I said.

"Okay," said Dave, "good luck. I just talked to Peggy, who's our assistant manager? She's been here like forever. She remembers Michael Warner. He kept his boat moored here up until a couple years ago. A Bertram, right?"

"Yes," I said, "that's right. A Bertram."

"Okay. Peggy says Mr. Warner moved his boat over to the Kettle Cove Marina in Gloucester. That was two years ago last September, before I started working here. What happened was, they did a lot of renovations here? Built all new wharfs, expanded the restaurant, updated the security. Cameras and keypad locks and motion-activated floodlights, hired a night watchman. Fees nearly tripled, and a lot of folks, I guess, went looking for something, um, less upscale. Give Kettle Cove a try. Here, I got their number. You got a pencil?"

"I owe you, man," I said. "Okay, I got a pencil. Shoot."

Dave read a phone number to me. "You'll probably talk to Sandy. She's a good kid. You can tell her it was me who gave you her number."

"Next time I'm up your way," I said, "I'm gonna buy you a beer. You have saved my scrawny butt today."

"Ah, don't worry about it. Glad to help."

After I disconnected from Dave, I let out a deep breath. This pretexting and social engineering was nerve-racking.

But I'd done it. I'd gotten away with it. Me, Phil, from Marine Engines in Beverly with a recall notice for engine parts.

I was glad Dave hadn't asked me which engine parts, or who manufactured them, or what was wrong with them. I wasn't sure I could name any part of a marine engine, never mind one that was a likely candidate for recall.

I leaned back in my chair for a couple of minutes. I decided not to be Phil anymore. I wasn't sure I wanted Dave and Sandy comparing notes on some guy named Phil.

I pecked out the number for the Kettle Cove Marina on my cell phone.

A woman answered. "Kettle Cove. This is Sandy. How can I help you?"

"Yeah," I said, "how you doin', Sandy. This is Frank, here at Danvers Marine, and I'm about to head over your way to take a look at Mike Warner's Bertram, but I seem to've lost the number for his slip. He says she's been running rough and he's in a big hurry to get it fixed. Help me out, willya?"

"Frank, is it?"

"You got it."

"That's funny," she said. "I saw Mr. Warner just a couple days ago, and he never mentioned anything about his boat running rough. It's a pretty old boat, but he takes good care of it."

"Well," I said, "he's trying to take good care of it now. I got the work order right here in my hand, which means I got a job to do. I just need his slip number so I can take a look at her, you know?"

"Hang on there a minute, Frank," Sandy said. "Let's see what I can do for you."

I waited with my fingers crossed.

She came back on the line a minute later. "Frank? You there?"

"Yep. I'm waiting."

"Do I know you?"

"I don't think so," I said. "My loss."

"Where you from? Danvers Marine, you said?"

"That's it," I said. I held my breath.

"Hm," she said. "I don't think we've ever done any business with you."

"Well," I said, "it's about time we did, hey?"

"Sure," she said. "I guess so. Thing is, I'm not supposed to give out information about our clients. You know what I'm saying?"

"Oh, absolutely," I said. "I understand. I could be anybody. It's just, I been trying to call Mr. Warner, and all I get is his voice mail, and I'm really backed up over here. I don't wanna get you in trouble. All I need is the damn slip number."

Sandy paused. I was afraid I'd blown it. Then she said, "Well, okay, Frank. What the hell. I don't see any harm. You wanna write it down?"

"Yep," I said. "I'm ready. Fire away."

"Mr. Warner's Bertram is in slip G-9. You've been here before, right?"

"Not lately. You know how many marinas there are on the North Shore, Sandy? I been to all of 'em one time or another. After a while one starts to look like all the others, you know what I'm saying? You better remind me how to find G-9."

"Sure," she said, "okay. Slip G-9 is on wharf G, which is the last one out off the main dock. Even-numbered slips on the left, odd numbers on the right. So G-9 is the next-to-last slip on the outside on the right. Make sense?"

"Got it," I said.

"You know Mr. Warner's boat?"

"One of the other guys used to work on it," I said, making it up as I went along. "He quit, so now it's me. A Bertram, is all I got written down here."

"A Bertram, right," Sandy said. "She's a thirty-eight-footer. *Dot Com* is her name. White with blue trim. Nice old boat. Sleeps four. Mr. Warner and his wife have been going out quite a bit lately. They do a lot of fishing. Funny that he never said anything about her not running right. I mean, folks usually mention it to me if somebody's coming over to look at their boat."

Dot Com, I thought. A cute name for a boat. So the dot-com boom was how—and when—Mike Warner made his money. I wondered if he was one of those people who hit it big, didn't get out soon enough, and was now finding himself squeezed.

According to Dalt, Mike had exhausted his resources trying to track down his missing son. A boat could be a giant money pit.

"Well," I said to Sandy, "all I know is, he's in a big hurry. I got a rush on this. The fishing must be pretty good these days."

"Very good, what I'm hearing."

"Okay, well, thanks a million, there, Sandy. I'll be over some-time this afternoon, take a look at Mr. Warner's boat."

"You've got to sign in at the office," she said, "get the secu-rity code. When you do, be sure to say hello."

"You bet," I said.

I hung up the phone and blew out a long breath. That had been way easier than I'd expected. Gordie always said you couldn't overestimate the gullibility of the American public, and the billion-dollar annual sales from telephone and e-mail solicit-ing and television infomercials bore him out. He said, tell some-body you're a reporter or, even better, a novelist, and they'll just spill out their life story to you. Mostly, Gordie said, people like the idea of being helpful, and they're flattered when somebody asks them for help.

Dave and Sandy were both nice, friendly, helpful people. Why should they mistrust Phil with the recall notice or Frank the marine-engine mechanic? They were just good old boys trying to do their jobs.

I printed out Mapquest directions to the Kettle Cove Marina in Gloucester, then went out to the kitchen. Henry, who'd been snoozing on the daybed in my den, scrambled after me. I found some sliced ham and made myself two ham-and-cheese sand-wiches. I ate over the sink. Henry sat on the floor beside me. He looked up at me. Patience and loyalty and love glowed in his liquid brown eyes.

I gave him half a sandwich. He swallowed it in one gulp, then resumed gazing hungrily at me.

"That's all you get," I said. "The rest is mine."

He lay down, dropped his chin onto his paws, and refused to make eye contact.

"It's all about food with you, isn't it?" I said to him.

He rolled his eyes up, looked at me for a minute, then sighed and closed them.

"Listen," I said to him, "I'm going to be gone for a while this afternoon, and you can't come with me. Sorry."

His ears flattened against his head. Henry was a master at reading intonation and body language. The only word I'd just spoken that he understood was "sorry." He'd learned to equate "sorry" with disappointment and abandonment. Flattened ears meant he was worried and depressed.

I reached down and scratched the sweet spot on his forehead. "I'll be back before you know it," I told him. "You guard the house, okay? Don't hesitate to bark at strange noises."

He narrowed his eyes at me, then got up and walked back into my den.

I'd have to make it up to him. He'd been abandoned quite a bit since Evie left.

I followed Henry into the den. I changed into a pair of my most faded and threadbare blue jeans, a green work shirt, an old pair of sneakers, and a blue windbreaker.

I threaded the leather holster for my big Leatherman multi-purpose tool onto my belt. It unfolded into a sharp three-inch blade, or a Phillips or flat-head screwdriver, or pliers and wire cutters, or can and bottle openers, or a saw blade, or a file, or an awl. I put a cigarette lighter and a Mini Mag flashlight into a pocket in the windbreaker. I set my cell phone to vibrate and slipped it into my pants pocket. I draped my binoculars around my neck. From the vast hat collection on my closet shelf I found a faded and fish-blood-stained cap with the picture of a big oceangoing sportfishing boat on it.

I didn't know if this outfit would enable me to pass myself off as a marine-engine mechanic. For one thing, aside from the Leatherman, I didn't have any tools. Nor did I have a business card, not to mention the fact that I drove a four-year-old green

BMW instead of a panel truck with the Danvers Marine logo on the side.

I figured there'd be some more social engineering and pre-texting in my future before I managed to get a look into the cabin of the old thirty-eight-foot Bertram called *Dot Com* that was owned by Mike Warner and moored in slip G-9 in the Kettle Cove Marina in Gloucester.

TWENTY-FIVE

Thursday-afternoon commuter traffic was what I expected—bumper-to-bumper, stop-and-go all the way from Mt. Vernon Street to Cambridge Street, then on Charles out past the North Station in Boston, over the bridge on Route 93, and all the way to Beverly. When I picked up 128 east, a straight shot out to Cape Ann, the traffic seemed to thin out a little.

The rain had been just a misty drizzle in the city, but as I traveled north and east it became a steady, hard summer rain under a low oatmeal-colored sky.

I guessed I was ten or fifteen minutes from Gloucester when something vibrated against my thigh. It felt like an angry bee had bumbled into my pants pocket, and it took me a second to realize it was my cell phone.

Adrienne? Dalt? Teresa?

The kidnappers?

I remembered that I'd called Becca Quinlan in the morning. She hadn't called back. Maybe it was her.

I pulled over to the side of the road, turned on my emergency flashers, fished the phone from my pocket, flipped it open, and said, "Yes?"

"Hey. It's me. Your wayward girlfriend." Evie.

My throat got tight, just hearing her voice. "You're hardly wayward, honey." I paused. "I can't even begin to tell you how good it is to hear your voice."

"You, too," she said. "You doing anything?"

"Nothing important," I said. "Nothing as important as talking to you."

"I called your office. Julie said you'd taken the day off. Are you okay?"

"I'm fine," I said. "A mental health day, you know?"

"You're not home, either," Evie said. "I tried our house. I thought you'd be home."

"Nope," I said. Her next question would be: Where was I on this rainy evening, then, if not home? I surfed my mind frantically for a believable lie. Everything I came up with sounded false. "I'm not home yet, no," I said lamely, a lie itself, of sorts, implying that I was on my way home from somewhere instead of on the road trying to track down a kidnapper. "So do you have some news?"

I waited. She didn't say anything, didn't follow up on the where-are-you question.

"Talk to me, babe," I said finally.

"Ah, shit," she said. "I'm trying to be all upbeat and brave and sweet for you, and it's not working."

"You don't have to pretend anything for me," I said. "Tell me what you know."

"It's bad," she said. "Bad, bad. I expected it, you know? But still, when you hear it . . ."

"I'm sorry" was all I could think of to say.

"They wheeled him into the operating room at seven this

morning. Ed. My daddy. It was supposed to be what they call exploratory, meaning they didn't know what the hell they were going to find. All the wonders of modern fucking medicine, and half the time diagnosis is still a mystery. He was in there all morning. Nobody told me anything. Me, a big-time hospital administrator, and they made me feel like a bag lady who'd snuck in for the crappy coffee. I finally got to see him in recovery just a few minutes ago. He's still unconscious. All pale and thin and hollowed out and hooked up to machines." She sucked in a breath, let it out. "I'm sorry. I'm kind of a mess. It's been a long day. You gear yourself up for the worst thing, but deep down inside you believe that it's going to be something better than that, as if you can fend off the really bad things by inventing worst-case scenarios. You understand what I'm saying?"

"Sure," I said. "It's like, if you can make yourself imagine it, it won't happen that way."

"Yeah," Evie said. "Well, I'm here to tell you, sometimes it does."

"Tell me."

"Worst-case scenario," she said. "They didn't know what they'd find. Or at least, so they said. Maybe they knew all along. A lot of the time they just don't tell you what they think. I've been around doctors enough. I asked all the right questions, and I got all the predictable evasions." She paused and blew out a long breath. I could hear that she was smoking a cigarette. "It's a stage four pancreatic cancer. That's the worst stage. It means that it's spread all over the place. Lymph nodes. Other organs. He's going to die. The doctor said he couldn't operate. Only about one in five of these things is operable anyway, he said, as if that would make me feel better. He might want to do chemotherapy or something. He wanted me to thank him, I think. Funny thing was, I almost did. Your father's going to die, lady. Oh, thank you so fucking much, kind doctor."

"I wish I was there with you," I said.

"No," she said. "It wouldn't do any good. You can't help me. I'm sorry. That sounded shitty. Do you understand?"

"Sure," I said, although I didn't.

"I'm going to stay here. With him. Until . . ."

"Okay," I said.

"It might be six months. Maybe a little more, but probably less. They can't tell me."

I was sitting there in my car on the shoulder off Route 128 on the way to Gloucester. My headlights were on, and the windshield wipers were swishing back and forth. Raindrops were pattering down on the roof and dancing on the hood. When the cars and trucks went slamming past me, my little BMW rocked in their wet backdraft.

I didn't know what to say to Evie. She was my love, and I couldn't think of anything to say to her.

"Brady?" she said after a minute. "Are you there?"

"I'm here, honey."

"I do miss you, you know."

"I miss you, too."

"And Henry," she said. "You'll give him a hug for me, okay? Tell him I love him."

"I will."

"Hey?" she said.

"What?"

"Please don't think about coming out here."

"Okay," I said. "I understand."

"No," she said, "I mean really. It would be just like you to show up sometime."

"I won't if you don't want me to."

240

She was quiet for a while. Then she said, "What's going to become of us?"

"We're solid," I said. "We'll be good."

"I don't know," she said. "I can't think about us right now. I'm sorry."

"I want you to do what you have to do," I said. "Don't worry about me. We'll worry about afterwards when the time comes."

"That's the thing," she said. "I'm not. Not worried about you, I mean. I'm worried about my daddy. And about me. I can't even think about afterwards." She paused. "I've got to go. I want to get back with him. I just stepped out to the parking lot for a minute. I needed a cigarette. I didn't want the damn doctor to know he made me cry. And I wanted to call you. I wanted you to know what's going on."

"I'm sorry it's bad news."

"Yeah," she said. "Me, too. You be good, okay?"

"Of course. Always."

"Don't worry about me," she said. "I'm doing what I need to be doing."

"Okay."

A pause. "Hey, Brady?"

"What, honey?"

"Look," she said. "If you want to . . . I mean, this is going to be a long time."

"If I want to *what*?"

I heard her blow out a breath. "Have a life. Jesus, Brady. I want you to live your life. Go out, have fun. Life is too short. If you don't believe me, ask my father." She hesitated. "You know what I'm talking about. I know you do. Do I have to say it?"

I laughed softly. "You want me to see other people? Is that what you're saying?"

"It sounds kind of high-schoolish, doesn't it?" she said. "But, yeah, I guess that's what I'm saying. Really. If we're—what did you say? solid?—if we're solid, it won't make any difference."

"I don't want to see other people," I said.

"Listen," she said. "Here's the reason I'm calling. I'm here with my daddy and he's dying and he's full of regrets for the time he's wasted, the things he didn't get to do, the possibilities he didn't pursue, the life he didn't live. I have made this choice. To be here with him. Because I know I'd regret it for the rest of my life if I didn't. I want you to make your choices, too. I don't want you to have any regrets. I don't want to be responsible for your life. I don't want to have to worry about you. Do you understand what I'm saying?"

The rain seemed to have softened. It sounded like mice scampering around on the roof of my car. "I understand, honey," I said. "I appreciate what you're saying. I'll do what I want to do, okay?"

"Promise?"

"I promise."

"Except," she said, "no matter how much you might think you want to come out here, don't. Please."

"Okay."

There was a long pause. "Love you," she said.

"I love you, too."

After Evie disconnected, I sat there holding my cell phone in my lap, as if she might call right back to tell me she'd changed her mind, that she was coming home.

Or at least to say, "*I* love you." When she said it without the personal pronoun, a sentence with no subject, it sounded . . . impersonal. Glib and insincere.

Right about then I wished I had a cigarette of my own to smoke.

242

TWENTY-SIX

By the time I turned onto the road leading to the Kettle Cove Marina, the premature gray gloom of a sunless evening had begun to settle over the damp landscape. It pretty much mirrored my mood.

Evie didn't want to have to worry about me. She didn't know when she'd be coming home. She wasn't thinking about me. She didn't want to see me.

I found myself resenting a dying man. I was jealous of the attention poor Ed Banyon was getting from his daughter.

Get over it, Coyne. Be a man.

A weatherbeaten wooden sign reading "Kettle Cove Marina" marked the entrance. I stopped there on a rise of land to survey the layout. There was no gate at the entrance, no guardhouse, no security camera. You could just drive right in on a gravel driveway that sloped down to a big sandy parking area along the curving edge of the water. A ten-foot chain-link fence ran along the entire outer edge of the lot, separating it from the water and the maze of docks where the boats were moored. There was a barred steel gate at the entrance to the long wooden pier that reached out into the cove. Evenly spaced at right angles off both sides of the pier were narrower wooden docks. The boats were tied up in their slips against these docks. If I'd done my math right—seven wharves, twenty slips per wharf—when the marina was full, it could handle 140 boats. Now it appeared to be a little more than half full. I assumed that this time of year a lot of people would be out fishing or otherwise enjoying a ride on the sea, if they didn't mind a little rain.

From the crest of the slope where I was stopped, I could see out past the end of Kettle Cove to the mist-shrouded ocean. It looked black and choppy and cold.

Off to the left of the parking area was a low-slung shingled building. I guessed it housed the office where Sandy, my unwitting accomplice, worked, and probably a coffee shop and a bar and rest rooms. Behind it was a larger hangar-like building for dry-docking and working on boats.

Right now, a little after six on this rainy Thursday afternoon, it all looked deserted. There were about two dozen vehicles parked randomly in the lot. I saw no people getting into or out of any of them, nobody walking on the docks, no boats pulling in or pulling out. The floodlights atop the tall poles around the rim of the parking area had not yet come on. The only sign of life was the glow of lights from the shingled building.

From where I had stopped in my car at the top of the slope by the entrance to the parking lot, I lifted my binoculars and scanned the boats that were moored there. Rebecca said that Mike Warner's Bertram was in slip G-9, on the outside of the outermost dock on the right.

I focused on the most distant row of boats and located her. Through my binoculars past the swish of the wipers on my windshield I could make out her name—*Dot Com*—in blue block letters on her stern. She had a wide, open deck, a sleek, curving bow, and round portholes on the side of the cabin. White, trimmed in pale blue. She looked solid and well cared for and seaworthy. She was a thirty-eight-footer, Sandy had said. Bigger than most of the other boats moored here.

I drove down the driveway and tucked my car between a pickup and an SUV at the corner of the lot farthest from the office, where I hoped it wouldn't be noticed.

I got out, locked up, and patted my hip and my pockets. Leatherman, flashlight, cell phone. My binoculars hung from my neck. I tucked them inside my windbreaker to keep them dry.

I skulked along the chain-link fence in the shadows, keeping the parked cars between myself and the office building.

When I got to the gate leading out onto the main pier, I tried the latch. Locked, as expected. There was a keypad on the post beside the gate. Sandy had mentioned a code. Those who paid to moor their boats here would know it. I didn't.

I walked slowly back along the fence, looking for a way to get under, through, or around it. It seemed to go on and on, and I was beginning to get that hopeless feeling of having come so far only to be thwarted at the end, when I heard a car door slam and then some loud male voices from the opposite side of the parking lot.

A big SUV had driven in. Its dome light was on. Three men had climbed out, and they were standing there unloading the back of their vehicle. There were a couple of coolers, some tackle boxes and bait buckets, a tangle of fishing rods.

The three guys were laughing and talking loudly, as if they were happy for an evening away from their wives and had already made a start on the beer in their coolers.

I headed in their direction, moving slowly, trying to time it. I let them finish unloading, lock up their SUV, and start lugging their gear to the locked gate, and then I fell in behind them.

One of the guys put down the cooler he was carrying, pecked at the keypad, and pushed the gate open. He held it for his two companions.

I came along right behind them, and he held it for me, too. "Hey, thanks," I said as I walked in through the gate.

"No problem," said the guy.

"Gonna try the stripers?" I said.

"A little fishin'," he said, "a lot of beer."

His buddies laughed.

"What could be better?" I said.

And I was in, just as easy as that, no soshing or pretexting required.

I followed the three fishermen down the wooden pier. They turned onto the fourth dock on the left.

"Well, good luck," I said to them.

"Yeah," said the guy who was lugging the rods. "Good luck yourself."

I kept going toward the end of the central pier, then went out onto the fifth pier on the right, pier E, which was two down from pier G, where Mike Warner's Bertram was moored. I found an angle between the moored boats where I could see *Dot Com*. She looked deserted. No lights lit her deck or glowed from her portholes. I scanned her with my binoculars and detected no movement except her gentle rocking in the swells that rolled in from the ocean.

Well, if this excursion to Cape Ann was going to be a big fat wild goose chase, I wanted to find out sooner rather than later.

I glanced back toward the gate, then walked quickly to *Dot Com*'s mooring.

Up close, she was an impressive craft. Thirty-eight feet is a lot of boat. She had a spacious wheelhouse over a big forward cabin and a wide rear deck with a fighting chair for big-game fishing.

I slipped my little hand-sized Maglite from the pocket of my windbreaker and shone it around the deck. There were a few coiled lines and some bumper buoys and a big fish locker. About a dozen rods were racked in the ceiling of the wheel-house. Everything was clean and neat and bare. Mike Warner kept his boat shipshape.

I glanced around again, feeling furtive and sneaky. Then I hopped aboard, which made me an instant trespasser.

The wheelhouse was a couple of steps up, over the cabin where the galley and the berths and the head would be. It was surrounded by glass and gave a high, wide view of the ocean. There were a lot of shiny chrome knobs and levers and switches and buttons and beer-can holders. There were lights and radios and microphones, radar and sonar and fish-finder screens.

The steering wheel was the only mechanism I was pretty sure I knew how to operate. The watercraft I was most comfortable in were propelled by oars and paddles.

The distant, muffled roar of a marine engine echoed through the misty rain from somewhere out beyond the marina, and a minute or two later the wake hit *Dot Com* and slapped against her hull. That sound reminded me of why I was there.

I crawled out on the narrow walkway that curved along the starboard side of the cabin to the bow. I crouched awkwardly by one of the portholes and shone my flashlight inside through the thick glass. The cabin featured a lot of blond wood paneling and shiny chrome fixtures and red vinyl upholstery. Against the opposite wall I could see what I guessed was the narrow door to the head, a folding table, and part of a berth.

A big piece of cloth was balled up on the berth. It looked like a pale blue bedsheet.

The porthole gave me a narrow angle. I could only see a small section of the cabin through it. I moved to a different one, which enabled me to see the other end of the berth where the boat narrowed at the bow. A small bookshelf and a locker were built into the wall at the head of the berth.

I crept around to the port side of the cabin and again shone my little light inside. From this side I could see part of the other berth on the opposite side of the cabin. It was covered with a lumpy brown blanket. The lumps got my attention.

I moved down one porthole. Through that one I could see clearly that the lumps under the thin blanket were what I suspected—the outline of the lower half of a person's body. Hips, thighs, knees, calves, and feet.

The next porthole gave me an angle to see Robert Lancaster's shoulders and head. His body was covered up to his chin with the brown blanket. The bottom half of his face was plastered with silver duct tape. His eyes were closed. He appeared utterly motionless.

I focused my light on his blanket-covered chest. I could not see it rise and fall. If he was breathing, I couldn't detect it.

I tapped on the porthole with the end of my steel flashlight. The sound would ring loudly inside the cabin.

Robert didn't even twitch.

I scrambled back to the deck. A hatch with double doors led down to the cabin. I yanked on the latch. It was locked, of course.

I looked quickly around the marina, mindful of the fact that I didn't belong here. The boat with the fishermen was pulling away from its slip. Its engines roared. Otherwise, the place seemed deserted.

I pounded on one of the doors with the heel of my fist. "Hey, Robert," I said as loudly as I dared. "It's Brady. Are you okay?"

I put my ear to the door. I heard no response.

The latch on the double doors opened by a key. The lock looked like the one on my front door back home. I took my Leatherman off my hip, pried open the knife blade, wedged it into the crack between the two doors, and tried to force the lock.

It wouldn't budge. I pounded and pried and levered at it, with no luck. The hatch doors remained stubbornly and solidly closed and locked.

My friend J. W. Jackson, a retired cop, once found a set of lock picks at a Martha's Vineyard yard sale and used them to teach himself how to pick locks. But he hadn't taught me.

Where was J. W. when I needed him?

Panic and fear clenched at my chest. Robert was lying in there. I didn't know if he was alive or dead or somewhere in between, but it felt as if every second I wasted was a tick off his young life.

I prowled around, looking for some kind of pry bar, which I realized was an unlikely tool to find on a boat. A battering ram would do. Anything to get that hatch open.

I found something that might do the job in a locker in the stern. It was a small anchor such as you might use with a dory or a much smaller powerboat—too small for a thirty-eight-foot Bertram, but just right for me. It had long curving tines.

I untied it from its line, took it over to the hatch that opened into the cabin, forced one of the anchor tines into the crack between the two doors, curled it around behind one of the doors, and levered it.

The door creaked and groaned. I put all my weight into it,

and the wood around the lock cracked and splintered and broke away, and the doors popped open.

I put down the anchor, ducked my head, and went down the three steps into the cabin.

The wet heat and the sour stench of sweat and rot and urine came blasting out at me from inside the cabin and staggered me back a step. I guessed that Robert had been locked down there all day—maybe for several days—with virtually no ventilation, while the sun's heat blasted the exposed boat and the ocean's humidity filtered in through the cracks. It was an oven in there.

I took a deep breath and ducked back into the cabin. I went over to where Robert was lying. I shone my flashlight on his face. His skin looked unnaturally white and papery. His few days' growth of black whiskers made it look even paler by contrast.

I used the scissors on my Leatherman to cut the tape. Then I peeled it off his mouth. His lips were cracked and scabby. Festering sores on both corners of his mouth oozed pus.

"Robert," I said. "Hey, buddy."

His eyes rolled under his lids, but he did not open them.

I grabbed his arm and shook him. "Hey," I said. "Wake up, man. Come on."

His eyelids fluttered, and then he opened his eyes. They looked cloudy and unfocused.

"Robert," I said. "It's Brady."

He seemed to look at me, but I couldn't tell if he recognized me. Then his eyes closed.

His throat clenched in a dry swallow.

The galley occupied one corner of the cabin. I opened the half-sized refrigerator and found a bottle of Poland Spring water. I took it over to Robert, cradled his head in one arm, and poured some on his lips. His tongue came out and licked. I tilted the bottle against his mouth, and he swallowed a little of it.

I was afraid that if I gave him too much water he'd choke, or if he did get it down, he'd vomit.

I poured water over his face. His eyes opened. They looked blankly at me, then closed again.

I patted my pants pocket, found my cell phone, fished it out, and dialed 911.

It rang several times before the operator said, "Where are you calling from?"

"Kettle Cove Marina in Gloucester. I'm on a boat in slip G-9. I've got a man who is severely dehydrated. He might have heatstroke. He's barely alive. It's possible he's been drugged. He's been locked up in the cabin of this boat. Come quickly."

"Say again where you are, sir."

I took a breath and repeated what I'd said.

"Who is this?"

"My name is Brady Coyne. I'm a lawyer. I'm here, on my cell phone. Tell Horowitz. Lieutenant Roger Horowitz, state police. What should I do for this man? I'm worried he's going to die."

"Wet his skin. Try to cool him down. Give him air and water. Don't try to move him. We're on our way."

I snapped my phone shut, then went to where Robert was lying and peeled the blanket off his body. He was wearing a pair of blue jeans and a dirty white T-shirt—the same clothes, if I remembered correctly, that he'd had on when he made the CD five or six days ago. His clothes were drenched with sweat and smelled of urine. Duct tape encircled his chest and held his arms at his sides. More tape bound his legs together from his knees to his ankles.

I cut through the tape and ripped it off. Then I cut off his T-shirt. I emptied the bottle of water over his torso.

His chest moved. It looked bony and shrunken. But he was breathing.

I gripped his hand. "Robert," I said, "listen to me. Help is coming. Hang in there, all right?"

He gave my hand a little squeeze.

I went over to the refrigerator, found another bottle of water, and tipped it against his mouth. Most of it ran off his chin.

But his tongue moved over his lips, and he swallowed.

Then I heard some voices. They came filtering through the misty evening air. Hooray. The EMTs were here. That was quick.

I wondered why I hadn't heard their sirens.

I went up to the deck and looked back toward the parking area. Darkness was settling over the harbor. All I saw was the interior lights of a van that was parked at the far end of the lot.

No red lights twirled on its roof. It was not an emergency vehicle.

I lifted my binoculars and focused on it.

The rear hatch was open, and two people were unloading things from it. A man and a woman.

The woman was blond. She was wearing a dark windbreaker and a pink cap.

Kimmie Warner.

The man was Mike Warner.

It looked like they were unloading provisions for a long sea voyage.

As I watched, a third person came trotting across the parking area toward them from the direction of the office. It was a woman. She was wearing a yellow slicker with the hood over her head. Under the slicker, her bare legs winked in the gray half-light.

252

Sandy, I guessed, coming out to tell the Warners that the mechanic from Danvers Marine, Frank was his name, seemed like a nice guy, he'd called about the engine problem you've been having with *Dot Com* and said he was coming out to take a look at it, though it didn't look like he'd made it today.

TWENTY-SEVEN

I ducked back into the cabin and went over to where Robert was lying on his berth. "Hey," I said. "Robert. Listen to me."

He didn't even twitch.

I grabbed his arm and shook him. "Come on, man. We don't have much time. Help me out here. Wake up."

His eyelids fluttered, then opened. He looked at me, blankly at first, and then he seemed to focus on me.

"Can you understand what I'm saying?" I said.

He gave a small nod and made a dry grunting noise in his throat.

"Okay," I said. "Good. Mike and Kimmie are coming. I'm not going to leave you. I called 911. Help is on the way. You just lie there and pretend you're asleep, all right?"

He blinked and nodded.

"I'm going to put the tape back on your mouth and pull the blanket over you again. It's just for a few minutes. You've got to hang in there, all right, pal?"

He opened his mouth, then closed it. I put my ear close to it.

"Water," he rasped.

I gave him another sip of water. Then I found a strip of duct tape that I'd cut off him and pressed it back over his mouth. I pulled the brown blanket up to his chin and patted his cheek. "Hang in there," I said.

I went up top and looked back at the parking area. The dome light still glowed from inside the Warners' van. Sandy in her yellow slicker had left, but Mike and Kimmie were still there unloading their stuff.

I couldn't let them take their boat out to sea before the EMTs arrived. If they did, I guessed it would be all over for Robert. I didn't know what they had planned for him, but judging by the condition I'd found him in, it wasn't good. I guessed they intended to dump him overboard. I had to find a way to delay them.

I didn't dare shine my flashlight around the boat, even inside the cabin. Mike and Kimmie would see the lights glowing in the portholes from the parking area.

High on the paneled wall inside the cabin under where the steering wheel was located, I found a two-foot-square metal panel. It was set flush in the wall. The latch was padlocked.

I used the anchor tine to rip the padlock off, and the panel door swung open.

I cupped the business end of my flashlight in one hand, turned it on, and shone it inside. Running down between the walls of the boat—from the wheel back to the rudder, I guessed, but what did I know about it?—were half a dozen twisted-steel cables.

I unsheathed my Leatherman, opened the wire cutters, and went to work on one of the cables. It snapped with a satisfying ping.

I hacked through one other cable, folded up my Leatherman, and went topside for another look.

The dome light was no longer shining from the Warners' van. I raised my binoculars and saw them heading across the parking lot for the gate. They were both loaded with duffels and shoulder bags and coolers. Once they went through the gate, they had about a fifty-yard walk up the pier to slip G-9.

I didn't have much more time.

I returned the anchor, my indispensable tool, to the locker in the stern. Then I went down into the cabin. I picked up the balls of duct tape I'd peeled off Robert and the empty Poland Spring bottles and threw them into a trash bin in the corner.

I pushed the metal panel door closed on the wall. There wasn't much I could do about the jagged scratches and bent latch where I'd pried off the padlock, but in the dim light from the portholes, in spite of the missing lock, I thought it might go unnoticed for a little while.

"Hang in there, buddy," I whispered to Robert. "Everything's going to be okay."

Then I went up the three steps to the deck. I pushed the double hatch doors shut. The wood along the edge was splintered, and they wouldn't close and latch properly, of course. The anchor tine had taken care of that.

Mike and Kimmie would notice that right away.

I hoped they'd think that some burglar—maybe a guy posing as Frank the mechanic from Danvers Marine—had been in the marina breaking into the boats.

It was possible, of course, that they'd think it was somebody like me who had tracked down Robert.

It was too late to worry about what they'd think, so I didn't. I just worried about buying some time for Robert.

The lights on the tall poles in the parking area and spaced out along the central pier were starting to come on. They bathed the marina in dim orange light that was slowly becoming brighter.

When I looked back toward the gate, I saw that the Warners were now halfway up the main pier, coming my way. I could hear their voices, Mike's deep and rumbling, Kimmie's soft and a little whiny. Their tones made me think they were having a quiet disagreement, but I couldn't make out any of their actual words.

I wondered if they were accusing each other of calling the boat dealer about some engine problem that they hadn't told the other one about.

I hopped off *Dot Com*, looked around quickly, then ducked onto the small center-console fishing boat that was parked on the other side of the dock opposite slip G-9. I crouched there behind the console in the shadow cast by the light on the pole.

A minute later Mike and Kimmie turned onto Pier G, and I heard Mike say, ". . . no choice. So tough."

"This is stupid," Kimmie said. "There's got to be a better way."

"What's your plan?" Mike's voice was an angry growl.

"I don't know," she said, "but we can't just—"

"What the hell did you think was gonna happen?"

"Sometimes," she said, "it's like I don't even know you."

"You're in this as deep as me," he said, "so you better not even think about crapping out on me."

I peeked around the side of the console. Mike had climbed into the boat. Their gear bags and coolers were piled on the deck, and Kimmie was handing things down to him. The deck was only about eight feet wide. I was that close to her.

"So," Mike said, "if you didn't make that call—and I sure as hell didn't—who did?"

"How would I know?" she said. "You're the one who takes care of that. Sandy probably just misunderstood. Anyway, I—"

"*What the fuck is this?*" Mike was looking at the splintered doors on the cabin hatch.

Kimmie hopped into the boat and went over to the hatch doors. She looked at them for a minute, then pulled them open and ducked into the cabin. "He's still here," she said from inside.

"Is he breathing?" said Mike.

There was a pause. Then Kimmie's voice said, "Yes. Barely." She came back onto the deck and stood in front of Mike with her hands on her hips. "We've got to get him to a hospital."

"Oh, yeah," he said. "That's a great idea."

"He's gonna die, Mike."

"You just figuring that out? Come on, honey. We're a team, remember? Get the gear stowed below while I get us under way. See if there's anything missing down there. The security at this place sucks."

"You're a monster," she said. But she grabbed a big duffle and wrestled it down into the cabin.

A minute later she reappeared. "Nothing missing that I can see."

"So what the hell happened?"

"Maybe somebody broke in to see what they could steal," she said, "and when they saw poor Robert, they just got the hell out of there."

"Yeah," said Mike, "or maybe it was your mechanic pal taking a look at our engine."

"How many times do I have to tell you?" she said. "I didn't call any mechanic."

"Just get us untied," said Mike. "We gotta get out of here."

"What about Robert?"

"We're not changing our plan now," he said.

"We can't just—"

"Are you forgetting who got Jimmy into gambling?" he said. "Let's see how that son of a bitch likes losing his only son."

"That was your plan all along, wasn't it?" said Kimmie. "It wasn't about the money. It was revenge. It was about Jimmy."

"He was your son, too, honey. We're in this together."

"I'm not a murderer, Mike. I didn't bargain for this."

"Yeah, well, the money's not bad," said Warner, "you gotta admit that."

"Jesus Christ," said Kimmie. "You make me sick."

"We'll have plenty of time for this interesting discussion later," said Mike Warner. "Right now, though, let's get moving. Bring in the fucking lines, will you please?"

Kimmie mumbled something I didn't catch, then jumped out of the boat and began untying the lines from the cleats on the dock.

Mike went into the wheelhouse, turned on the boat's interior and running lights, and started up her engines. They grumbled and burbled. They sounded smooth and strong.

I looked back toward the parking area. I hoped to see a caravan of flashing red and blue lights coming down the driveway.

But I saw nothing, nor did I hear any distant sirens.

I peeked back at *Dot Com*. Mike had gone below, and Kimmie was crouched on the dock just a few feet from where I was hiding. She had her back to me as she coiled the lines.

I had to do something. It was pretty obvious that if they got away from the marina and out to the high seas, they'd dump Robert overboard. Then they could turn north or south. It was a big ocean with a coastline of nooks and crannies. They could go anywhere. The Caribbean, Canada, Central America. They had a big oceangoing boat and a quarter of a million dollars in untraceable bills.

I took a deep breath, then slipped around the console of the little boat. I hopped up onto the dock and slapped my hand around Kimmie's mouth before she could react. I yanked her back against me. I was rough with her. I wanted to hurt her. I wanted her to be afraid.

She reached up with both of her hands, scratching and grabbing at my fingers. She gurgled and grunted in her throat, but I kept my hand tight against her mouth, and the rumble of *Dot Com*'s engines drowned her out.

I jammed the end of my little Maglite hard into her back. "Don't even breathe," I growled in her ear, "or I'll blow you away. Cooperate and I won't hurt you. Got it?"

She nodded. Her hands fell to her sides.

I dragged her backwards to the edge of the dock where the little center-console boat was moored. I didn't know what I expected to accomplish except maybe a little chaos. I just wanted to buy some time.

Mike revved *Dot Com*'s engine a couple of times, then let it idle.

I could feel Kimmie trembling against me. I had taken her by surprise. She had no idea who I was or what I wanted.

"Step back and down into the boat," I whispered to her. "No noise. If you fuck with me, you're dead."

I stepped backwards into the boat, bringing Kimmie along with me. Then I dragged her behind the console where Mike couldn't see us.

I jabbed her again with the steel flashlight. "Not a peep," I hissed.

I peeked around the side of the console and saw Mike start to come down from the wheelhouse. "Okay," he said as he stepped onto the deck. "We're all set. Let's go."

I pulled my head back before he could spot me.

"Hey!" he said. "Where the fuck are you? Come on. We gotta

take off now." A pause. He was looking all around. "Kimmie? God damn it, this is no time for games. Get your ass on the boat."

Just then I heard the sirens. They were distant and muffled, but they were approaching quickly.

"Jesus Christ," Mike said. "The fucking cops are coming. I'm warning you, lady. I'm not going to wait for you. Where'd you go? Dammit, Kimmie. What the hell are you trying to do?"

I was standing behind Kimmie, using the front of my body to press her against the side of the console. My left hand was clamped around her mouth. With my right hand I kept the end of my flashlight rammed hard against her back.

I turned my head to glance back at the parking area. A line of vehicles was turning down the sloping driveway.

My hand on Kimmie's mouth must have slipped when I turned to look, because that's when she bit me. Her teeth clamped down hard on the base of my thumb and sank into my flesh, and the pain shot up my arm and hit the center of my brain like a hot knife. "Ow!" I yelled. "Jesus!"

Kimmie rammed her elbow into my solar plexus and twisted away from me, and before I could react, Mike was on me. He levered his forearm around my throat and smashed my face against the cockpit. I felt my nose crunch, and then my legs melted, and I fell hard onto the deck.

I lay there for a minute waiting for the world to stop spinning.

When I pushed myself to my knees and looked around the corner of the console, I saw that Mike was at *Dot Com*'s wheel and Kimmie was standing beside him. Then the burble of the engine changed pitch. The boat's transmission made a soft clunking sound, and *Dot Com* eased backwards.

Another clunk, and she began to pull forward out of her slot.

I braced myself against the console of the little boat and managed to stand up. Behind me in the parking area, there was a chaos of lights and voices and thumping car doors and squawking radios.

Then a voice on a bullhorn called: "Michael Warner. Kimberly Warner. This is the FBI. Remain where you are."

I heard Mike mumble, "Fuck you." He eased *Dot Com* forward until she'd cleared her mooring slot along the dock. Then he gunned her engines. She shot forward, headed for the channel that would take them through the harbor out to the ocean. The channel curved like an **S** and was marked by buoys. Along both sides of the channel were moored boats too large to park at the side of a dock—big sailboats and oceangoing sportfishing boats and luxury yachts mingled democratically with working lobster boats and commercial fishing craft.

This channel, like all channels in harbors where there's a lot of boat traffic, was marked with "No Wake" signs. Mike Warner was ignoring them. *Dot Com*'s engines were roaring, and she was throwing a lot of wake as she sped through the channel.

Once they got outside the harbor, they could turn left or right and shut off their lights and dump Robert overboard. Within a few hours they could drop anchor in any one of a thousand rocky coves and hidden harbors all the way from Bar Harbor to Block Island. In a few days Mike and Kimmie Warner could be in Nova Scotia or Costa Rica.

If the FBI was calling the Coast Guard right now, it was too late. Mike would be far beyond the reach of their helicopters and cutters by the time they got mobilized.

I crawled up onto the dock. I crouched there on my hands and knees and shook off a wave of dizziness. Blood was gushing from my nose and dripping onto the planks. My head hurt and my hand throbbed.

After a minute I pushed myself to my feet. As I watched, Mike and Kimmie Warner's speeding boat started to turn toward the right. It was veering out of the narrow harbor channel. The big old Bertram inscribed a wide curve, and without slowing down, she plowed into the side of a chunky old steel-sided trawler. The hollow crash echoed over the water.

A few minutes later the dock around me was swarming with people. There were uniformed cops and plainclothes cops and EMTs, local and state and federal cops, all talking into telephones and two-way radios and yelling at each other.

Out in the harbor, *Dot Com* appeared to have bounced off the trawler. I could see that her bow was smashed, and she was slowly settling into the water.

A uniformed cop grabbed my arm and turned me around. "Did you see what happened?" he said.

I nodded. When I tried to speak, I realized that my mouth was full of blood. I turned my head and spat a big gob onto the deck. "There are three people on that boat," I said. More blood trickled into the back of my throat. I hacked and spat again.

The cop peered into my face. "What happened to you? Are you all right, sir?"

"There's a boy in the cabin of that boat," I said. "He's too sick to move. He won't be able to get off by himself."

The cop touched my shoulder and pointed out at the water. A white runabout with its searchlights blazing was speeding into the harbor, heading toward the site of the collision. The letters USCG were painted on its side.

"That was something, though, wasn't it?" the cop said. "The guy driving that boat must be pretty drunk."

"It was something, all right," I said. "I hope they get there before she explodes."

We watched as the Coast Guard boat pulled alongside *Dot*

Com, which was listing on her side. Her bow was tilting low in the water. It looked like she was going to sink any minute.

A hand gripped my biceps. I turned.

It was Roger Horowitz. "Jesus," he said. "Take a look at you. What the hell happened?"

"I'm all right," I said. "It took you long enough. Robert Lancaster is on that boat. He's practically dead."

Horowitz nodded. "You got some explaining to do, Coyne." He handed me a handkerchief. "Clean yourself up, why don't you? You're a mess."

TWENTY-EIGHT

Fifteen or twenty minutes later the Coast Guard boat pulled up beside the pier. As Roger Horowitz and I stood there watching, a waiting crew of EMTs lifted Robert Lancaster onto a gurney and wheeled him down the dock to an emergency wagon, which then peeled out of the parking area with lights flashing and sirens shrieking.

Then two uniformed police officers took Mike and Kimmie Warner off the boat. Their hands were cuffed behind their backs.

Horowitz touched my arm. "I'll catch up with you," he said. "You better get your face looked at, see if it's salvageable." He turned and headed down the dock to the parking area.

I blew some globs of clotted blood out of my nose into Horowitz's handkerchief, then went over to the Coast Guard boat. One of the officers was standing there on the pier.

"Is he all right?" I said to him.

He turned to look at me. "Which one?"

"The boy. Robert Lancaster."

"He's alive," he said. "Barely, by the looks of him. He was

267

unconscious. The hull of that Bertram was half filled with water, and he was kind of sloshing around in it."

"Where are they taking him?"

"Addison Gilbert here in Gloucester. It's the nearest hospital."

"What about the Warners?"

"They're okay. Their boat looks like it's a goner, though."

"Thanks for saving them."

"We get hurricanes, missing fishing boats, kids swept out to sea by the undertow. This was pretty tame." He looked out over the harbor and smiled. "Damnedest thing, though, the way that guy suddenly veered out of the channel and plowed right into that old trawler, wasn't it?"

I smiled. "Damnedest thing."

I wandered up to the parking area, found a private rock to sit on, fished out my cell phone, and called Dalt. When he answered, I told him that Robert had been rescued and was en route to the Addison Gilbert Hospital in Gloucester. I told him he'd probably want to get there as soon as he could.

"Are you saying . . . ?"

"He's in pretty bad shape," I said. "But they're taking care of him. I'm sure he's going to be fine."

I heard him exhale. "What can you tell me?"

"Not now, Dalt. It's a long story. I'll meet you at the hospital. Why don't you call Teresa. I'll fill all of you in when I see you."

I was heading to my car when Horowitz caught up to me. "So you're a hero, huh?"

I laughed. "Yeah. Look at me."

"You're a disaster, all right."

I showed him my left hand. Blood was seeping from the smile-shaped wound made by Kimmie Warner's teeth. "She bit me. I probably need a tetanus shot."

"What I noticed about that woman," said Horowitz, "maybe it should be a rabies shot. Listen. We gotta have your story."

"You will."

"No time like the present, Coyne."

I nodded. "Mike and Kimmie Warner kidnapped Robert Lancaster and extorted a quarter of a million dollars from his family in ransom money. They were holding him hostage on their boat."

"That's a start," he said. "I got a feeling there's way more to it than that."

"Of course there is. I've got to talk to my clients first."

"Your clients being?"

"Robert Lancaster," I said. "The victim. And his family."

He narrowed his eyes at me, then nodded. "The sooner the better, okay?"

"What about the Warners?" I said.

"We got them in custody. We're holding both of them. Not sure how cooperative they're gonna be. We got a lot of questions. We need to know what you know, Coyne."

"Not now," I said.

I drove to the Addison Gilbert Hospital, and when I went into the emergency room, a nurse—she was quite tall and very pretty and about seven months pregnant—told me that Robert Lancaster had been taken to intensive care. When I asked her how to find the ICU, she narrowed her eyes at me and said I wasn't going anywhere until somebody examined me.

Now my head and my left hand were both throbbing with every beat of my heart, and I'd begun to feel dizzy and nauseated. So I allowed the nurse—she told me her name was Brooke—to steer me to a curtained cubicle. I lay back on a narrow bed on wheels. She said she'd be right back, and she was. She had a clip-board. She asked me a lot of questions. Her interest seemed to center on my health insurance.

After I signed the form, my pregnant nurse washed the dried blood off my face and hand. She said a doctor would be with me shortly, patted my shoulder, and left.

I guess I dozed off, because the next thing I knew a gray-haired woman with glasses down on the tip of her nose was shining a light in my eyes. "Mr. Coyne," she said. "How do you feel?"

"Okay," I said. "Fine."

"You don't seem to have a concussion," she said. "I want to take a couple of stitches in that gash on your nose. When did you have your last tetanus shot?"

I shook my head. "I have no idea."

She stitched up my nose and slapped a Band-Aid over it. She washed out the wound on my hand and bandaged it. Then she stuck a needle into my arm, wrote out a prescription, and handed it to me. "You might not need this," she said, "but if the pain gets too bad, it'll help. It's got codeine in it, so don't drive." She put her arms under my shoulders and helped me to sit up. "How're you doing?"

I took a couple of deep breaths. "I'm okay. Little headache."

"Is there somebody who can drive you home?"

"I'll be all right," I said. "Thanks."

I found my way up to the intensive care unit. It was marked by a closed door and a sign suggesting that the only way to talk to anybody was by ringing a doorbell.

I rang the bell, and after a while a nurse opened the door.

"Robert Lancaster is in there," I said. "I'm his lawyer."

"Only immediate family is allowed in here without the pa-tient's permission."

"So ask Robert," I said.

"We can't do that right now," she said. "Sorry." And she closed the door.

I found a little waiting area, and Dalt and Teresa and Jess arrived about a half hour later. The ICU nurse let Teresa and Dalt in to see Robert.

Jess stayed in the waiting room with me. "What happened to you?" she said.

"I fell down."

She rolled her eyes. "That's what my husband told me the night those thugs beat him up. He said he tripped on some stairs."

"We men don't like to admit that anybody could beat us up," I said.

A few minutes later Teresa came out with tears welling in her eyes. Dalt's jaw was clenched. They sat down with Jess and me. Teresa said that Robert looked like death. He was unconscious and riddled with plastic tubes, she said, and hooked up to about a dozen machines. He was dehydrated and he'd been drugged.

Dalt didn't say anything. I wondered what he knew, or had figured out, about Mike and Kimmie Warner.

I asked them to release me from my commitment to confidentiality so I could talk frankly and fully with the police and get to the bottom of what had happened.

Dalt and Teresa both nodded and said, "Sure. Of course."

"They'll want to talk to both of you, too," I said. "You, too, Jess. Just tell them everything."

Jess decided to go looking for a coffee vending machine. Teresa stood up and said she'd go, too, and I was left alone with Dalt.

"Mike and Kimmie," he said after a minute. "I can't believe it. So those thugs who beat me up weren't the ones who took Robert after all."

"Nope. It was your brother-in-law."

"Son of a bitch. Guy pretends to be your best old buddy and all the time he's holding your son hostage, extorting money out of your mother. I don't get it." He arched his eyebrows, asking me to explain.

I said nothing.

"He's been a strange man since . . . what happened to Jimmy," said Dalt slowly. "There's an emptiness about him. He's hollowed out. You wouldn't notice it unless you knew him before, when Jimmy was alive. It's like his soul is gone." He looked up at me. "That's what this is about, isn't it?"

"I don't really know, Dalt," I said. "I could only speculate."

"This was Mike's way of evening things up between us," he said. "Between him and me. He lost a son, so it's only fair that I should. See, he's always blamed me for what happened to Jimmy. He's jealous that I've still got my son. He thinks Jimmy got into gambling because of me."

I looked at him. "What about you? What do you think?"

He shook his head. "You can be a prick sometimes, you know that?"

I shrugged.

He turned his face away and gazed off into the distance for a minute. Then, without looking at me, he said, "It's complicated, isn't it? Who knows what makes people the way they are? I guess the only way Mike could live with Jimmy being gone was to have somebody to blame. I understand that. Do I blame myself?" He turned and looked at me. "Sure. I think all of us who were close to Jimmy have found ways to blame ourselves. You think, if I'd only said or done something at one time or another, if I'd listened to him more closely, asked him the right question at the right time . . . you think maybe this wouldn't have happened. You

272

could have prevented it. You can't help second-guessing yourself, you know?"

I nodded. "I know. It's what they call having a conscience."

"The money, too," Dalt said. "Mike and Kimmie have spent everything they had trying to find Jimmy. I don't know how many trips to Nevada they've taken, how many investigators they've hired . . ." He shook his head. "When Jess understands all this, she'll be devastated. Her own sister. Jesus."

I went to the nurses' station and rang the bell. One of the nurses told me that a doctor was with Robert. She promised to remind him to talk with Dalt and Teresa afterwards.

Roger Horowitz was sitting in the waiting room with Dalt when I got back. He had a magazine opened on his lap. Dalt was turned away from him.

When Horowitz saw me, he stood up, grabbed my arm, and steered me into the corridor. "Let's talk," he said.

"I don't want to do this a million times," I said. "We can talk now, or we can go to some police station where they have one-way mirrors and video recorders and a good cop to offset you."

"Now is fine," he said. "We got those two in custody. Warner and his wife. They're the ones who'll get the one-way-mirror treatment. And, of course, I'll have to get our victim's story."

"You're not talking to Robert without me."

He cocked his head at me. "Why the hell not?"

I smiled. "Nice try, Roger."

He shrugged. "We found a trash bag full of cash stashed in a forward locker on that boat," he said. "Looks like a couple hundred thousand dollars. I bet you know something about that."

I nodded. "I bet I do."

Just then Jess and Teresa came back. Jess was carrying a tray that held some Styrofoam cups. She gave one to me. "Black, right?"

I took it from her. "Right. Thanks." I turned to Horowitz. "This is Teresa Samborski. Robert's mother. And this is Jessica Lancaster. Dalt's wife. Robert's stepmother."

Horowitz nodded and smiled at them. "We'll want to talk with both of you."

"Who are you?" Jess said.

"Horowitz," he said. "State cops."

Jess pointed her chin at the waiting room. "I'll be in there with my husband."

Horowitz and I found a little alcove off the corridor where we could sit, and I told him the whole story—how Robert Lancaster's addiction to high-stakes poker had dug him a deep hole of debt with Paulie Russo, how Russo sent his thugs to beat up Robert, how when Robert couldn't come up with the money, they beat up Dalt, Robert's father. I told him I'd made Robert promise to lay his cards on the table, so to speak, with his parents, and soon after that he disappeared. I told him about Dalt finding the CD and the cell phone inside his Sunday *Globe*, about his mother, Judge Adrienne Lancaster, putting up the quarter-million-dollar ransom, about me stuffing it into a trash bag and dropping it off a bridge into the Merrimack River. I told him how I'd connected some clues from the CD with my discovery that Mike Warner owned a boat, and how that led me to the Kettle Cove Marina, where I found Robert unconscious and wrapped in duct tape in the cabin of Warner's Bertram.

"That's about it," I said. "You know the rest."

"Why'd Warner do it?" said Horowitz. "Besides the money."

I told him about what had happened to Jimmy Warner, how he'd disappeared in Las Vegas after he and some of his college friends had succeeded in scamming the casinos.

"So it's some kind of sick vengeance," said Horowitz. "An eye for an eye, a son for a son."

I shrugged. "Something like that, I guess. That and the money."

"Snazzy detecting, Coyne," he said.

"Yes," I said. "I thought so."

"There's a lot you're not telling me," he said.

"Not all that much, actually."

"About Robert," he said. "Our victim."

I shrugged.

"So now I'm going to ask you a bunch of questions."

"I assumed you would," I said. "I'll probably refuse to answer many of them."

"You being a slimy shyster lawyer."

"But a snazzy detective," I said.

It was close to two o'clock in the morning when I got home. Henry was happy to see me. He whined and barked and wagged his entire hind end, and I knelt down so he could lick my face and I could hug him and scratch his ears.

After I let him out into the backyard, I headed for the stairs leading up to our bedroom, where Evie would be sleeping on her belly, hugging her pillow, but would want to hear all about my adventures, so I'd drop my clothes right there on the floor and slide onto the bed beside her and lift her hair away from her neck and nuzzle her throat and stroke her hip until she moaned and mumbled and rolled onto her side . . .

I stopped with one foot on the bottom step. Evie was gone. Our bed upstairs was cold and empty.

For a moment I'd forgotten, and it felt good. For that moment I felt complete again.

I woke up a little after nine on Friday morning and had a moment of panic. Julie was going to kill me for being late.

Then I remembered that I'd declared an Office Holiday, a four-day weekend for the busy law practice of Brady L. Coyne, Esquire.

When I went downstairs and let Henry into the backyard, I saw that Roger Horowitz was sitting at the picnic table. He was wearing his brown suit and reading a paperback book.

TWENTY-NINE

Henry went over and sat beside him so that Horowitz could scratch his ears.

"Breaking and entering," I said.

He looked up at me. "I entered," he said, "but I didn't break. You gotta get that lock fixed." He jerked his thumb at the door in the garden wall that opened to the alley.

"Been here long?"

"Started to worry," he said. "You slept late."

"Want some coffee? It's all brewed."

"I thought you'd never ask."

I fetched two mugs of coffee, took them out, and sat across from him.

He took a sip, then cocked his head and looked at me. "Your nose is all swollen. Your eyes, too. How're you feeling? How's the hand?"

"Good," I said. "I feel good."

"Sleep okay?"

"Took a couple aspirin." I smiled. "Nice of you to come all the way to my house to see how I was feeling."

"Sure," he said. "What are friends for?" A manila envelope lay on the table by his elbow. He opened it and slid out about a dozen eight-by-ten black-and-white photographs. They were mug shots. "Recognize any of these guys?"

They were men in their twenties and thirties. Two African Americans, one Asian, one Hispanic, the rest Caucasians. Several of the white guys had moles on their faces. I pointed at one of them. "Him," I said. "Mole-face Louie. He's Paulie Russo's enforcer. The one who gave me the kidney punch. He beat the crap out of Dalt Lancaster. Robert, too. The one, I assume, whose face was delivered to me in a shoe box."

Horowitz nodded. "His name's Malatesta. We can't find him."

"That's because he's dead," I said.

"I know. Point is, we can't track him down. Russo says he hasn't seen him for a couple days, doesn't know where he is. That's what everybody says. We got no leads, no corpus delecti, no nothing."

"Corpus delecti." I smiled.

"It means delicious corpse."

"I doubt it," I said.

He slid the photos back into the envelope. "I just wanted to be sure we were talking about the same guy."

"He's under a concrete foundation in Southie or chained to four cement blocks on the bottom of the harbor channel," I said.

Horowitz shrugged. "I'm sure you're right."

"I assumed this was Mendoza's case," I said. "She's the one who's got the face in the shoe box."

"Member of the Russo family? Everybody's case. Feds're interested, too. We're all trying to cooperate." He took a swig of beer. "They're saying Robert Lancaster will be moved out of intensive care this afternoon or tomorrow morning. I imagine you'll want to visit him."

"Of course," I said. "He's my client, also my friend. I care about his health and his well-being."

"About what time do you think you might go?"

I shrugged. "Midafternoon tomorrow, I guess."

"I'll meet you there at three."

After Horowitz left, I pulled on a pair of hiking boots and left my cell phone on the kitchen table, and Henry and I drove to Bolton Flats.

Henry had a long rambling run. He flushed a pair of mallards from the brook, a few meadowlarks from the fields, one bobolink from a patch of briars, and dozens of robins and sparrows and red-winged blackbirds from the bushes.

Yesterday's rain had washed the clouds out of the June sky. The air tasted clean, and I felt good. I had a long muscle-stretching walk and managed not to think about much of anything except the sweetness of the air in my nostrils and the honesty of the sweat on my forehead.

We stopped at a farmstand at Nine-Acre Corner in Concord on the way back, and I bought a loaf of rosemary-and-olive bread, two pints of strawberries, and three bunches of fresh-picked local asparagus.

I ate hunks of bread dipped in olive oil, roasted asparagus spears drenched in butter and drizzled with melted Vermont cheddar, and strawberries sprinkled with brown sugar. If Evie had been there, she would've insisted that we have slices of chicken breast and a salad of spring greens with the bread and asparagus, and she would surely have whipped some cream and baked some shortcake for the strawberries. But Evie wasn't there.

After dinner, Henry and I watched the ball game in the living room, and I fell asleep on the sofa.

Robert had a private room on the second floor of the Addison Gilbert Hospital in Gloucester. He was sleeping when I got there a little before two on Saturday afternoon. Aside from an IV drip, all of the other tubes and wires had been removed from his body.

I pulled a chair up beside him and poked his shoulder.

His eyes blinked, then opened. He turned his head and looked at me. "Hey," he said. "Brady."

"How're you feeling?"

"Not so bad. Tired, mainly."

"Ready to tell me all about it?"

"I guess so."

"Do you want me to act as your lawyer?"

He blinked. "Do I need a lawyer?"

"You tell me."

He looked at me for a minute, then nodded. "I guess I might."

"All right," I said. "You got me. Lieutenant Horowitz will be here in a while. He's with the state police. He needs to talk to you. But first I want you to tell me your story."

He nodded. "Where do you want me to start?"

"That time we met at Dunkin' Donuts, you promised me you'd talk to your family," I said. "Instead you disappeared. Start there."

"My first thought, honest to God, was, join the army, go to Iraq."

280

"Of course," I said. "Get yourself blown up. Solve everything."

"Well," he said, "it would've, right?" He waved his hand in the air. "I couldn't face my father. I wanted to get it taken care of without him knowing what I'd done. I didn't want to disappoint him. That was probably stupid, but it's what I was thinking. I was pretty panicked. So I called Uncle Mike."

"Your father's best friend," I said.

Robert shrugged. "I felt I could trust him. He was the only one I thought I could trust. He always treated me like a man, not a kid. I told him I was in trouble, needed his help." Robert smiled. "He said sure, anything. We got together, and when I told him that I owed those people a lot of money and I was afraid they'd come and beat me up or maybe kill me, he said he'd take me to his boat. I could hide out there, be safe until we figured out what to do. I made him promise not to say anything to my father."

"And he suggested you tap your grandmother for the money."

Robert nodded.

"That was Mike's idea?"

"Yes. But I went along with it. She's got tons of money. I figured if she knew I was in trouble, she'd do it."

"But you didn't just ask her."

"That was Uncle Mike's idea, too," Robert said. "He said it would be better if Grandma didn't know what I'd done, that she'd be ashamed of me. Because of my father, how he'd lost all his money gambling. Uncle Mike said that she'd probably cut me out of her will or something. He made it sound like what we were doing was for Grandma's benefit."

"So you agreed to pretend to be a hostage?"

"Right. I trusted Uncle Mike." He shook his head. "So he wrapped me up in duct tape and had me read this thing he'd written while he videotaped me."

"In the cabin in his boat," I said.

He nodded. "I didn't understand why we were asking for all that money. I mean, I only owed about fifty grand. But Uncle Mike said that it would be more believable if we asked for that much. So I did it. I read it just the way he wrote it." He looked at me and shook his head.

"Then what?" I said.

"Then he didn't take off the tape. Suddenly he was different. He said if I didn't cooperate with him, do everything he said, he'd kill me. He made me swallow some pills, and they knocked me out. After that it's all kinda fuzzy. I know he kept making me swallow pills. He didn't give me any food. Just water sometimes. He left me alone a lot, and mostly I slept. Next thing I really remember is being here in the hospital."

"What about Kimmie?"

"I remember she was there sometimes. This was after Uncle Mike taped me up and made me swallow those pills and everything, so it's pretty fuzzy. Sometimes Kimmie was the one who gave me the pills and the water."

"What you've told me is the truth, Robert?"

"Yes. It's the truth."

"If you had to swear to it in court . . . ?"

"Am I going to have to do that?"

"Probably."

He looked away from me for a moment. Then he said, "So am I in trouble?"

"Without you—"

"I know," he said. "If I hadn't been stupid in the first place, none of this would have happened. That's not what I meant."

"You conspired in a felony," I said.

"But—"

"You're also the only witness in this case. We'll see how it goes."

"You're my lawyer, right?"

"I am." I looked at my watch. It was almost two-thirty. "Lieutenant Horowitz will be here in about half an hour. I'll be with you when you talk to him."

Robert shrugged. "I'm more worried about what to say to my parents and my grandmother."

"Don't look at me, pal. I offered to help you with that once. Now you're on your own. I'm just a lawyer." I stood up and patted his shoulder. "Why don't you grab a nap so you'll be bright-eyed and bushy-tailed for the lieutenant?"

He closed his eyes. "Whatever my lawyer says."

I was in the waiting room when Horowitz arrived. A woman was with him. She was wearing dark tailored pants and a white shirt and shiny black shoes. Her blond hair was cut very short. The only thing that didn't fit was the makeup around her eyes and the multiple piercings on her ears.

Horowitz introduced her as Agent Loudon. She held out her hand to me. "FBI," she said. "Call me Grace."

I took her hand. "Family lawyer. Call me Brady."

"So," said Horowitz, "we're gonna get Lancaster's statement now. You gonna join us?"

I shook my head. "He doesn't remember much," I said. "They had him drugged, beat him, starved him. He was all dehydrated when we found him, which raises hell with your electrolytes, messes up your memory. It's all fuzzy and confusing to him. Blurry, you know?"

"You're saying he'll make a poor witness?" said Agent Grace Loudon.

"No," said Horowitz, "he's saying he wants something. So whaddya want, Coyne?"

I spread my hands. "I'm worried, in his condition, that he'll say something that you guys will take the wrong way."

Horowitz narrowed his eyes at me, then turned to Agent Loudon. "He wants immunity for his client."

She cocked her head and looked at me.

I looked right back at her.

"Immunity?" she said.

I shrugged.

"We already got this whole scenario pretty much figured out," she said. "We know your client conspired in a scheme to extort a quarter-million dollars from a judge. I don't see how we can grant him immunity."

"Well," I said, "I don't see how I can allow him to talk to you, then, risk incriminating himself." I shrugged. "I'm sure you've got plenty of good witnesses anyway. You don't need Robert Lancaster."

Agent Loudon looked at me, then smiled. "Hang on a minute, please." She grabbed Horowitz by the elbow and dragged him out to the corridor.

They were back about five minutes later. Grace Loudon sat down beside me. "Lieutenant Horowitz says, knowing you the way he does, we might make more progress if we didn't play games with each other."

"I don't play games," I said.

She smiled. "Assuming Robert Lancaster's role in all of this was what we understand it was, and assuming he cooperates fully in our investigation, I'm prepared to recommend to the federal prosecutor that we do not charge him with any crime."

"You willing to put that in writing?" I said.

"In writing?" She shook her head. "Certainly not."

I looked at Horowitz and arched my eyebrows.

He nodded.

"Can we shake on it, at least?" I said.

Agent Grace Loudon smiled and held out her hand.

We shook. "Good enough for me," I said.

Robert was lying there with his eyes shut and his hands folded peacefully on top of his blanket.

I poked his shoulder. "Wake up," I said. "You've got guests."

His eyes popped open. He looked at Grace Loudon, then Horowitz, then me. "These are the people you want me to talk to?"

"Yes," I said. "Lieutenant Horowitz, state police, and Agent Loudon, FBI. You don't have anything to hide."

"I don't?"

"No. Just tell them everything. I'll be sitting right here. If they ask you something, um, inappropriate or irrelevant, I'll interrupt. If you want to consult with me before answering a question, we can do that. And if I hear you lying or exaggerating or doing anything but telling the truth, I'll help you get back on track. Okay?"

"Okay," he said. "I want to get it off my chest."

THIRTY

Roger Horowitz came to my house six days after Federal Agent Grace Loudon deposed Robert Lancaster in the hospital. It was a sultry evening in late June. I cooked us cheeseburgers on my backyard grill, and we ate them with bottles of Sam Adams lager at my picnic table. Horowitz sneaked pieces of his burger to Henry, who knew a sucker when he saw one and sat expectantly beside him the whole time. We talked about the Red Sox and hybrid automobiles and the upcoming mayoral election and the weird weather we'd been having.

When I brought out the coffee, Horowitz said, "Michael and Kimberly Warner have agreed to plead guilty. Robert Lancaster will not be called upon to testify. Thought you'd want to know."

"They made a deal, huh?"

"Kimberly Warner caved," he said. "Spilled out the whole story. When her husband heard about it, he talked, too. They'll both spend some time in federal prison. Him a few years more than her." He shrugged. "The prosecutor decided there was no purpose in dragging the family through the mud."

"Judge Lancaster had some input, I imagine."

"I don't know about that," he said. "Wouldn't be surprised."

"Good deal all around, then, huh?"

He shrugged. "The victim survived, and the ransom money was recovered. The judge will get it back when the feds decide they don't need it for evidence. It could've been a lot worse."

"They were going to kill him, you know."

He shrugged. Can't prove it. Neither of 'em would admit to it." He took a sip of coffee. "So how are they doing?"

"The Lancaster family?"

He nodded.

"Robert's back at school finishing up his summer classes," I said. "When that's done, his father's taking him to Idaho for a week of trout fishing with my son Billy, who's a guide out there."

"They're doing good, then."

"They're both compulsive gamblers," I said. "Same as alcoholics. They'll have to fight it all their lives. We'll see."

We sat there in comfortable silence for a few minutes. The sky over the city was darkening, and the stars were beginning to pop out.

"Any news on the guy with the missing face?" I said.

"Louie Malatesta?" Horowitz shook his head. "No faceless dead bodies have turned up. No one's been spotted walking around without his face, either. Nobody knows nothing. Be nice if we could nail Paulie Russo for it, but I'm not holding my breath." He leaned forward and peered at me. "You notice the giant elephant that's been clomping around here in your backyard?"

"Huh?"

"The most obvious thing that we haven't talked about?"

"Oh," I said. "Evie."

He nodded.

"She's in California with her father," I said. "He's dying of pancreatic cancer. They've given him maybe six months."

"So how's she doing?"

I shook my head. "I don't know."

The next day around four in the afternoon I drove directly from Judge Adrienne Lancaster's big Tudor in Belmont to Paulie Russo's headquarters in the North End with a red gym bag decorated with a Nike swoosh on the seat beside me. I called Paulie from my car to tell him I was on my way.

One of his associates was waiting for me on the delivery platform in the alley. He frisked me and peeked into the gym bag. When he was satisfied that I was neither armed nor wired, he said, "Okay, Mr. Coyne. Mr. Russo's waiting for you." He held the door for me, then followed me up the back stairs.

Paulie looked like he was about to go play a round of golf. He was wearing a blood-colored polo shirt and vanilla-flavored linen pants. A pair of wraparound Ray-Bans was perched on top of his head.

He stood up when I walked in. I went over to his desk, dropped the gym bag on it, and sat down.

Paulie picked up a tall glass that was coated with condensation and took a long swig from it. I could hear the ice cubes clink against his teeth. When he put the glass down, he said, "Iced tea with crushed mint leaves, little splash of bourbon. Want some?"

"No," I said. "Thanks." I pointed my chin at the gym bag. "Aren't you going to count your money?"

"No need, Mr. Coyne. I trust you."

"Sixty grand," I said. "Six bundles of hundreds. That covers it, right?"

He nodded.

"Including interest."

"Whatever." He waved his hand in the air. Sixty thousand dollars didn't mean much to Paulie.

"Now the Lancaster family is clear of you," I said. "Agreed?"

"That's right," he said.

"If you ever let Robert Lancaster anywhere near a game of yours, or Dalt, either, for that matter . . ."

"We got a deal, Mr. Coyne. I gave you my word. You don't need to threaten me."

"It wasn't a threat," I said. "All I meant was that I'd be very disappointed if I found out that you were not to be trusted."

"You don't need to worry about that," he said. "Sure you don't want some of this iced tea?"

"I bet it's good," I said, "but I can't stay." I glanced around the room. One thug was standing by the door, and another was leaning against the wall off to the side of Paulie's desk. "So where's Louie?"

Paulie looked at me. "Who?"

"Your associate. The guy with the wart on his face. Malatesta."

He shrugged. "I don't know who this Louie is." He lifted his chin at the goon by the door. "You know some Louie Malatesta?"

"Not me," said the goon.

I smiled. "My mistake, I guess."

On the Wednesday evening before the long Fourth of July weekend, Henry and I were out in the backyard watching another Red Sox game on the portable TV. I'd been watching a lot of baseball lately.

In the years we'd been together, Evie and I had always taken

290

an extra day on each side of the Independence Day holiday week-end to get away, sometimes to an out-of-the-way B and B in northern Vermont or New Hampshire, once to a rented cottage on Cape Cod, and the past couple of years to Martha's Vineyard, where we stayed with J. W. and Zee Jackson. Wherever we ended up, we fished, we poked around antique shops, we explored flea markets, we ate in nice restaurants, we stayed up late and slept late, we went to the movies when it rained, we read paperback novels, and we made love on a blanket under the moon.

This time, though, Evie was in California, and the long week-end loomed like a black thunderhead on my horizon.

The last time I'd actually talked with her was when I pulled to the side of Route 128 on my way to Gloucester the night I found Robert Lancaster on Mike Warner's boat. The soft June rain had been pattering down on the roof of my car, and Evie told me she didn't know when—or even if—she'd be back. She wanted me to live my life, she said. She was calling to set me free of her.

I'd tried to call her many times since then. It had been about two weeks, and in all that time, she never once answered her phone.

At first I left what I intended to be casual, unthreatening mes-sages. "Hi, babe. Just want to say hello and see how things are going," or, "Thinking of you, kiddo. Hope Ed's doing okay."

After a while, I stopped leaving messages. I let it ring, listened to her familiar voice mail message—"It's Evie. I can't come to the phone. Leave a message and I'll get right back to you"—and then hung up. Leaving no messages was better than having her ignore them.

She had not gotten back to me. Not once. I wondered if she returned other people's calls, if it was just me.

I suspected it was just me. That was her message.

It was about time I got it.

My cell phone sat on the picnic table beside my empty bottle of Long Trail ale. I never went anywhere without that phone anymore, just in case.

I picked it up. Evie's cell was number one on my speed dial. I thought about it, then pecked out the Jacksons' number.

J. W. answered on the second ring.

"It's Brady," I said, "and I wonder if you and Zee want to do some fishing this weekend."

"Always," he said. "We'll do some eating and drinking, too. Just tell me what ferry you guys'll be on."

"Guy," I said. "Just me."

J. W. didn't say anything for a minute, in case I chose to elaborate, which I didn't. Then he said, "Okay. Great. The stripers have been biting at Lobsterville, and the blues're blitzing off all the beaches, and the martinis show up every afternoon on our balcony. We'll have some fun. Bring Henry. Zee loves that dog."

"Henry would like that," I said.